Marlen

(Book Two)

Christopher Coleman

Prologue

AS ALWAYS, TIME WAS the enemy. Not bad luck or people or ambition—the scapegoats she often turned to in crisis—but time. Time was always flowing relentlessly, unaware of its destruction, like a herd of buffalo striding across a plain of anthills.

The men would be coming soon, and if they found her here alive, there wasn't even the sliver of a chance of her survival. She would be the one to make sure of that.

Her mind went to the Source and her mouth watered instantly. Even in her current state, with death looming above her like a buzzard, ready to descend upon her at any moment, she couldn't keep her mind away from it. It was the smell, she now realized, that triggered the thought. That candied aroma of her former prisoner still lingered in the damp air of the cannery, wafting down from the top floor in subtle waves. It wasn't that exact smell though, the one she had grown to lavish over all those weeks while the young woman lay trapped and shackled in the back room of her cabin; this smell was mixed with the even sweeter fragrance of another. Her daughter. Gretel.

Gretel.

The silent sound of the word in her mind elicited a tingle in her shoulders and groin.

The witch lay mangled on the stone floor, the fall from the loft leaving her body a twisted heap, with arms and legs pointed at unnatural angles. The top half of her body felt like it was on fire; the bottom half she felt not at all. At the crest of her head, she could feel the pressure of the weapon used to strike her only hours earlier, the weight of it unstable and sickening. There was no pain at the entry point, but the damage was certainly unimaginable. *My head and face have been through a lot over the past few days*, she thought, belching out a deep, hoarse cough, a sound representing both laughter and disgust.

You must go. Now. They're coming.

The voices registered as whispers in her brain, urgent and quick, not unlike the manner she imagined deranged women in institutions had heard just before they sunk their children, one by one, below the waterline in the bathtub.

The witch tried to open her eyes, but they felt sewn shut. She tried again but felt only the stretch of her closed eyelids. She wiggled one finger on her right hand, then two, tapping them on the floor, the tips splashing in the shallow pools beneath them—her blood, no doubt, and judging by the depth, not an insignificant amount. She made a fist, barely bringing her hand together at first but then progressively working up to a tight clench. She relaxed her grip and stretched her fingers wide before slowly bringing them to her face, using her thumb and index finger to crush the crust of caked blood from her eyelids. She could now see the handle of the weapon staring at her, taunting her from an inch away, the business end of the thing still clinging tightly to her skull.

She resisted the urge to pull it away, fearing the hemorrhaging that would ensue.

Moving only her eyeballs, the woman surveyed her surroundings, glancing wildly from wall to stairs to ceiling to floor. This last area—the floor—was a horror show, and the newly risen sun hid none of the massacre. The fallow, brown ground where she lay was now a dark purple lake of viscous blood, the color matching perfectly that of her palms and sleeves.

The woman maneuvered her hand under her cloak and then reached down toward the top of her thigh, touching herself lightly at first, and then, feeling nothing, grabbing her leg with the force of panic. Her leg muscles tightened reflexively with the clench, bringing a sigh of hope and relief to the woman. She had feeling in her legs. She was not paralyzed.

They're almost here, the voices warned again. *You'll die here. Die here.*

The last two words drifted away, but she followed them until they disappeared from her thoughts.

"I will not," the woman spoke aloud, her warm breath bouncing back at her off the base of the hammer. "I'll never die."

The woman inhaled to her lungs' capacity, and on the exhale rolled herself flat against the floor, chest down, before pushing herself to her knees. She stretched her back straight and stared up through the opening of the loft, listening for life. They had long since gone, of course, the women, but she would never again assume anything.

The ditch. Get to the ditch.

She thought of her cabin and the holes she had dug following her Source's escape, just after resurrecting her life with the most brilliant taste she would ever know. The instinct to dig had been odd, but she'd followed it, using her newfound strength to move quickly through the sod and dirt. She'd buried some of the potion there, and now she needed to find her way home to drink it.

The witch finally stood, the effort of it immense considering the trauma her body had suffered. But the potion seemed to have staved off any truly debilitating injuries. And as long as she was mobile, she had a chance.

She walked to the door of the cannery and opened it slowly, half-expecting one of the Morgan women—or perhaps a System officer—to be standing outside, waiting with pickax in hand to finish the job they had come so close to completing. But there was only the clean, cool air of the Back Country, and as it entered the cannery, the feel of the breeze on her wounds was exhilarating. She walked outside the boundaries of the dilapidated structure to the openness of the cannery grounds and listened again for anything that may indicate her odds of escape—sirens, voices, gunshots—but she heard only the sounds of the morning.

She strolled to the chain link fence and stared through to the lake, reliving last night's hunt. She had lost control. Lost sight of her goals. Lost her chance at Gretel.

She retraced her steps back past the cannery and began to ascend the hill at the rear of the grounds. With the industrial hammer still projecting from the top of her head, she imagined she must have looked like some type of mythical woodland beast, the kind hundreds of people claim to have seen but which is widely dismissed as legend by the rest of the world.

She had not a clue what the top of the hill held for her, but at this point, it was her only chance of escape. If it was more fencing, like that which ran along the front of the cannery, she would be in serious trouble. In her condition, she couldn't conceive lifting herself six inches off the ground, let alone the eight or ten feet that was necessary to clear a fence. She'd fly again one day, but not today.

Halfway up the hill, she saw the shape of a roof come into view, and soon after, the warehouse. There was no fence barring her from the structure, and this, she acknowledged, was a small sign of hope. And when she slowly pushed open the back door of the warehouse and saw the corpse of the man who had started her on this latest path of addiction and murder, she knew Life had returned for her.

CHAPTER ONE

"THERE IT IS. I TOLD you it was here."

The woman's eyes sprung open and she caught her breath at the apex of an inhale. Voices. Voices and footsteps. Her mind deciphered the sounds even before she was fully awake. There were three of them. She knew it instantly. Three intruders. Pre-adolescent. She could detect the pitch of their voices and their vibrations through the ground.

"It really is here," another boy replied. "I can't believe it. I didn't think it was true."

The woman turned her head toward the sound of the words and was greeted by one of the earthen walls of her bunker. She could feel the rays of the sun beaming through the grass canopy that had so effectively camouflaged her for what must have been, at this point, months. Maybe even a year. These young travelers on the perimeter of her yard were the first to come since those days immediately following the horrific night in the cannery. The first she had detected anyway. It was likely others had come and gone during her deepest of slumber, and now the thought of laughing gawkers defacing and stealing her property made her gag. She thought back to the first days of hiding, the days when the men had come for her, scouring her property and desecrating her cabin. But they had come to do more. They had come to take her as their prisoner. To rob her of her potion. And, no doubt, to kill her.

The potion.

She felt beside her and touched the small jar that still contained several viable ounces of the elixir—the extraordinary brew that had allowed her to rest and heal. The grave had been her shelter and concealment, but the potion had allowed her to go without food and water, to get perfect—almost—once again. Perhaps these plodding boys had awoken her a few weeks earlier than the optimum recovery time, but her mind was clear and her body lithe. She felt fresh. Reborn.

The woman stood in the ditch and peered over the ledge, pushing the twigged canopy up with the top of her head, stooping slightly to keep her eyes at a level barely above the dirt wall that surrounded her. Through the foliage in the distance, she could only see the shoes of the intruders, but she could tell by their voices they weren't much older than twelve. She held her breath for several beats and then exhaled slowly, never blinking the eye that remained. Her left eye had been beyond repair; the combination of the ceramic bowl and hammer claw had proven too costly. She had feared the damage would be permanent, agonizing over the dire possibilities during her grueling trek from the Back Country, and she now accepted the obvious truth of it. But it was only an eye. The rest of her seemed to have healed quite well. She blinked her eye fully now, feeling the bulge of the orb beneath her lid, savoring it setting in its socket. There will be a price to pay for the other one, the woman thought. Revenge. A smile followed this last thought as the literal manifestation of the biblical metaphor took hold in her mind.

"Wait," one of the voices uttered. It was the third boy this time, younger and more frightened than the others. "What if she's there? What if she's waiting for us?"

The woman listened closely to the reply, ready to strike if the answer was inadequate, ready to erupt from the ground like a tarantula if the boys suddenly became spooked and began the first movements and utterances of flight. Instead, she smiled wildly at the sound of the other boys as their crackling voices spilled into mocking laughter.

The first boy coughed out a few more chortling breaths and then said with defiance, "She's dead, you pillock. Her skeleton is at the bottom of a lake somewhere in the Back Country."

"So everyone says, but how do you know that's true? If they never found her body, how can you know?"

"Because the girl killed her. And her mom was there and saw the whole thing. They saw her dead body splayed across the ground as they left. That's how I know. Are you the only person from the Southlands who hasn't heard the story?"

"I've heard the story, but back to my same question then: where is the body? Why is there no body?"

"How many laps do you want to take around this 'body' track? Hmm? I don't know where the body is exactly. It was probably dragged off and eaten by dogs. Or something. The System doesn't seem too concerned about it, so why are you?"

"I'm not concerned about it, I just..."

"Or maybe," the first boy interrupted, "maybe they did find the body and the System is covering that whole night up. Did you think about that?"

"No." The boy paused, indicating he was considering the explanation. "But why would they do that?"

"Because that's the kind of crap they do! I don't know. It doesn't matter." The first boy's tone was curt now, irritated, and any more talk about the body's location was likely to propel him into raw anger.

The woman groaned in ecstasy.

"And anyway, she's not here. How could she be here? She was killed in the Back Country, not here at her cabin. Think about things before you spit up your stupid theories. Besides that, the System has probably been through this place a million times by now. The cabin is empty. There's no one here waiting for us."

The boy paused, and the woman could almost see his eyes widen and his chin jut out slightly, taunting another challenge.

"But...I guess if you're scared, you should stay back here. I honestly don't give a crap. I knew I shouldn't have brought you along."

The woman listened intently, in some ways hoping the boy would call the bully's bluff and keep away from the property. So soon after her hibernation, she was somewhat concerned she would only have strength for one of the boys right now—maybe even two if she was quick with the first. But three would be a definite challenge, so if one of them had to escape, she'd rather it be the sensible one. Not that she was more concerned about him than the others, she just figured the more prudent boy would be too frightened to tell his tale to anyone who mattered. At least not for a few days anyway. And by then she would be gone. By then she would have started hunting again.

"I'll go with you," the boy relented. "I was only saying."

The witch watched as the three boys came into full view, clearing the last of the branches and crossing the threshold of the tree line. They stood motionless, standing in the clearing that bordered the side of her home. The woman could now see them clearly. They were average in height and build, gangly and unsure in their movements, typical mannerisms of boys that age. She could no longer see them below their knees, their shoes and lower legs now completely enveloped by the ryegrass and thistle that had overtaken the property. They look like apparitions gliding over the weeds, she thought.

"Let's go," said the first boy, the leader, the one who, moments before, had mocked his frightened friend—or possibly brother, which, if that were true, would give her less time if he escaped. His voice was quick and full of energy and adventure, and the witch knew that if they headed toward the back of the house, he would be her first victim. It was always the eager ones who made the most mistakes. Bless their hearts.

The thought of new prey now elicited ecstasy. She licked her tongue across the bottom of her top row of front teeth, groaning as she did so. The sound was low and guttural, starting deep in her chest and rattling up through her throat. The noise came out in a loud rumble, louder than she had intended, and she saw the boys stop and pivot, now facing toward the backyard and the ditch where she was lurking. She ducked below the brim of the narrow channel, the canopy closing the small gap, and waited, listening for the scatter of terrified footsteps. If they did run, she stood poised to attack. This was a gift she wouldn't deny herself.

"What was that?" a voice asked, his tone playfully suspicious. It was the second brave boy in the group, the other teaser, and his question was clearly directed toward the coward with the intention of pushing the boy into panic.

"Oh that was definitely her," the leader declared. "I mean, what other explanation could there be? The Old Witch of the North lives!"

The second boy laughed at this and said, "You're crazy, Tomas." But the fear behind his brave veneer was now detectable to the woman. She could almost smell it.

"Okay, well what was it then?" It was the coward this time, he making no pretensions at bravery. "We should leave. There's probably bums back here anyway. Or wild animals."

"Or..." the leader replied, "wild bums! Terrifying wild bums!"

The first two boys burst into laughter, loud enough now to veil the woman if she chose this moment to attack. But she restrained herself, not quite confident that her legs were charged and ready for a guerilla attack at this distance. Soon, but not yet. Instead, she waited and listened, trying to anticipate the boys' next moves.

"Well something is back there. You heard it. And I'm not going to find out what it is. Have fun being brave; I'll have fun being alive."

"Leave then. Bye. Don't forget your bottle, baby."

The witch couldn't tell which one of the bullies supplied this last taunt, but there was a malignancy in the tone that was unmistakable. It was the sound of the rotten men she'd known all her life.

Suddenly the bullies began laughing like rabid jackals, and the woman could hear the coward's footsteps trotting off and diminishing into the distance, a slow gallop at first and then breaking into the trod of a full sprint.

"Do you still want to check it out?" said the second in command.

"Of course. Why wouldn't I? Wait a minute. Don't tell me you're scared too."

"Shut up, Tomas. I was just asking." There was a pause. "You're such a whaling prick."

"Stop pouting and come on then. Of course we're going to check it out. Let's see if this crazy bitch has something cool in her attic or something."

"Wait. You want to go inside? I don't know about that. I mean, maybe we—"

"You are scared! Ha! I knew it."

The woman could imagine the look of gleeful satisfaction on the face of the leader, his dominance once again established by the apprehension of his companion.

"Go off with Billy then! You can probably catch up! Ha! I don't care. I'll go alone. Faggot."

"Shut up, Tomas!" the second boy screamed, the fury in his voice real.

The witch's eyes opened wide, and the trace of a smile returned to her face.

"Or what?" Tomas replied. The words were threatening, daring.

"You don't want to find out."

"Really? You won't do crap. Pussy."

And with that, the scuffle was on. The jocular conversation of the adolescents was replaced with grunts and screams and slaps of skin.

With the delicacy of a new mother rousing her infant, the woman pushed up on the canopy and slid it aside, just far enough so she could clear her head fully from the ditch. Fascinated, she watched the boys as they grappled themselves into a human knot of head and leg locks, pinning each other helplessly into a stalemate of limbs. She rotated the canopy further, with less care this time, and then nestled her foot on an earthen step that had formed naturally on the side of the trench. Effortlessly, she propelled herself to the ledge of the ditch and then pulled herself easily from the grave.

Now on level ground, the woman strode steadily toward the boys, focused and menacing; her dark cloak and the cake of mud on her hair and face made her appear like an encroaching black blot against the sun-filled landscape. The boys, still caught up in the scrap and whines of their own meaningless struggle, took no notice of the evil that was now less than twenty yards from them.

It wasn't until the old woman's blade-like thumbnail pierced the back of the leader's head, just at the neckline, that the second boy knew what was happening. His scream lasted only a second or two, but it was loud enough to be heard by a third boy who was now sprinting in terror through the woods of the Back Country.

THE BOARDWALK THAT led to the defaced cottage was warped and mildewed, and the witch recalled the day—a day that to her seemed like decades ago but was probably only a year or two past—when she lay dying, lamenting the universe as the energy of Life seeped from her bones and organs, bringing blackness to her mind. It had seemed so final that day, death so absolute in its certainty. Until the moment when the gift of Anika Morgan was presented to her in the form of a desperate scream from miles deep in the Northlands forest. It was the moment of her rebirth.

She recalled how expertly she had stalked her prey that night, seeing all the moves clearly in her mind hours before executing them. And when she'd captured her Source and finally learned the secret of Anika's family and the power of Life in the cells and blood of all of them, her mission became clear: to take all of them—Anika, Gretel, and Hansel—and become truly immortal.

She'd done well at first, killing the father and disposing of the nurse. The latter killing, that of the Orphist, had not come without a struggle. The woman had been fierce and heroic in her efforts before finally succumbing to a strength and brutality the witch thought impossible for her ever to possess.

And then she was there. So close. So near to her destiny, only a movement or decision away from seizing the women, both of them, and finalizing the greatest power ever conceived. They had been trapped, positioned there just for her, hopelessly sealed in that cannery by the lake; the old woman needed only to use the cunning and patience she had imparted that first night in the forest.

But it had ended in disaster. The Morgan women escaped, and she had been critically wounded in the process.

In the end, it was her great failure, and now, as she stood on the porch of her decrepit shack of a home, she knew that if she didn't find the family again, her failure would be fatal.

The woman opened the large wooden door that led to her cottage and stepped inside, proceeding directly to the kitchen. It was evident—mainly due to the presence of the many sets of large, dusty footprints—that more men had walked through her house in the past six months than had ever walked through in the home's existence. She'd been right that she'd missed some of the invaders who'd come during her slumber, but things inside weren't quite as different as she expected. A few remnants of the round black crock remained on the floor by the counter, and the witch's eyes widened for just a moment. Was it possible that some of the potion...?

No. Of course not. She reined in the idea. What she hadn't collected the day of the escape had long since dried away or been eaten by vermin. It was never going to be that easy.

The woman again fantasized about the power of the brew at its full potency after the bile of Gretel Morgan was added to the already powerful mélange.

She had work to do, and it started with finding them. The Morgans. All of them. Finding out where they had gone. She had no idea where they might be just now, but she knew there was someone who would.

CHAPTER TWO

GEORG KLAHR LIFTED the dusty rag from his back pocket and snapped it once, watching the dust scatter to the wind before methodically wiping his face. The sweat began collecting on his brow almost from the moment he stepped off the porch this morning, and he was forced to stop every minute or so to clear it. It was the hottest day of the year, no question about it. He only had about another half hour in him, and by that time, the sun would have peaked. He knew he was stronger than most men half his age, but he didn't want to push his limits. Amanda had been through enough; nursing her husband back from a stroke was more than even she could handle.

The thought of his incapacitation invoked a vague image of Heinrich Morgan, and then a clearer one of Gretel. It had been nearly a year since the day she and her family left for the Old Country, and the Klahrs hadn't heard a word from them since, a fact about which Georg had grown slightly angry. Anika had written them the mysterious letter before they left, detailing where they were headed, and emphasizing that they were not to be contacted unless absolutely necessary. He'd not had a chance to question this clause—the letter had been given to him just before the Morgans departed on their quest—and as difficult as it had been these last eleven months, neither Georg nor Amanda ever felt there was proper cause to disobey it. Amanda had cried on and off for several days after Gretel left, and as the months ticked by, her worry had only ripened.

The girl couldn't call? Or send a letter?

Georg stuffed the damp rag back into his pocket and stared across the lake at the Morgan property. He closed his eyes and thought of that day of death and carnage. Of the spectacle he had witnessed. Of the woman—witch—who had attacked him. And of the things he hadn't done to save the nurse. He had failed her, and he now lived with that thought every day, just as he would until the day he died. He squeezed his eyes tightly and shook the memory clear. Not now. It was too early in the day to descend into this thinking.

"I'm leaving, Georg."

Georg spun to see his wife stalking the back porch, studying her lavender and jasmine, sniffing them gently before moving on to tease up her hydrangeas.

"What's that, dear?"

"I'm leaving for a bit. Got some things to buy for the garden. Don't want you out here too much longer. Hottest I've felt it in a long while." Amanda Klahr stopped and stared defiantly at her husband, imparting the seriousness of her statement.

"Would you like me to go instead? To the store?"

"I would not. If you do my hobbies for me, they're no longer my hobbies."

Georg smiled. "All right then. Be safe, will ya?"

"Course hon. Always am."

Amanda paused and stared at her husband, as if waiting for the answer to her question before she asked it. Finally, she said, "Have you seen Petr today?"

Georg forced a smile. "Not yet. He'll be around soon."

Amanda nodded, gave one last pluck to a rose bush, and then faded from the porch into the cottage.

Georg stared his wife back into the house, wincing at the sucking sound of the sliding glass door sealing behind her. He closed his eyes and sighed. Petr.

Petr Stenson had worked at the orchard for almost a year and a half, and after the death of his father at the hands of the faithless she-devil, there had never been a question as to where the boy would live. The Klahrs had never given a second thought to taking the boy in. He was an orphan now, his mother having died years earlier, and both Georg and Amanda had grown to love him like a grandson.

But the new arrangement had been difficult, and the truth was they hadn't expected such a dramatic shift in Petr's behavior, at least not so immediately after becoming their responsibility. Georg realized this was probably a naïve way of thinking, given the boy's age and the trauma he'd been exposed to, but the adoption itself was only a formality—Petr had essentially been living with them anyway—so they both thought the transition would be less rocky.

But Petr now stayed out late most nights—sometimes even all night, as in the case of this previous evening—and his friends were not of the type the fathers of the Back Country hoped their daughters would marry. Neither he nor Amanda suspected Petr was getting into any dire trouble, but his pattern of disappearing was becoming a concern.

But Georg knew it wasn't the recent living arrangements or even the death of his father that was the most trying on Petr. It was losing Gretel.

Georg opened his eyes and turned back to his work, lifting the hoe high above his head before slamming it into the brittle earth. He loved the power and ferocity of this move—whether with the pick, the axe, or the hoe—and from that first day when spring quietly snuck a day in in March, he had come to the orchard every day, building his strength this way for hours at a time. Georg Klahr's days of working the harvest had been effectively done years ago, so during the season, as he continued his violent work of chopping an empty field, the workers simply watched with odd fascination while they did their business of picking the blossoming apples and pears.

Georg raised the hoe again and slammed it to the earth, unconcerned what the migrant workers may have thought. Or what anyone thought. He was training. Getting strong. Building the muscles of his shoulders and biceps and thighs. Working his lungs until they burned and tormented him. And if he ever got the chance again, he would kill without consideration the person who threatened him or his.

"Georg."

He registered his name and the voice that spoke it, but the sound didn't quite file as real, as if it were uttered from a dream.

"Georg!"

Georg barked out a scream this time, lurching toward the sound of his name and raising the hoe high above his head, directing it toward the intruder. He stopped before swinging it, blinking wildly at the boy standing before him.

"Petr?" Georg was frozen, his eyes now dilated in madness, the garden tool still poised to strike. "Petr, I'm sorry. I was deep in thought...work."

Petr grinned slightly and nodded. "I know those thoughts, Georg. Trust me, I do."

Petr had recently gone from using the moniker "Mr. Klahr" to "Georg," and Georg was still not quite comfortable with it. It was fine, of course—"Mr. Klahr" seemed too formal for their relationship, and "Dad" or "Grandad" wasn't right either—but Petr's use of the title somehow put him on a level of adulthood that Georg wasn't ready for. Thankfully, Petr hadn't yet made the transition to "Amanda," and Georg quietly hoped he never would.

"Where were you last night? Mrs. Klahr was worried." Georg now held the hoe down by his waist, gripping it in front of him casually with both hands.

Petr frowned and looked away. "I needed to be away last night."

Georg waited for more, and when he got nothing, he said, "Searching?"

Petr looked back at Georg, whose eyes were set in marble. "She's alive."

Georg frowned at the statement, but this time he resisted the urge to diminish the boy's beliefs further with a shake of the head or a snicker as he'd done dozens of times since Petr first declared his theory.

"I know you don't believe that, and that's your choice, but she's alive...or at least...she didn't die that night in the cannery. Not the way they said she did."

"Gretel was there, Petr. And Mrs. Morgan. Gretel was the one who ki—" Georg stopped, not wanting to attach Gretel to the violence that had occurred that night.

"They didn't see her die, Georg," Petr replied. He was delicate with his words, detached from the emotion of the events. "They saw her fall. They saw her lying on the ground. But they never saw her die. They jumped from the cannery window and never saw—"

"Where is she then, Petr?"

"It's a big world out there, Georg."

The theory, which Petr had recited to Georg within the first month of moving in, was that the witch was alive, and she would be coming once again for Gretel. Likely Anika and Hansel too, but Gretel for sure. This discussion, which they now had once or twice a month, never reached the point where Petr told him exactly how it was that the woman was still alive or where she had been living. Or why the System had her officially listed as dead. When Georg had asked Petr about this last part, Petr had simply laughed at him and replied something sarcastic like, "Yeah, you're right Georg, the System would never do anything like that. No way."

Georg supposed he had a point there.

And here they were again, back in the throes of the subject, speeding down the bumpy road to nowhere. Georg decided to veer off. "Where were you searching last night?"

Petr was clearly caught off guard by this indirect validation of his belief, but he answered calmly. "It's better you don't know."

Georg nodded and let the tension of the words set in. Finally, he said, "You know that you aren't the only one who misses her, right? You know we love her too. And that Mrs. Klahr still cries at night. Not every night, but often, out of the blue, because she misses her and has no idea whether or not she's okay."

"But you know where she went! That's what I don't get. Why don't you just find out if she's okay?"

Georg felt the sting of the boy's words, accusatory and hurt.

A tear rolled down Petr's cheek. "Why can't you just tell me? Why don't you trust me? Still?"

Georg grabbed Petr by the back of the neck and pulled him to his chest, holding him there for a few beats. "We do trust you, Petr. With our lives. But this secret is not ours to give to anyone. Including you. Mrs. Morgan was explicit about that."

Petr pulled away and looked hard into his guardian's eyes. "But what happens when something happens to you? How do I tell Gretel? How will I get in touch with her?"

"What do you mean, 'when something happens to us?' Nothing will happen to us. Not any time soon anyway. And we will hear from her soon. I believe that. Gretel is fine. She's fine. She's doing what you're doing, that's all. She's searching." He smiled. "And if something does happen to me, then Aman—Mrs. Klahr will know how to get in touch with her. And she will, I promise. We just have to wait for her a little longer, Petr. We swore we would, so that's our only real choice right now."

Petr gave a reluctant nod, never releasing Mr. Klahr's gaze. "Just stay careful, Georg. Please stay careful."

Georg flashed a wide smile at this warning, holding the hoe up to his chest, gripping it tightly with both hands. "You sound like Mrs. Klahr." His smile softened, and then, "I promise I will be careful. Too old to push myself too hard."

"Not that, Georg. Keep doing that. Keep getting stronger. You need to stay careful because this isn't over. She is alive. I know she is. And we're going to have to be ready."

CHAPTER THREE

THE WOMAN ESTIMATED the trek to the Back Country would take two full days if she followed the road; it would be a little more than half that time if she took to the woods. There were pros and cons to both routes, but after weighing them all, it was clear that the forest was the only option. It wasn't so much the time that made the difference for her, it was the fear of being seen and questioned by some curious citizen. Or the System. In a manner as graceful and violent as any predator on the planet, she rid herself of that ambitious Officer Stenson, but it was still possible—probable even—that others in the organization were eager to challenge the miracle. Any organization as cliquey and testosterone-laced as a police force certainly didn't keep secrets well. And once word leaked of her sempiternal recipe, there would be more than one or two lionhearts who would risk it all for a taste of the magic.

And there was the more pressing issue of the boys.

She had slaughtered the two troublemakers, but the third had run off. It was only a matter of time before he told of his escapades with his friends on her property. Maybe it wouldn't be immediately, but eventually he would tell, especially when his friends—or brother—didn't show up for dinner and the parents started asking questions. The local police would then come search the property, and the System wouldn't be far behind.

And what if they found the bodies?

This was perhaps a dangerous prospect, but perhaps not. Based on the boys' conversation, the discovery of their bodies wouldn't much matter. From what she could determine, her case had been closed. She was dead in the minds of the world. No one would suspect she was responsible for the disappearances or murders of two kids this many months after she herself had been slain and presumably hauled away by a pack of wild animals. Any heinous acts discovered on her property would surely be attributed to some copycat fanatic who had fallen in love with her story, an avid follower of the infamous tale of Anika Morgan.

That was all true, of course, unless someone spotted an old woman cloaked in a dark robe, ambling down a deserted road in the Northlands. In that case, there may be a few more questions.

No, her route would have to be through the forest. She would never again take the silly risks she took at the beginning of this saga.

The woman decided she would start out at night, which would mean she would arrive around dawn on the second day. That was the plan. Sleep would be short along the way, and only during the day. She would walk all night. She'd bring food and enough water for a day. There would be no time to waste foraging. If she encountered any hikers or hunters along the way, she would assess their threat and deal with them as necessary. She didn't foresee the need to kill anyone else, but the option for such measures was always available to her.

There would also be no opportunity to harvest the young boys. Her instincts had propelled her to kill them, to flaunt her newfound strength and agility, but there was no time or resources to use them. The act was senseless in retrospect, but it was almost automatic. Just as a philanderer might cheat on his beautiful spouse, even when there was sex to be had at home, she too was driven by a similar instinct, albeit one that was far more gruesome and lasting. It had been the first challenge of her resurrection. Practice for the ultimate game. A not-so-dry run of the performance ahead. She knew now for sure that she was still capable and virile, and that the hibernation had only enhanced her desires.

The woman opened the back door and descended the rotting steps to the yard. She surveyed the edge of the forest, narrowing her eyes suspiciously at the empty shadows that lurked there, and then walked briskly back to the ditch where she had slept for the last many months. She peered into the empty space in the ground and focused on the dirty glass vial and the liquid inside. The container sat propped up in the corner of the narrow space, and the swig of potion that remained was barely noticeable through the film of time and soil. There were perhaps three last sips remaining. It was enough to keep her alive for two years or more, enough to keep her at this strength for three or four months.

She sat on the edge of the hole and eased herself back inside. She had to admit, the construction of this trench was very impressive, especially considering that it had been an ad hoc endeavor, done almost as an afterthought. In the end, however, it was the reason for her survival, being perfectly camouflaged with the landscape of her property.

The System fools obviously suspected nothing. She had listened closely when they came, the villainous trove of men who tromped around her property and barked inane orders and benign discoveries to each other. None of what she heard from the thieves concerned her whereabouts; instead they focused on the girl—Anika. They tried to figure the whys and hows of the whole capture, hoping to corroborate the facts her Source had no doubt revealed in the aftermath. What they weren't intending to do was dig. Anika and Gretel were both alive; there wouldn't have been any reason to put resources into digging up a yard searching for bodies that weren't missing.

Except for hers perhaps. Her body had not been found.

The cannery was obviously empty when the System arrived, and no detective worth his badge would have believed her body was dragged off by wolves or stray dogs. Their likely conclusion would have been that, despite the undoubtedly gruesome description of the night's events given by her Source, the witch had survived the attacks of the Morgan women. The evidence would have been obvious. The handprints around her bloody landing spot. The trail she no doubt left behind on the stone floor as she made her way back to the open field. Even the most inept detective would have deduced she made it out alive, and without evidence of a second set of prints or a smattering of bloody paw tracks, she had made it out alone.

They were looking for her during their investigation, she now realized. Of course they were. Now that she thought it through, she had no doubt. But they hadn't looked underground. They would have never thought to dig. It was illogical.

Besides, making it out of the cannery alive was one thing. Traveling from the Back Country to her cabin in the Northlands was another thing altogether. The System obviously knew she made it out of the cannery, but they likely assumed she died soon after, somewhere beyond in the closest forest.

Now, here she was, back in the ditch, considering whether to bury the boys here or to take them far into the woods and bury them, eventually to be dug up and devoured by feral woodland creatures. It would take a lot of effort, the dragging and digging and such, but with the third boy possibly reliving his story right now, the System would be returning soon—sooner than she originally calculated, and probably with dogs. And they would be looking for graves this time. Everything would be exposed, including real evidence that she was still alive.

The woman grabbed the vial and snuck it into the pocket of her robe, nestling it to the bottom fabric and pulling the drawstring taut on her pocket. She climbed her way back to ground level and looked despairingly at the perfect grass canopy and the stilts of wood that kept it aloft over her during her sleep of recovery. That would now have to be retrofitted. She couldn't leave such an obvious trace. And so she made another decision. She would take the boys to the woods and bury them.

But first she had a hole to fill.

CHAPTER FOUR

CARL DODD SPED PAST the fallen tree for the fifth time today, and probably the thousandth time in the past eight months. He hadn't missed a day since he last walked off the property with the rest of the System officers, having spent the better part of two days searching a wide perimeter surrounding the tiny house. When he later indicated on his official report that no evidence of the woman had been found, he was, of course, lying.

He couldn't see the cottage from the road at this vantage point, but each time he passed the rotting oak, he knew it was there, just beyond the foliage, hiding. He'd measured the coordinates precisely, so he always knew where he was in relation to the ramshackle hut, but it was at this point on the stretch of highway that he was closest. Right here at the tree.

On most occasions, as it was on this day, the road was as desolate as the Sahara. But on those rare occasions when he came across another car, Dodd always stopped it, pulling the motorist over under the guise of a warning about speeding or swerving or to inform the driver that there was no trouble, it's just that the vehicle fit the description of some other vehicle that had been stolen from a surrounding area. In truth, he couldn't remember the last time he'd read a report of a car being stolen anywhere outside the Urbanlands, but who were they to question him?

He would keep looking for her. Keep waiting for her to emerge. If she was alive, which he was almost positive she was, he wouldn't let her sneak away.

"Dodd, where the hell are you?"

Dodd glared at the radio, wishing he could reach through the receiver and strangle the wretched cunt on the other end. Leave me alone!

When he started with the System twelve years ago, he didn't give much of a damn about the job; today what he felt was nothing short of disdain. He grabbed the microphone and pushed the talk button, pausing for just a moment to compose himself. "This is Dodd."

"Dodd, where are you?"

"Patrol. Out on Western right now. Something afoot?" Dodd released the radio button. "Because I've got a foot I'd like to put up your ass."

"What? Western? Why are you way out there? And where have you been? I've been calling you."

Lately Dodd had gotten into the habit of turning his radio off during these patrols. It was so quiet out here, and the constant crackling and blipping of the radio shook him from his concentration. He wanted all his senses clear when she finally surfaced.

"Dodd?"

"Yeah, I had to exit my cruiser for a few moments. Thought I saw something run into the woods," he lied. He hoped there wouldn't be any follow-up about his reasoning for being miles from his typical patrol area.

"Maybe you did," the voice on the other end of the radio replied. "There are some boys that have gone missing."

Dodd felt the blood clear from his head, and a knot formed instantly in his chest and gut. He swallowed. "Boys?" he said, trying his best to sound disinterested.

"Two. Both twelve years old. Went missing yesterday afternoon."

"Yesterday?"

"Yeah, I know, we just got the call from one of the parents. Let's just say none of them have plaques in the Parent Hall of Fame."

"Where?"

"You say you're on Western, correct? Depending on where you are on Western, they may have been right near you. The two missing boys and one other. The third boy is the one who finally reported the other two missing."

"Where?" Dodd repeated, this time with a bit more snap.

"You remember that old cabin, right? The Witch of the North?" The dispatcher put a spooky spin on the title.

If the woman on the radio said anything after that, Dodd didn't hear it. He suddenly couldn't breathe, and for a few moments he was afraid he might pass out. He pulled the car to the shoulder and closed his eyes, focusing on the news he had just received and the work that lay ahead.

"...so the boy thinks that..."

"I'm on my way."

DODD PULLED UP TO THE cabin six minutes later and hopped out of his cruiser without any concern about who or what might be lurking. He wasn't ignorant to the possibility of danger, and he knew intimately the story of Officer Stenson and the brutal end he met. In fact, Dodd was one of the first officers on the scene after the whole story was told, witnessing with his own eyes the crumpled body and mangled neck of his fellow agent. He wouldn't have called Stenson a friend exactly, but he remembered the sadness he felt for him. All that time invested in the woman and her promises, only to be used as fodder.

Dodd walked to the first step of the front porch and then veered left toward the side of the house. Some of the brush had been trampled, but it was impossible to tell who had caused it. Raccoons? Children? An old woman?

He unbuckled his side arm and rested his palm on the butt. He strode at a normal pace toward the backyard, keeping his head on a swivel until he reached the place where the pit should have been.

The awning had been spectacular in its camouflage. The seamlessness of the grass roof, reinforced by wooden beams and plywood, gave no indication that the ground had been altered in anyway. No one, not even a skilled investigator, could have known about the ancient monster replenishing below. Her concealment was almost absolute. If he hadn't been looking for it, not the grave exactly, but for something similar, he would never have seen it either. Even now, having studied the ground and landmarking the spot for months, he couldn't find it.

Officer Dodd smashed the long stick into the ground where he believed the roof was, expecting the sound and feel of a wooden plank or thin plywood. Instead there was only earth.

But he was sure it was here.

Dodd dropped to his knees and examined the ground more closely. The overgrown brush made the grass line difficult to follow; if this was the floor, this was the only perspective from where he would be able see it. He crawled a few feet to his left, where he thought the tomb was, and finally saw it: a small pile of dirt mounded up about six inches off the ground. He ran his fingers through the mound and then realized what had happened. Dodd was at the spot, exactly, but the woman was gone, and the tomb where she had lain for all those months had been filled. She was on the loose, and he had let her escape.

CHAPTER FIVE

WE HAVE TO GO BACK.

Gretel's eyes snapped open and began blinking frantically, obediently trying to locate enough light in the dim surroundings to see, desperate to remind their master where she was. It didn't take long, as the moonlight lit the far side of the room. Gretel could see a lump of wool blanket in the shapes of knees and feet. Hansel. She was aligned again, aware now of her place in the world.

This wasn't an every-night occurrence for her, this frantic, late-hour disorientation, but for the last two weeks, it was most. And it was always triggered by the same five words. We have to go back. The phrase came not in a dream, but audibly, as if whispered to her by a ghost. There were no real phantoms muttering to her, of course, and the phrase was neither menacing nor panicked, but there was the weight of truth to it, something not to be ignored, and with her newfound lessons in the magical ways of the cosmos, she'd be damned if she would cast it aside.

Gretel glanced at the clock and saw it was quarter past two in the morning—too early to get up and too late to attempt going back to sleep, so she did neither, and instead lay still in her musty, yet comfortable bed, pondering her next move. It was time to tell her mother. She would do it tomorrow.

Gretel clicked the knob on her bedside lamp and a dull halo of light appeared. She peeked over at Hansel once more and then, seeing no movement, reached beneath the bed and pulled out the book. She opened it absently, randomly fingering a page amongst the first hundred or so and began reading. This was a common practice of hers now, as common as any devout Christian would read the Bible on a Sunday afternoon. And with no less reverence.

Gretel still couldn't believe the book she was reading was the same one she had first spotted in the cellar of her grandfather's house so many years before, and the same one that had brought so much disruption and tragedy, as well as intrigue and travel, to her quiet, rural life. And misery. She must never forget the misery.

But here it was. *Orphism*. As cold and black as ever. Not just in her possession, but clear and accessible, translated almost completely without gaps or discrepancies. The village elders, the ones who had fled the mountains of the ancients generations earlier, had been intimately versed in the language of the book and had translated the symbols without any coaxing or suspicion or fear. Gretel had thought they were almost amused at the request, flattered even, that there were those who still existed in the world with an interest in the ways of their people.

Gretel was never quite sure during those translation sessions if they believed in any of the book's powers. Her mother seemed to think they didn't believe and that they valued Orphism only for the tradition and culture it contained. But Gretel had her doubts about that theory. She thought maybe they truly did know of the book's power, yet instead of cowering from it the way those of the modern world had been conditioned to do, they simply accepted it as a part of life. Like the vastness of space or the depths of the sea, both contain agents capable of awesome destruction, yet neither cause angst or fear for most people from one day to the next.

Gretel flipped through the pages, scanning the decorative block lettering and words without reading them. She considered how often she had done this casual page surfing after first taking control of the book, before she could read a word, before she knew of the magic it contained. How the book had comforted her throughout her mother's disappearance and how it had given her the hope she needed that one day her mother would come home. There was something about the feel of it that was so palliative. To her, it was always more about the physical book than it was the meaning inside, even after she learned of the power in the words.

She flipped farther into the pages until she reached the first page of the book's 'Back.' That was how she thought of it now, and even that word sounded a bit too ominous. The Back section contained the recipe, and though she and her mother had insisted to the elders that—for obvious reasons—they not fully decrypt the section, they couldn't bring themselves to destroy it either. Neither Gretel nor her mother had any affection for the Back, but there was an unspoken fear about the consequences of such desecration, even to something as inherently evil as the torturous recipes. Even when the elders had offered to decode it, they had done so reluctantly, and when her mother had refused, they moved on quickly, never questioning why.

But Gretel and her mother knew the truth: the Rosetta Stone had already been decoded. Gretel could likely decipher anything that hadn't already been translated.

Gretel turned toward a noise that sounded like it was coming from the kitchen, which, in the tiny home they had been renting for almost a full year now, meant only steps away. She lowered the book down onto the nightstand and got up from her bed, grabbing her robe and wrapping it tightly against her. She opened the door quietly and stepped into the foyer, where she was met instantly by the ambient light of the overhead lamp that hung above the dining table.

Her mother was sitting in one of the three chairs surrounding the table, her back to Gretel. It was clear something was wrong, and it wasn't just the fact that it was late. She was leaning forward, slumped almost, with her elbows jutting as if her hands were folded across the table in prayer. Her shoulders were rising and falling in small jerks. She was crying.

"Mother?"

"Gretel..." Anika didn't turn around, but Gretel saw her throw the backs of her hands to her face in a panicked wiping motion.

"Mother, what's wrong?"

"Nothing, honey. I'm fine."

Gretel walked toward her mother and then around to the other side of the table. She sat in the opposing chair and leaned forward, studying her mother's face closely.

Anika smiled weakly at her daughter, the smear of tears comically obvious. "Why are you awake?"

"Mother, what's wrong?" This time, Gretel's voice quivered and was laced with anger.

Anika Morgan closed her eyes and covered her face with her hands, leaning back in the chair and tilting her head toward the ceiling. She let out an exasperated grunt. It was the sound of frustration, the refrain of someone who couldn't seem to catch a break. "Oh Gretel. I love you so much. I love you and your brother so much. You know that, right?"

"What...is...wrong?"

"I'm sick, Gretel."

Gretel sat staring at her mother but said nothing.

Still gazing at the ceiling, Anika shook her head in disbelief. "I can't believe it," she said, almost in a whisper.

"Sick? How sick? You seem well to me." Gretel instantly felt the magnitude of her mother's statement. Whatever this was, it was beyond a simple case of the common cold.

"It's probably bad, Gretel." Anika now looked deeply into her daughter's face, the compassion in her eyes teetering on despondency. "It's probably pretty bad." The last part of her sentence was a throaty whisper.

"Probably?"

"I'll know for sure in a day or two, but the doctor thinks...he's pretty sure it's some kind of cancer."

The word smashed against Gretel like a violent wave, and she dropped her mother's gaze. She wanted to run from the room the way she'd done the day her father told her that her mother hadn't returned home from Deda's. That she was hours late and no word had come in from the road. Gretel had known instantly that day that something was wrong. She had known that day that what her instincts told her was accurate, and she was equally certain now as she sat across from her mother.

But Gretel didn't run. Instead she said, "You saw a doctor? Here? When did you see a doctor?"

"Three days ago. I—"

"Three days?" Gretel shouted. She instinctively looked toward the room where Hansel still lay sleeping. She lowered her voice slightly. "Three days? Why are you telling me this now?"

Anika shook her head in quick, epileptic movements, the expressions on her face morphing, attempting to hold back tears. She mouthed, "I'm sorry," but no sound came out.

"And what 'doctor' did you see? Was he wearing a grass skirt and carrying a staff with a skull screwed to the top of it?"

Anika chuckled. "No, Gretel. I went to the city. I saw a real doctor."

Gretel started to argue again but stopped short. It was wasted effort. Her mother was the strongest person in the world, and she would fight cancer or tuberculosis or any other sickness with every gram of strength left in her cells and with every resource available. If she had reached this point in the cycle of tragedy, this place of despair and sadness, she hadn't arrived without knowing all the odds and options. There was nothing Gretel could offer to make either of those things more favorable. This was the new reality of her family, unfolding as she spoke, and Gretel had to accept and deal with the facts as they were. There was no space for wishes or fantasies. Or even lingering hope.

"The doctor knew in minutes, but he ran tests to be sure. I'll know how long I...I'll know soon."

Gretel stayed silent, letting her new existence set in and take hold. All that mattered now was what she could do, either to help her mother get better or ease her dying. There was no time for self-pity or delusion. And Hansel, she had him to consider too. "What do you want to do about Hansel?"

"I'll tell him when I know for sure." Anika grabbed Gretel's hand and squeezed it lightly. "We'll tell him together."

Gretel thought about how this news would play out with her brother. Obviously, he'd be devastated, but it wouldn't be as bad as before. Nothing could be as bad as the uncertainty and mystery during the time their mother was missing. The discord and turmoil in the house with their father and Odalinde had been unbearable at times. There had always been hope, of course, especially in the beginning, but the trauma of that experience to Hansel could never be equaled. Even if there was no hope this time, at least they would all be together. And if their mother was dying, that was a normal part of life that children often had to accept. They could love each other until the end. Besides, Gretel knew there was always hope with cancer, even if sometimes it was only a sliver. People recovered sometimes. Not always, and the odds changed depending on the type and stage, but sometimes cancer disappeared forever. There were miracles.

Gretel thought of Odalinde, and the dull ache of loneliness and yearning set in. Even though they had only known each other for a short time, Gretel missed the woman badly, and this revelation from her mother now brought that feeling closer to the surface.

"There's another thing, Gretel." Anika squeezed her daughter's hands, encouraging her to look in her eyes.

Gretel took in her mother's stare again.

"I want you to contact the Klahrs." She paused, and then, "And I want you to go home. You and Hansel. I want you to go back to the Back Country."

"What?"

"It's time, Gretel. I can't imagine how sick with worry those sweet people are. God knows I'm worried about them. I can't imagine what they're going through. I had planned to contact them months ago, but..."

"Okay, we'll go. I was going to talk to you tomorrow about leaving. I've been having...dreams. More than dreams, really. About going home. So, let's leave. All of us. Now. Tomorrow. We'll set sail back home, check on the Klahrs, and then go directly to the Urbanlands where you can see better doctors. We can—"

"No, Gretel. Just you and Hansel. I'm not going."

Gretel's mouth hung open in midsentence. She blinked twice in disbelief. "What? Why? What do you mean?"

"You remember why I didn't want to contact the Klahrs, right?"

Gretel remembered. She had wanted to write them the day they had arrived in the Old World and finished setting up in the apartment. The letter she had given the Klahrs on the day they left gave strict instructions for the couple not to contact them except in the case of an extreme emergency.

Her mother was still skittish, for obvious reasons, that there were others connected to the terror that she and her family had been subjected to. If there were others in the community, or the System, or even her own extended family who were involved with the 'Gretel and Anika Morgan Ordeal,' those individuals would have feared having their names surface and the risk of being dragged down to a System barracks where they would be forced to answer questions in a small room with a bright, unshaded light. Anika and Gretel didn't specifically know of, or even suspect, anyone else was involved, but if there were indeed others, those folks wouldn't have known which person knew what, and nefarious individuals like that didn't often take chances if it meant the difference between freedom and spending their lives in prison. So, Anika had held fast to her insistence that communication be dark. At least for a while.

The Morgans had traveled well. The trek—first by car to the coast and then by ship across the ocean to the Old World—had been mostly tranquil. At times, even fun. Neither Hansel nor Gretel had ever seen a body of water larger than the Back Country River, so for most of the first two days, and periodically throughout the rest of the two-week voyage, the two children stared spellbound at the never-ending sea. Gretel would never have believed the world was big enough to hold so much water.

During the remainder of the trip, with not much else to do, the Morgan family spent most of their time in conversation, most of which began with Anika Morgan inquiring about how everyone was feeling. Gretel knew her mother's fears: that her children had suffered some irreversible spiritual collision and would spend the rest of their long lives floundering. This concern was reasonable to Gretel, and frankly, Gretel had the same worries about her mother, but Gretel wasn't quite ready for therapy. That day would come, but not yet. She was still exhausted from the upheaval and madness of the past several months, and she hadn't come close to formulating any of it into coherence, at least not any she could verbalize. Instead, she held back, listening uncomfortably as Hansel and her mother recounted their experiences. Her mother's forays into stories of her imprisonment were particularly hard for Gretel, and she would find herself leaving their cabin to find air on the ship's deck. How she wished she could live there, traveling on the water constantly, never again being moored to the earth where evil and pain lurked. Perhaps it lurked here on the ocean too, but whatever lay in wait, beneath the waves or above, she hadn't encountered it yet. And that was enough for her.

Eventually the family's dialogue would swerve from counseling sessions to reminiscences of an earlier life. Of fonder memories and better times. And about their father. It was during one of these remembrances that Gretel spoke, finally telling her mother through a barrage of tears that she'd forgiven him. She forgave him even before he died. Hansel had too, but had been afraid to say so, fearing his sister would hate him for it.

Anika hadn't quite reached the point of forgiving her husband, but she was trying.

In the end, all the bonding had been effective, and by the time the Morgans reached the coast at the far end of the ocean, Gretel, Hansel, and Anika were energized about what lay ahead. They were ready to put the past year behind them and study a whole new chapter in their family's story, one that had been lost and buried over the centuries. And finding the source for these data hadn't taken long. The few clues Gretel had learned from Odalinde, as well as those her mother had gotten from Deda, were effective enough to set them on the path to discovery.

By their second day in the Old World, Gretel and her family located the first of the Aulwurms—the surname of her mother's family—living as merchants and fisherman just a few miles from where their ship had docked. And by the end of the first week, they had found a translator and were actively decoding Orphism into English. It was almost unbelievable how fast everything moved. At the rate they had been going, Gretel expected they would stay no more than a month, two at the most.

But that was not to be.

As the last words of the ancient script were deciphered and the mysteries of Orphism steadily unraveled, Anika began stalling their return, making excuses that her children's schooling would be interrupted, or that so much movement in such a short time would unbalance them.

The delays were fine with Gretel at first, and she looked forward to a few more months in the Old World. She had fallen in love with the charms of the architecture and language of the myriad cultures that had emerged as clusters in the tight geographies of the Old World. And the warmth and love their ancient relatives had shown them touched Gretel deeply, and the thought of leaving them so quickly made her melancholy. And then there was the food. She would have stayed in this place another year just for the food.

What Gretel had not handled well was the order from her mother to not communicate with the Klahrs. It was torture. Mr. and Mrs. Klahr were her family too, and she loved them as much as she did Hansel and her mother. They had given her a life when Gretel was desperate and all seemed lost. When her family was starving and her father had lain physically and emotionally useless in his bed, it was the Klahrs who gave Gretel a job and food and purpose. They had helped her find freedom, not just in her work and responsibility, but in the form of rowing, the hobby that had seen her through the days when her emotions had reached their breaking point. When she was forlorn about her father and Odalinde and their ill-fated marriage, the Klahrs had given Gretel hope and friendship and advice.

Those were three things she needed now, as she sat in a rented Old World apartment listening to her mother reveal her malignant fate.

"Do you remember what I said, Gretel?"

"Of course I remember. I think about it every day. You told me not to contact the Klahrs. You said you didn't want to put them in danger." Gretel recited these lines as if bored from the repetition, and then added with spooky sarcasm, "Conspiracies were afoot."

"That's right." Anika stared with cold seriousness at her daughter. "You can mock it, but that is true."

"And what if they were in danger? How would you know? Are they in danger now? What if it is true and someone else was involved in what happened? What if they'v come for them? How could we help them if we never knew about it?"

Anika dropped her eyes in a gesture of remorse. "We couldn't." She met her daughter's eyes once again. "But you and Hansel were all I cared about. Protecting you is the only thing that mattered."

Gretel wanted to argue further but couldn't. "I know," is all she said.

"But it's time now. It's been long enough. I want you to go back and make sure the Klahrs are okay. I really am worried about them."

Gretel nodded in agreement, and then her expression turned from a look of understanding to a look of pleading. "But why can't we all go? Why aren't you coming with us?"

Anika raised her hands up as if fending off a person who has accidentally stumbled toward her. "Okay, I know. There is something I've been keeping from you."

Gretel gave a bemused look. "You mean other than that you have cancer?"

This time Anika let out a laugh, which devolved quickly into a look of disbelief and sadness and then quiet weeping. She beckoned her daughter from her chair, and Gretel got up and walked over to her with tears streaming down her face. She hugged her mother and both cried softly into each other.

"I'm sorry, Gretel. I'm sorry this is happening. I promise 'l fight it. I promise I won't quit on you and your brother. 's why I'm staying."

t how can I go?" Gretel whispered. "How can I leave 'f you're sick? How can I leave you to take care of

"I'll be okay for a while." Anika paused for a moment, as if considering whether to say the next line. "And maybe longer."

Gretel pulled back from the embrace, confused. "What does that mean?" she asked, searching her mother's face for an answer.

"I know what the doctors will say. I know the treatments they'll offer. Sometimes those treatments work, but often they don't. I have a feeling, though, that with the conventional treatments, for me, there's even less of a chance than most. And I think that will be true no matter which doctors I see. Here or at home."

"So why not come then? Why don't we all go home?"

"Because here, in this place, there are other possibilities. You know this well. It's why we came here. For answers. Maybe not to this particular problem but...almost in a way... this is what we were seeking when we left."

Gretel's eyes widened and her throat tightened. Her voice crackled as she said, "You mean...?"

Anika looked at her daughter, confused for a moment, and then, finally understanding the implication scolded, "Gretel, no! Not that! I would never..." Anika took a breath and smiled. "I'm sorry. I don't blame you for thinking that. Especially since your father... But I would never hurt you Gretel. Either of you. Ever. I would die this second to keep either of you from suffering a single day of pain."

"I didn't mean you'd do that to us, Mother, but I guess I...I don't know any more." Gretel let out a long breath, relieved for the moment that her mother had not fallen under the spell of the potion that had been the source of most of their misery for the last year.

"What I mean is that since we come from this line of re-markable people, this clan of innovators whose strides and discoveries have been almost completely quarantined within their own culture, perhaps they have a remedy for this. Isn't it possible they cured cancer centuries ago? Yet instead of un-folding the methods to the world, the secret has been frozen in time, locked in the shroud of hills and trees of the Old World. I know I'm stretching my hope, Gretel. I know that. And the possibility of this being successful is more slight than I'd even like to discuss. But I must try. Why wouldn't I try? For you and your brother, I have to try."

"Where will you go?" Gretel could hear the determina-tion in her mother's voice, the vitality in her eyes.

"I don't know exactly, but into the mountains. To the source. They're still there, the ancients, the originals, and to hear others tell it, they've been untouched by time."

Gretel could feel the dubious expression erupt on her face. "But why not try the elders here in the towns? Maybe they have answers."

"I've asked them, Gretel. I went to them first. But the el-ders who translated the book for us have been outside the tribes for generations now. They've been...domesticated." Anika smiled at this notion. "But you were there. You heard en they spoke of the others, the Aulwurms in the moun-who never left. They spoke of them with a reverence ·eserved for gods and kings. Do you remember?"

·mber."

·g to try to find them."

"I'll help you then," Gretel pleaded. "Hansel and I will help you."

"No." Anika's response was instant and powerful. "This is my journey, and I have to begin it soon, before I get very sick and have no strength to go. I've arranged a guide and translator, so I won't be alone."

"But..."

"I want you to do as I say, okay? You'll set sail for home soon, and when you arrive, you'll find the Klahrs and watch over them. And your brother too, of course." Anika paused. "And Petr."

Gretel felt the blush on her cheeks at Petr's name and felt foolish for the reaction. Here she was, learning that her mother was dying and trekking off to the mountains of the Old World for a remedy that likely didn't exist, and Gretel was getting flush at the sound of a boy's name. But it wasn't just any boy. It was Petr.

"I'll...I will. I'll watch over them."

"And Gretel," Anika studied her daughter's face, making sure she had the necessary attention for what she was about to say. "Always assume you're in danger."

Gretel shook her head, slightly confused. "Danger from who?"

Anika pushed her daughter gently away from her and held her eyes. "From whom," she corrected, "and I don't know exactly. Maybe no one. But..."

"What mother? Who?"

"She may be alive."

Gretel inhaled and froze. The blow she'd felt earlier when her mother said the word "cancer" was dwarfed by the force she felt from her words this time. There was no doubt as to who "she" was. Gretel didn't even ask. "Why would you say that?"

"Listen, you know that before we left, just before we came here to live, I spoke with Petr. You remember that. I just wanted him to know that I was sorry and that I was thankful that he was okay."

"Yes, so?"

"So he said something to me just before we left, something I never told you because it was strange and superstitious and...scary, really. I tried to dismiss it, but it has stayed with me all this time. And now I think that what he said is the real reason why we didn't leave here months ago. Why I never let you reach out to the Klahrs."

"About the...woman?"

Anika nodded slowly. "The body. They never found her body."

"What? How...how did he know that?"

"His father was a System officer. Someone must have told him."

"But the report...they said she was dead. Not missing."

"I think she is dead, Gretel." Anika paused and then added, "But she may not be. Just, when you get back, be careful. Be more careful than you've ever been in your life."

CHAPTER SIX

THE WITCH STOOD ON the bank of the lake where, only months earlier, she had impaled the neck of the Orphist and ended her protracted life.

She had made it to the Morgan property in just under two days, just as she had estimated, and the moon that now shined directly above her seemed to celebrate the accomplishment by casting its beam down on her like a spotlight. The trek had been mostly easy, especially considering the woman had only been to the Morgan home once in the past, and on that occasion, she had driven in a System car along the Interways.

But she had been born into an older world during an era when people were connected to the Earth, and their senses were more calibrated to time and direction. She had known the general coordinates of the Morgan house, but as she moved closer, she recognized specific trees and smells; she could taste the water of the lake in the air and hear the plopping of frogs and fish. It was intoxicating to be so attuned to the world.

She thought again of the dead Orphist. Odalinde the Orphist. Were it not for her, the witch knew undoubtedly, the Morgan women would have been batched and blended long ago, and their liquefied parts would be energizing her body at this very moment. Things hadn't happened that way, however. Odalinde had saved them, ultimately giving up her ancient, immortal life so that they could live. The old witch couldn't help but respect her valiancy and sacrifice, and the remembrance of Odalinde's death made the woman wistful. She remembered that moment on the bank of the lake and the twinge of sorrow she felt just after she tore her razor-edged nails through the front of Odalinde's neck. But there had been no time to dwell. Gretel and Anika had launched their boat off toward the cannery, escaping with their platelets and their bile of life.

At the time, naturally, the witch's focus turned to the mother and daughter; but now, as the old woman measured her surroundings at the water's edge, she thought of her isolation in this world of new religions and mortal men. Other than herself, Odalinde was perhaps the last of the remaining Orphists in this new land. The old woman knew the ancients, her mother's people, still existed in the Old World, barricaded behind secret landscapes in the forests and mountains. But in this land, the religion was almost dead. She'd never even known of Odalinde's existence. Perhaps in a different century they'd have become allies. Lovers even.

Across the lake, the woman studied the faint outlines of the trees that formed the Klahr Orchard. It was there that the children had fled during her battle with Odalinde. The Klahrs had been their refuge that day. The owner of the orchard—a man named Georg, she would learn later—was the man who'd threatened her, aiming his shotgun and barking demands at the old woman, attempting heroism in a world of cowards and indifference. He had failed, of course, but she sensed during that brief, intense confrontation that a mean-

ness—or even fury—existed in the man. A fury reserved only for his enemies, which she, no doubt, was one. There was
no question of that. But Georg Klahr would know one day
soon what it meant to be her enemy. He would know all too
well.

The witch made a low, growling sound as she envisioned
the horrific man and his wife sleeping in their bed. If she
wished, she could easily kill them now without either of
them ever knowing she was there.

But killing the Klahrs wasn't the goal. The goal was to
find Gretel. And despite all the pleasure she would get from
the feel of soft flesh between her fingers and the smell of
blood as it mixed with cotton linen and the wood of the
floorboards, the quick death of the Klahrs wouldn't help her.

She climbed the earthen steps that led from the lake to
the Morgan house, taking long, purposeful strides. She felt
young and spry now, and she suddenly couldn't wait for the
daylight to arrive. She reached the back of the house and attempted to slide open the door of the basement, eager to begin her search of the home. It was locked, immovable. The
woman had no expectations that the Morgans would still be
home. Given the trauma they endured, it would have been
shocking to find them still living in the place where Heinrich
Morgan had betrayed his wife and children before meeting
his death on the property's gravel driveway.

She'd hoped they were living across the lake with the
Klahrs, but as she stood next to the stone outer wall of the
home's lower level, she sensed the family had not only left the
home, but also the Back Country entirely. She wasn't quite

sure where this sense arose, but that was part of her new magic.

What she hadn't known when she set off from her cabin two days ago was whether other occupants had taken up in the Morgan home—renters or transients—and it was a bit of a risk to arrive so openly on the property, even under the cape of night. But she wasn't careless. She was prepared to act. Had there been others, she would have rid them as she would any infestation, quickly and with as little mess as possible. The consequences of any extermination would have made her plan a bit more elaborate, that was true, but elaborate plans were not impossible to carry out; they just required more attention to detail.

The home was vacant, however, so her worries had been unnecessary, but she wouldn't allow herself to get negligent. She would stay in the home only as long as necessary, until she learned where the Morgan women had gone. Then she would follow them. Her hope was that she could achieve this knowledge without anyone discovering she was ever there, but she would keep close watch on the Klahrs, just in case. If there were no clues in the Morgan home, she was certain to find some in the minds of the elderly neighbors.

The woman walked from the rear of the house and up the hill to the front porch. She climbed to the top of the staircase, where she turned around and surveyed the front of the Morgan property. She closed her eyes and thought of the day she'd first met Gretel and her brother Hansel, as well as Odalinde and that officer's son, Petr. It was here, on this spot. She'd felt such power that day, standing high above them all like a god, controlling Heinrich like a puppet while mesmerizing each of them with her newfound youth and clarity. The moment had been fleeting, but even now, almost a year later, she basked in the ecstasy of the memory.

Gretel, however, had been brazen that day, and the depth of character and strength she emanated during their encounter had disconcerted the old woman. She wouldn't have said she felt scared of Gretel that day, not exactly—especially considering the presence of the Orphist and the attention she was sure to garner at some point in the encounter—but the old woman knew instantly that Gretel was unique. Barely a teenager, she was sure to be a formidable foe.

The woman reached for the top of her head where Gretel had lodged the horns of the iron hammer. She swallowed intensively at the memory of the pain and suppressed the urge to gag. She grimaced, glowering into the woods beyond the yard, picturing in her mind the violence she would produce. Whatever fear she may have had for the girl during that first meeting, hate and revenge now eclipsed.

As did the hunger.

Above all was the hunger for the girl's body. And the life it promised.

The witch turned toward the front door and tried the knob. It too was locked, but there was some give to it, some promise of letting her pass. She would work at it, and if she couldn't get through that way, she would find a window or crawl space. She would find a way in. It was fate, and fate never failed her. For now, though, she needed to rest, to restore her thoughts and polish her plans. Gretel and Anika were out there.

CHAPTER SEVEN

"WHY DON'T YOU STAY, Petr? Relax a little." Ben Richter stood tall in the back of the pickup truck with two fishing poles flanking him. "Sofia's coming." He paused and then said, "Well, she'll come if she knows you're here."

Petr ignored his friend and continued unloading the last of the gear, consisting of a tackle box and a cooler.

"Petr!"

"What?" Petr flinched. He looked around, expecting some impending danger. "What's wrong?"

"Did you hear me?"

"No, what happened?"

Ben rolled his eyes and shook his head slowly. "I said you should stay because Sofia is coming."

Petr dismissed this news with a slight shrug and flitter of his head. "No." He lightened his pitch. "I mean, I'd like to, but I can't."

Ben was bemused. "Why? It's Sunday morning, you're sixteen years old, and the sexiest girl in school wants to hang out with you by the fishing hole. Where do you have to be that is more important than that? And don't tell me church because I know damn well that's not the truth."

"I just can't; I have to go."

"I know. You said that. I asked you why you can't stay."

56

"Look Ben, I just can't. I just need to borrow your truck for a few hours. That was the deal. If the deal's off, then let me know and I'll figure something else out." Petr stood staring at his friend, waiting for the reply.

"You're an asshole," Ben said casually, a look of examination on his face as if he was just, at this moment, discovering this truth.

Petr closed his eyes and sighed. "Look, Ben, I'm sorry. I just have something to do this morning, and I can't really talk about it. That's all. Can I borrow your truck or not?"

"No," Ben said, and then tossed Petr the keys. "Pick us up at noon. Don't forget. That truck is our only way home. Sofia Karlsson will be none too happy about walking eight or nine miles in a wet bathing suit. Although that might make me kind of happy."

"I thought she wasn't coming unless I was here?"

"Yeah, well, when you don't show, I'll tell her something must have come up." Ben smiled. "It's kind of true."

Petr smiled back at Ben and then climbed into the driver's seat and started the ignition. He rolled down the window and said, "Tell Sofia I said hi," before driving off through a brume of dust.

"Yeah, sure," Ben said to no one.

As he got about fifty yards down the unpaved road, Petr could hear the word "asshole" being yelled behind him.

THE SYSTEM BARRACKS was over two hours from the lake, and Petr knew he'd never be back by noon. He had agreed to the arrangement as a condition for using Ben's truck, but he knew it was never to be. If he reached the barracks and immediately turned the truck around and headed back to the fishing hole, he might have made the time. But those weren't Petr's intentions. He planned to take whatever time he needed until he found someone in the System with answers to the whereabouts of the woman who killed his father and tortured the mother of the girl he loved.

From what Petr knew about his father's former employer—which, the more he thought about it, was surprisingly little—they didn't tell many tales out of school, so Petr knew he had his share of work ahead. But he was determined to get some answers or get tossed out trying.

Petr thought of Ben and frowned. He had knowingly lied to his friend, but he hadn't done so lightly. Petr knew fully the importance of a solid reputation in the Back Country, and particularly for him since he was a relative newcomer to the area. But this trip was critical and worth a couple of dings to his trustworthiness. He would make it up to his friend later.

The Klahrs owned a truck, of course, and Petr had weighed the advantages and likelihood of Mr. Klahr allowing him to use it. Ultimately, however, Petr thought better of it, knowing Georg would never have let Petr use the lone farm transport for his fruitless quest. At least not this quest. Not for him to chase down the System in some wild attempt to uncover the fantasy conspiracy of the century. Petr could have come up with a different story, of course, one about a girl or a job or something, but he hadn't become desperate enough to lie directly to the Klahrs. Not yet. He would evade and disguise and camouflage as often as needed, but not flat out lie. He realized that he might reach that juncture at some point in the future, but Petr had managed to avoid that place for at least another day.

He drove Ben's truck east on the Interways, away from the Back Country and toward the Urbanlands. The System barracks sat just outside the western border of the Urbanlands, only a few miles from where Petr was born and raised. It was so strange to Petr. It hadn't been two years since the day he first visited the Back Country, but it felt as if he'd lived there his whole life. Two lives, even. The Urbanlands and his parents now seemed like characters and places he had read about in a book.

He had first come to the Back Country with his father for a meeting at the Hengst Academy—a private school to which he'd been condemned for behavioral reasons. That meeting was now a forgetful blip in Petr's childhood memory, an experience that he was sure to look back on years later and wonder whether it had really happened.

The subsequent stop at the Morgan house, however, had altered his life forever. He would never forget that night. It was where Petr met Gretel for the first time, an encounter which ended with him watching Gretel's initial girlish timidity turn to strength and loyalty after he accidentally insulted her. He looked back on the encounter now and realized it was during that episode that he fell in love with her.

Love at first fight.

Here, again, as with every day since she left, something in the landscape of Petr's world reignited thoughts of Gretel. Sometimes the trigger was a concrete thing, tangible and real—the Morgan house, or perhaps her primitive canoe sitting bleakly, covered in leaves and age on the back of her property—other times it was a word or a thought that arrived violently in his mind, snapping his focus back to her, as if punishing him for straying.

She was the real reason he was on his way now to confront the System. About that he was sure. When Petr began his plan to search for the truth of the witch's disappearing corpse, he told himself that his father was the reason—that he had a responsibility to him to ensure the woman was truly dead and that justice had been served. But that wasn't entirely true. Maybe not even mostly. He had cared deeply for his father. Despite the aloof and demanding nature of the man, Petr had always felt love from him. But his betrayal was devastating to his legacy, and it had cushioned Petr's feelings of mourning considerably. Or perhaps those feelings had just been transmuted from grief into something else, something more closely resembling anger.

With Gretel, his purpose was different, his pursuit more urgent. Petr loved Gretel. It was a feeling that swelled with each day that passed. If there was any chance she was still in danger, even if that chance was remote, he was going to protect her and push through any barriers to do so. She, too, deserved justice for what the witch had done to her and her mother, but with Gretel, Petr wasn't motivated by justice. Justice didn't inspire the same frenzy to action that preservation did.

As he approached the barracks, Petr mentally rehearsed what he was going to say once inside. He had to be confident, stand tall, and look into the eyes of everyone he spoke with and state his purpose for being there with expectancy in his voice. Most of the agents and administrators in the System knew who he was, of course. The son of the officer murdered by the immortal witch of the Northlands was not going to fly under the radar in this building, but in some ways, it worked to Petr's advantage. When he told them his suspicion, that the Witch of the North was alive, they would internally dismiss it as the misguided notion of a vigilante—a grief-blinded idea from a child consumed with his father's death.

They would think that, but they wouldn't ignore him.

His father's death entitled him to be heard. And even if most of them rolled their eyes at him in their hearts, they would still talk to him, if only to appear sympathetic. And when they spoke, if there was a cover-up about the details of the woman's death, someone would let it slip, and Petr would hear it immediately. He was certainly as familiar with the official report as anyone in the System, including the officers first on the scene.

On the other hand, if the reports were accurate and the woman was dead, he'd accept it, move on, and try his best to contribute to his life at the Klahr orchard in the depths of the Back Country. He would continue to miss Gretel and ache for her return, but he would be content in the knowledge that she was no longer the subject of a hunt.

Petr knew the truth, though. The witch was alive.

The call had come three days after the night in the cannery. The voice on the other end of the line had been that of a woman, though it was not feminine either in tone or language. She spoke quickly and directly, without introduction, and said only five words before immediately hanging up. The call lasted maybe ten seconds.

Have you seen her body?

The message was cryptic and out of context, but Petr never had any doubt as to the meaning of the rhetorical question. They had never found her. The System officers on site at the cannery the following morning never discovered a body. She was alive. And Petr wasn't the least bit surprised. He'd seen her in the flesh, terrifying and wicked, her strength beyond what any human could possess, her giant white teeth enveloping her face when she smiled. He had no doubt Gretel had injured her in the cannery, perhaps badly. But not mortally. No, she was alive, and it was now his duty to find her. To find her and kill her, forever this time.

Petr pulled Ben Richter's truck slowly into the lot of the barracks and parked in one of the isolated spots at the back, keeping his distance from the massive chrome cruisers that lined the front of the broad, charmless building. He felt his bladder and bowels strain, and the recent memory of the witch pulling back that black tarp to unveil his father's cruiser flooded him. She had been so measured and cocky that day, taunting him, completely void of sympathy or fear as she descended from the top of the porch staircase.

He sat quietly in the pickup truck and took five or six deep breaths, slowly and deliberately, until he felt somewhat composed. This was a technique he'd discovered recently, this deep breathing, micro-meditation method, and it had gotten him through many of his more solemn days. Sometimes it took ten breaths, sometimes two, but the pause was critical, and it grounded him to the moment.

He stepped from the truck and walked to the front of the System barracks, passing a pair of disinterested officers as he climbed the steps to the large, glass doors of the entrance. The height of the doors suggested the building was designed for some ancient race of giants, long dead perhaps, their stronghold now overrun with a human police force known as the System. These types of designs were no accident, and they certainly helped to disseminate the System's reputation as towering, futuristic soldiers—men of few words and many weapons. Of course, Petr knew the truth—that they were just regular people of ordinary size, and he would always just laugh and shake his head when his friends in the Back Country spoke of them mythically.

Petr stepped into the lobby and was immediately struck by the modernity of the place, as he always was since his days as a small child. A wall of televisions showing a rainbow of young people acting out various public service announcements greeted him, the subtitles suggesting they were giving tips on things like safety and civic responsibility. Along another wall, more TVs showed news programming and weather forecasts, as well as a running account of all the crimes that had been prevented because of the System's diligence. Petr could never quite figure out how anyone calculated "prevented crimes," but there it was on the monitor, its electronic form somehow making it seem more official.

What Petr didn't see were people. When he had last been there with his father years ago, and every time before then, an officer was always at the front, about twenty paces beyond the doors, positioned in a way that naturally drew visitors to the desk as they entered. But this setup was different. Instead of the scowling heavyset woman of his youth, there was an electronic bulletin board containing a digital listing of all the departments and their locations within the building. It seemed like a strange adaptation for a police barracks, but in a way, Petr was relieved, since he could now advance farther into the building without having to dive right into his theories about the zombie witch.

He perused the barracks' electronic directory for a few seconds and decided he would just head to the farthest area at the back of the floor, looking for someone important who'd be willing to talk to him. Perhaps he could get straight to the captain. And if he did happen to get that far, surely the teenage son of a fallen officer warranted a few minutes of his time.

Petr started toward the large frosted door at the far end of the barracks when he felt a hand fall on his shoulder.

"Can I help you find something, son?" a man's voice asked.

"Don't touch me!" Petr blurted, shuddering the hand from his back and spinning toward the assailant.

"Whoa buddy, easy," the man said in mock fear, "I'm just trying to help. Don't swing."

Petr vaguely recognized the man, and the bemused look on the officer's face turned to a squint of searching, seamlessly replacing the scowl of mistrust.

"Petr?"

Petr nodded.

The man's playful tone dropped to a somber baritone. "Petr, how are you? I...what's wrong?"

Petr shook his head slowly, giving up the puzzle of the man's name. "I'm sorry, I don't remember your name."

"Dodd. Officer Dodd. Your father and I were friends."

CHAPTER EIGHT

HANSEL SAT QUIETLY in the far corner of the room he shared with his sister, his arms folded across his chest, his head tilted slightly forward in a posture of pouting.

Gretel had been watching him on and off for several hours now, occasionally asking him if he was ready to talk—about their travel plans, their mother, or any subject he chose—to which he simply responded, "No" or shook his head in dissent. Other than this single-word response, he said nothing at all.

"Hansel, it will be okay." Gretel tried again, not convinced of her own statement.

Hansel said nothing.

"We'll be back together before you know it."

"Why does she want us to leave?" Hansel finally blurted. "I don't understand."

Gretel had sat with her brother while their mother told Hansel about her sickness and about the hopes she had of tracking down those who could cure her. About the unknown journey she had to make—alone—to the isolated tribal lands of her ancestors. She had explained it all in the simplest way possible, which wasn't very simple at all.

"I'm not leaving you," she had told him. "I'm sending you home. And I have every intention and belief that I will join you there one day. One day soon."

But their mother's optimism hadn't penetrated either of her children. She had found a pair of their distant kin—or so they claimed—to take her on the journey. One was to navigate and another was to translate upon arrival. Gretel normally would have felt extremely distrustful of this arrangement, like her mother was being lured into some con to be robbed and raped. But the trust she felt for these distant Aulwurms was deep, and it seemed like, in a matter of only a few months, they had come to love Anika like a daughter.

But despite their sincere intentions, Gretel didn't feel great about the prospects of success for this upcoming journey her mother was about to take. The Old World Aulwurms were always so positive and philosophical, but it was unclear to Gretel if they even understood what their mother sought, let alone how and where exactly she would find it in the mountains beyond the borders.

And then there was the journey itself; though not terribly distant as the crow flies, by the telling of it, the terrain and ascent could be rather treacherous.

Everything suddenly felt very vague to Gretel, and the more she weighed the odds of seeing her mother again, the more she suddenly wanted to join with Hansel and talk her out of it.

But that option was no longer on the table.

"It's time for us to go home, Hansel. And mother must try to live. It's as simple as that. We can't go with her where she's going, so we have to go back to our lives."

"I don't want to go back!" Hansel was crying now. "I never want to go in that house again!"

Gretel moved to her brother and put her arms around him. "We'll stay with the Klahrs for a while. The migrant workers should be gone by the time we get home. They'll have plenty of room for us. They'll be overjoyed we're home."

Hansel's sobs lessened just slightly.

"And you'll see your old friends. You really haven't made any friends here, so that will be nice, right?"

"I guess."

Gretel closed her eyes for a few beats, considering her next words, and then said, "Listen Hansel, I can't tell you for sure that mother is going to be okay." She paused to gauge her brother's reaction, and sensing none, she continued. "But I do know that this decision she's made will give her the best chance of being with us for as long as possible. We can trust her as far as that is concerned, right?"

Hansel nodded.

"We just have to trust her." Gretel said this last sentence to Hansel, but she was really speaking it to herself.

Hansel was quiet now, and Gretel kept him embraced.

"I get feelings sometimes Hansel, feelings that are almost impossible to explain. The only way I can describe it is that I can sense when certain forces in the world or the universe or something are guiding me toward what is true or right."

"What?"

"I'm not describing it properly." Gretel sighed and shook her head quickly as if to reset everything she'd just said and was now starting over. "Okay, remember when we were little and we would play hide and seek? And you would always accuse me of cheating because I would find you almost immediately?"

"You did cheat."

Gretel laughed. "I didn't! I just knew. After a while, I only pretended not to know, but I always did."

"But how?"

"I don't know. And that's just a small example. I've always just sort of known. Even when mother went missing, I always felt she was alive. I didn't know where she was, obviously, but I always knew I'd see her again."

"And you feel that now?"

"I can't promise you everything will turn out all right, I'm not some kind of seer who can see the future or anything like that, but I know these decisions are the right things to do. Mother has to go seek her cure, and we have to go home and be with the Klahrs."

"I do trust mother, Gretel, but more than that, I trust you."

Gretel smiled and gave her brother a final squeeze, holding back impending tears. "Good. Mother will be home from her appointment soon, and I want you to talk to her. As soon as she comes in. Tell her you can't wait until we're all home together again."

What Gretel didn't speak of was the witch, the idea of whom had jostled some divining rod within Gretel, some deep understanding that what her mother said may be possible and that Petr was right.

What if she was alive?

Was it even a possibility? Neither she nor her mother had descended the ladder that night to make sure she was dead. She hadn't even considered that the woman could be alive. Gretel had swung the hammer like an ancient god, connecting as cleanly and cruelly as she'd believed she was capable. But maybe that wasn't enough. The woman had demonstrated a strength that Gretel wouldn't have believed imaginable even in the strongest of men.

And she had flown. Never forget that part, Gretel, she told herself.

But she had also bled too. And her face had been badly deformed from the bowl strike during her mother's escape. And there was no question that she was exhausted outside the cannery that night as she sat and rested on the bank of the lake. She seemed like she could barely move. The woman had vulnerabilities, undoubtedly, and she and her mother—and Odalinde—had exposed many of them.

But none of those examples meant she was dead. Her weaknesses only suggested that the woman could die. Those were two very different things. Maybe a hammer wasn't enough.

Maybe, Gretel thought, the abominable crone needs to have her head sliced from her neck.

CHAPTER NINE

"OFFICER DODD?" PETR immediately was suspicious of the man in front of him and did nothing to hide it.

"That's right, Petr. You don't know me, but I know you. I meant to talk to you at your father's funeral but...well, there never seemed to be a good time. Anyway, I'm so sorry for your loss."

"You and my father were good friends?"

"Well, I guess I wouldn't say good friends, but we were friendly. He was a great officer. What happened...what she did to him...it could have happened to anyone."

Petr had thought a lot about his father's choices over the past year and came to a similar conclusion to that of Officer Dodd. Petr wasn't so sure anyone would have fallen victim to the temptations presented, but probably most would have. That belief subdued the sting of his father's failures only slightly.

"What are you doing here, Petr? You're a long way from the Back Country."

"You've kept up with my life, I see."

Dodd frowned at the implication that he was behaving like private detective. "Everyone here knows the story by now, Petr. And considering the folks you're living with were part of the story, yes, Petr, I know where you live."

Petr hesitated, first surveying Dodd's expression and then the station around him. "Is there somewhere we can talk?" he asked finally.

"Um, sure. My office is the third door on the left, just past the fountain. Have a seat in there. I have some things to finish up and I'll be right in."

Petr walked to the open door of Officer Dodd's office and glanced around the barracks one last time before entering, mildly curious as to what 'things' Dodd was finishing. He sat quietly in one of the two leather Carver chairs that faced Dodd's desk, which was a thick bulky piece made from some dark, coffee-colored wood. On each of the walls flanking the desk was a ceiling-high, half-filled bookshelf, both of which seemed to contain books devoted exclusively to policing.

Petr scanned the office, looking for family photos or memorabilia of some kind, but instead, he only saw the various framed awards and certificates of recognition that every officer in the System no doubt acquired over the years. Petr's father must have had at least fifty.

Dodd seemed like a real fun guy.

He's probably a bachelor, Petr thought. He seemed the type. The type who was friendly, but in a cold, creepy kind of way. The kind of man who would aggressively pursue any woman that showed him even the slightest interest, wearing her down until she was forced to tell him to screw off.

But it wasn't just that there were no family photos. There were no pictures at all in the office. No boating trips with buddies. No Mom and Dad at graduation. No Dodd and the dog at the beach. Yep, real fun guy.

Petr swiveled his head back over his shoulder to see if there was any sign of Dodd, and then, sensing nothing, he stood and walked to one of the bookshelves. He perused them slowly, looking at the titles of the books more closely—more out of boredom than anything—and saw nothing of interest to him. He walked behind Dodd's desk, for no other reason than to be irreverent, and made his way to the other side of the office and the opposite case of books. Police Procedures and Investigation, Advanced Law Enforcement, Police Firearms Tactics and Training. All in the same vein as the others. This guy is as square as a chessboard, Petr thought.

He looked up at the top shelf of the case and saw a lone book without any title on the spine. It was huge, boxy, and aged.

And black. As black as any object he'd ever seen.

"So what can I do for you, Petr?"

Petr pivoted toward Dodd and smashed his knee against the wooden desk. "Oww, dammit!" Petr's eyes filled with tears from the pain.

"Oooh," Dodd added, "that couldn't have felt good."

Petr looked at the officer and saw a meanness in the man's eyes, and maybe a trace of a smile.

"That's hickory. You'd be hard-pressed to find a wood more solid than that. Are you going to be all right?"

"I'm fine," Petr said as he backed his way into one of the visitor's chairs.

"It's your own fault. I told you to sit and wait for me in here, not explore."

"I'm sorry. I..."

"I'm just teasing, Petr. It's okay. I'm sorry. I guess I don't really know what to say to you. It's been a year, and I still can't believe it about Officer...about your father. How are you doing? Really?"

"Better." Petr couldn't have imagined anyone he would have rather talked to less about how he was coping with his father's loss. There was a frigidity in Dodd that no words could help warm.

Dodd stared at Petr, waiting for more, and then said, "You're a bit of a way from the Back Country."

Petr stayed silent.

"Is there something you need from us?"

Petr was right where he wanted to be when he set out just a few hours ago—in front of a System officer with the opportunity to ask all the questions he'd formulated over the past several months. But this didn't feel right. Dodd didn't feel right.

"I was hoping to speak with someone familiar with the case."

"Which case is that?"

Again, Petr saw Dodd's lips form just the hint of a curl, while his eyes stayed wide and locked. Petr couldn't have described precisely why, but he wanted to punch the man in his throat.

"The case," Petr replied, the light of his growing contempt for the man just beginning to shine through. "What other case would I be interested in?"

Dodd flinched, and his wide eyes narrowed by half at the boldness of the boy's words. He was almost glaring now, and his eyes never left the teenager sitting before him. "Of course. I'm sorry, Petr. I have so many cases I sometimes forget when I'm speaking with victims that..."

"I'm not the victim."

Dodd let the words linger without responding, and instead gave only a knowing nod. "Of course not. Families of the victim, I mean."

Petr supposed that was accurate, and so he let it stand. "There were reports that the woman's body was never found. That it somehow vanished from the site where Gretel killed her. I know that it sounds like a story kids tell in the school yard, but surely you've heard it?"

Dodd's pupils flashed for an instant, as if an old-time photo had been taken somewhere in his skull; the glint was so fast Petr wasn't sure if he had imagined it.

"Anyway, that's really what I'm interested in. Her body. If there's truth to the story."

Dodd stayed still for a beat and then closed his eyes and chuckled quietly, shaking his head as if, once again, he'd been worn down by the output of the rumor mill.

"I don't necessarily believe it, but my friends, they keep talking. You know how it is. So, anyway, I guess their talking got me doubting." Petr didn't take his eyes off Dodd, not even to blink. "Now I need to know for sure."

Dodd held the boy's stare, taking a more serious posture now. "I see."

"But again, sir, I don't want to waste your time. I would, though, like to speak with the person who was in charge of the case. Is in charge, I mean."

Petr knew about Dodd's involvement with the case. He'd read the public file and knew the officer was one of the lead detectives on the case and was on the scene at the cabin the day after it all came to a head. But he wasn't in charge of the case. In fact, judging by his mannerisms and attitude, Petr suspected Dodd had never been in charge of anything.

Petr also knew one other thing: Dodd was covering up something.

"Well, I'm not the overseer of your father's case, but I was—"

"I know about your involvement, Officer Dodd," Petr interrupted. "I'm very familiar with the case and am thankful for your contributions. But I was looking for a person with access to all the files."

Dodd was now visibly irritated by Petr's brashness and was probably embarrassed that he was getting badly beaten in their passive battle of words. Petr knew for the sake of progress he needed to walk things back, just a few steps to where they were a few minutes ago.

"I'm sorry, Officer Dodd, I don't mean to be rude, I'm just...I'm not dealing with any of this very well. I know there's nothing to the rumors. Of course I know that. But for my own peace of mind, to help me sleep and eat and just have a regular day, I need to know that she's dead. I don't need to see her body or anything. I just need to know. Who can tell me that? Please, I need to know."

Petr's words were sincere, if not the panicky way in which he said them. He wanted to speak with the lead investigator—the overseer, as Dodd put it—and to do so he would need to stir up some emotion. Petr knew he couldn't trust Dodd; a few minutes with the overseer and Petr hoped he would have a take on him as well.

"Wait here, Petr."

Dodd left for what must have been no more than three minutes, and when he returned he was followed into his office by an overweight man of about fifty, his slow pace and weary expression an indication of how much he wanted to be bothered with the inquiries of Petr Stenson.

The overseer, Petr presumed.

"Sir, this is Petr Stenson." Dodd's introduction went only one way.

"Hello, Petr." The overseer's voice was gravelly and deep, oozing authority.

Petr was immediately intimidated, but did his best to stay poised. "Hello."

"First, I'd like to express my deepest condolences."

"Thanks. And you are?"

"I'm sorry, I thought Officer Dodd would have told you." The large man glanced over at Dodd, admonishing his inferior's lack of etiquette with a brief stare. "I'm Officer Conway. I'm the overseer of this case. Do you know what that means?"

"You're in charge?"

Conway smiled softly, and Petr saw a kindness in the man's face. "Well, not of everyone." His smile straightened. "But when it comes to the case of the woman who murdered your father, yes, I'm in charge. Did you have some information regarding this case? As I'm sure you know, it's closed for now."

"I understand, but I was hoping we could talk privately." Petr avoided Dodd's face.

Conway looked over at Dodd. "Can you spare your office for a few minutes? You're working on the case of those missing boys, right? Maybe you can see if there is anything new on that."

Petr consciously registered the missing boys.

"Sure, of course," Dodd agreed. "It was nice meeting you, Petr. I'm sure we'll cross paths again."

Petr took the last sentence as a veiled threat, but out of context, they were innocent words of parting. Anyone watching wouldn't have blinked at them. And Officer Conway didn't.

"What's on your mind, son?"

Petr knew the man in front of him wasn't going to give him much time, so if he wanted to get his point out, he was going to have to do it immediately. This was a man he thought he could trust, and he took the plunge. "She's alive, isn't she?"

"What are you talking about, Petr?"

The lump in Petr's throat almost prevented him from repeating his question, but he kept going. "The witch. She's alive, right?"

"No. What? Why would you think that?"

"Did you ever see the body? Did you see her dead?"

Conway shook his head dismissively. "The reports stated that she was..."

"I know about the reports!" Petr shouted.

Officer Conway let the yell drift in the office without comment. There was no need to tell Petr to calm himself.

"I'm sorry, sir."

"I'm a very busy person, Petr. If you have some information about this case that you would like to share with me, I'll be happy to hear it. If not, I'll have to excuse myself."

"I don't have any information."

Conway raised his eyebrows and tilted his head as if to say, *Well, I guess that's that*.

"I have a theory."

"I'm sorry son, but—"

"Isn't that how it works? As detectives? When you don't know what happened, don't you weigh the evidence and formulate a theory?"

Conway frowned and lowered his head forward. "Yes, we do. When we don't know what happened. Unlike the case of your father where we know exactly what happened."

"Please, Officer Conway, just answer my one question honestly. For now, that's all I ask."

Conway grinned slightly, presumably at the for now part of Petr's request. "Okay, son. What question is that?"

"Based on everything you know about the case, is it possible she's still alive?"

Overseer Conway hesitated and stared directly at Petr, and Petr had his answer before the words were spoken. "I don't believe that to be true, Petr, but I suppose it's possible. Now, as I said, I've got a lot of work. You have yourself a nice rest of your day."

Conway sat on the edge of Dodd's desk with his arms folded, the last sentence an indicator that it wasn't Conway who would be leaving.

Petr stood and walked out of the office muttering his thanks, and he kept his eyes down as he exited the station and made his way to the truck. As he reached for the handle of Ben Richter's truck, he saw Officer Dodd in the side mirror. The officer stood pole straight, arms at his sides, staring at Petr. And from what Petr could tell, he was smiling.

Petr barely paused, and then in one motion opened the door and hopped in the driver's seat. He started the engine and headed back to the Back Country. As he drove, he thought how he wished he had stayed back at the fishing hole and spent the day with Sofia Karlsson.

CHAPTER TEN

GRETEL SPENT THE NEXT few days packing and planning her travel with Hansel. She hadn't brought much from home to begin with and had acquired virtually nothing during her time in the Old Country, so the packing part had been simple. The planning part was a little more involved, but not much. Their mother had already arranged passage for two with a private cabin on a transoceanic vessel known as the Schwebenberg, scheduled to depart on the last day of the month, which, though it was only days away, wasn't soon enough for Gretel. Of course, she wanted to be with her mother—and still spent a portion of her remaining days trying to convince her to come home with them—but with the seeds of danger for the Klahrs now planted, Gretel's anxiety was in full bloom.

And when the last day of the month arrived, she and Hansel were first in line at the dock before sunrise, suitcases in hand. They were going home. Finally.

Gretel's senses were mixed with love and longing. And danger. Her body raced with it.

CHAPTER ELEVEN

"GEORG, ARE YOU ALMOST out of there?" Amanda Klahr stood in their bedroom staring out across the lake to the Morgan property. As she did most nights, she thought of Gretel.

"Just another minute," Georg called from behind the bathroom door.

Amanda dimmed the lights to full darkness and continued staring out the window. The night was a black blanket, and she could only occasionally see a ripple of light off the lake. She closed her eyes, and when she opened them again she saw a beacon coming from inside the Morgan home. It was just an instant, a flash, and then it went dark.

Amanda moved closer to the window until her face nearly pressed against it. Her eyes were wide, disbelieving. Her urge was to call for her husband, but she didn't want to ruin the chance of seeing the light again.

And then it flashed on again, but this time it held steady. And it was moving now, clearly being walked about by someone inside.

"Georg." The words caught in her larynx and stuck there. She cleared her throat. "Georg! Come here!"

There was a scurry from the bathroom and Georg burst out, knowing undoubtedly the tenor of terror in his wife's voice. "What's wrong, Manda?"

"There." Amanda pointed across to Gretel's house. "It was inside the house, Georg. A light. It's out now, but it was there. I saw it twice."

"A light?"

"Yes, a light! A flashlight or...a lantern maybe. Wait for it. It will be back."

"Maybe I should go check on it."

"No!"

"Okay, okay. But why not? What's spooking you, dear?"

Amanda glanced over at her husband as if she'd been suspected of hiding something, and then turned back to the window. "Nothing's spooking me. Just don't go over there."

Georg stared at his wife for a few beats and then turned back to find the light. But it was out. At least for now.

Amanda would see it again later that night.

THE WOMAN KNEW THE risk the flashlight posed to her concealment, but she had been there almost two weeks and had yet to find any clue as to the whereabouts of the Morgan family. She was desperate for information. She was desperate to begin the blending process again. It was time to move forward.

Since her arrival, the woman had made watching the Klahr house her main activity, and she was pleasantly surprised at how easy it was to track the movements of their rote lives, which consisted mostly of gardening and field work. The man—Georg—spent his days like some deranged railroad worker, splitting the dry, empty ground with his pickaxe for what appeared to be no purpose; the woman seemed to do nothing at all, except for running the occasional errand at the market.

Petr, however, was a bit more mysterious.

From what she could tell, he wasn't home often. This wasn't necessarily a surprise—he was a teenage boy, after all—but her enhanced senses told her there was something beyond just schooling and social calls taking up his time. They told her it was something to do with her?

She couldn't trust this last feeling completely. Just as her physical senses were enhanced, she suspected so too was her sense of importance. Some might have called it paranoia or delusions of grandeur, but at least she was cognizant enough to recognize it. At least she was still aware of her addiction. And that was worth something. Perhaps there was no one looking for her. Perhaps nobody cared at all where her body had gone.

But that didn't feel quite right either. And her sense was that there were others beyond Petr looking for her.

The woman found the knob and instantly flicked the flashlight off before opening the door. There was enough ambient light outside for her to navigate the porch stairs and the yard, as well as the steps down to the lake; there was no reason to risk anything more than necessary. She tapped her toe to the first step of the porch and then began her descent of the stairs, breathing deeply the night air. It was still exhilarating, all these months later. She'd never dismiss the glory of oxygen again, not since she'd come so close to choking on her own skull.

The night was dark and quiet, but the woman sensed it was still too early. The Klahrs were old, but from what she had observed, they were the kind of folks who stayed up late and woke up at dawn. That was fine. She would use the hours to fine tune her strategy for this night.

The woman felt her way toward the back of the house and flicked on the flashlight for just an instant to get her bearings. She was at the top of the staircase of timbered railroad ties that led to the lake. She focused the beam of light to her left and shined it on the tarp covering what she had assumed over the past several days was some type of small boat. She had meant to uncover it days ago, but she'd been too afraid of exposing herself during the day, and at night she simply hadn't the energy. But tonight, she was rested and ready to explore it.

The witch had no doubt the boat underneath was the same one young Gretel and her mother had escaped in on that infamous night a year ago.

The woman mapped out her steps to the tarp and turned off the light, though at this hour she was becoming less and less worried about anyone spotting her. Only the Klahrs could have seen the light from this point on the property, and only then if they were scouting the house closely, which she couldn't imagine for what purpose they would be doing that.

She walked the estimated paces and could now see the outline of the tarp. It was definitely the canoe. She pulled off the tarp and flung it to the leaf-littered ground. Something scurried on the floorboards, running from side to side, trapped by the hull.

The woman closed her eyes and listened. She found herself enjoying the peace and tranquility of the Back Country, listening not just to the panicky imprisoned rodent but to the scurry of the mammals in the trees and the buzz of insects in the distance. For a moment, she understood the magnetism of normalcy, of life appreciated for these moments of natural intoxication. But these moments didn't last. Regardless of the struggle to grip them in her mind, to feel them with all the cells in her body, they always faded. Often within seconds.

Only her potion made it last.

And with the addition of the sweet brown honey from her distant kin—the glorious blood and lymph and inner fluids of Anika and Gretel Morgan—she could make the euphoria last forever.

The ancient woman was now trancelike as she stood over the canoe, undistracted by the tiny claw taps of the tiring animal below. She breathed deeply again, extending her neck forward as if smelling the air. She held in the breath and then opened her eyes, and a smile formed as she punched her arm downward, her hand clawed with nails extended.

The woman felt no resistance; she only knew she'd struck her target by the silence that followed. She lifted the mouse to her face and was disappointed at the size of the creature; with all that noise, she'd hoped for more. But it would have to do. She was hungry, and the Morgans hadn't left much behind.

Like a reptile, she swallowed the rodent whole. It wasn't her ideal method of eating, but she didn't see the point in wasting energy on skinning and gutting anything so tiny.

This was purely for sustenance. Her delicacies would come later. Perhaps even later tonight.

The woman grabbed the bow of the boat and pulled it toward the steps leading to the water's edge. The slope leading down wasn't too severe, and she managed the canoe to the shoreline with little fuss.

And then she waited. Another few hours maybe, and then she'd be on her way to discovering the whereabouts of Anika and Gretel and Hansel Morgan.

CHAPTER TWELVE

DODD READ OVER HIS notes one more time and then tucked the book deep into the glove box of the cruiser. It was his interview with the boy who had heard the screams of his friends coming from the backyard of the cabin. The cabin where the infamous woman of the Northlands once tried to make a meal of a young mother.

During the interview, which Dodd had tried to make casual and conversational, the boy's mother had sat in with her son—Franklin—while the father roamed from room to room, uninterested in the plot of the investigation, scoffing at the suggestion of foul play.

"The boys were no good," he had offered. "They ran away. It's as simple as that. If you knew the boys' parents, you wouldn't be considering any other possibilities."

"I've spoken with them, Mr. Blixt," Dodd had replied, just to keep the record straight.

"Well then, you know."

"And the screams, sir? What about the screams your son heard?"

"What do you mean 'screams?' Those boys are pranksters. They were only scaring Frankie. And they done it too. All of ya. Look at all of ya."

Had Dodd not known better, he may have considered Mr. Blixt a suspect, so eager to turn thoughts away from the idea that a crime had been committed.

But Dodd did know better.

He had questioned Mr. Blixt further, fishing for more details about the missing boys, gathering what theories he could to form a reasonable explanation for the disappearance of seemingly happy, if somewhat neglected, children. But Dodd had no doubt about the truth. He had been waiting for months for a call just like the one that had come across his radio two weeks back. And when it finally came, he had known instantly the woman was free from her hatch and had murdered the children coldly.

Obviously though, his report would have to say something much different.

And so, it had. After a week of searches from the local constabulary and a handful of volunteers, and then another week of searches and interviews from the System, Dodd had closed the case from his end and turned it over to the Department of the Missing and Absent. Dodd's official conclusion: runaways.

M&A would disseminate pictures of the boys, but the System searches would not continue. If the boys' bodies were ever found, it wouldn't be by his organization. He supposed the boys' parents could finance whatever search parties they could afford—maybe hire some hounds from a local hunter to go over the area around the cabin one more time—but judging by his official interviews with those folks, Dodd doubted there would be much to finance their own investigation. Dodd didn't care what they did now; he was clean of the case and could now focus his efforts on the only thing he cared about—finding the witch.

Dodd stepped out of the cruiser and walked to the area where Franklin had said he and his friends were when he ran off. It wasn't far from the pit where the woman had hidden for all those months. He'd been here several times during the investigation, of course, but he wanted one last look to make sure he hadn't bypassed anything noteworthy.

Finding nothing on the ground, he walked around to the back of the cabin and stepped into the house through a door that led to the kitchen. He walked to the counter where the residue of Officer Stenson's blood and brain nuggets remained. Despite the post-investigation cleaning of the place, the stains remained. Wood was a stubborn possessor of human fluid.

"Where did you go?" Dodd spoke aloud, clearly, as if the woman were standing in front of him.

He looked at the ground where the broken shards of the clay cauldron had been; he recognized the exact place by the stains. Stains of the broth. This was what it was for, he reminded himself. There it was, the brew of life.

He thought back to those first hours when he'd arrived on the crime scene, his initial nausea at the sight of Officer Stenson's body wickedly mauled on the kitchen floor.

And the book that sat so innocently on the counter above.

The huge weathered folio had sat spread like a prehistoric moth, beckoning to be read, teasing him with symbols and hieroglyphs that looked as if they had been rubbed from the inner walls of the Great Pyramids. He'd been entranced by the thing, momentarily taken out of the moment to some unknown past like an actor in a play, or a child steeped in the funhouse at an amusement park.

There had been no time to think; he had folded the book shut and grabbed it, covering it between his arms and chest, rushing the tome to his cruiser like a burglar, violating countless steps of crime-scene protocol.

He thought of the book now and the decision he had made to pull it from the shelf of his office and stash it beneath the passenger seat of his patrol car. The boy, Petr, had seemed drawn to it in his office, but that may just have been Dodd's own paranoia. Whichever, bringing the book with him had felt like the proper call at the time, and standing here now in the stale lair of this killer hermit only reinforced the feeling.

Dodd stared toward the front entranceway of the cabin. "Where would I go if were you? Maybe that's the better question?" He paused, giving his question sincere thought. "I'd bury those boys somewhere nice and safe, far from this place. Deep in the ground, but not so deep that scavengers wouldn't get to them within a few days. And then where?"

Dodd walked out the front door and stood on the cabin's porch for a moment, staring into the woods at the possibilities. He descended the staircase of the porch to the warped, faded boardwalk that met the bottom wooden step. He breathed in the crisp air and closed his eyes, bowing his head forward meditatively.

And then he had his answer.

Dodd opened his eyes and lifted his head and turned his whole body south toward the tree line.

"If I were you, I'd want revenge."

CHAPTER THIRTEEN

THE WOMAN SMACKED HER neck reflexively and instantly felt the splatter spread between her palm and throat. On the down stroke, the nail of her middle finger caught high on her cheek, slicing the skin wide and deep. She'd fallen asleep, and the mosquitos had taken advantage of the blood source. She'd felt the bites in her dreams, and now she wondered whether the potion had made her more attractive to the pests.

She was awake now, alert, panicked at the notion that morning was close. There was no sign of the sun yet, and she didn't have the feeling that she'd been asleep for long, but there was no way to be sure.

The witch stood and stared across the lake at the Klahr house. The structure was so still and quiet it looked abandoned. But they were there. Old and beaten by life. As vulnerable as a cricket in a spider's web. If she was going to go tonight, which was the decision she'd made earlier that morning, then there was no more time to waste.

She moved the boat into position and shoved it out on the water, hopping in deftly just as the stern end of the hull caught the waterline.

There was only one oar, and it took the woman a few moments to figure out the propulsion at first, but she adapted quickly, learning to alternate the oar from starboard to port with every other scull, moving the canoe effectively toward her target. And with the wind direction in her favor, she was moving at a speed that she figured would put her at the bank in little more than five or six minutes.

She held the flashlight between her feet, careful not to let it roll too far. If she lost the thing over the side or if the bulb broke, her upcoming mission would be far more difficult. By now she'd learned the nuances of the Morgan property; the Klahr orchard, however, was a much different story. She'd been able to study it a bit from across the lake, secretly, ducking behind branches at every chirp or plop of the water, and from what she'd learned, the landscape appeared to be an obstacle course of trees and uneven ground. And that assessment didn't include the ladders and tools that littered every farm as well as the vast collection of picking buckets strewn about the property, idly tossed aside by the pickers, now waiting in vain to be used for the next harvest that was still months away.

The witch felt the resistance from the bottom of the lake, the signal that she'd reached the bank of the orchard. She dug the oar into the muddy ground and raked the canoe up as far as possible to the shore, stepping over the bow carefully and stretching her foot as far as possible to avoid sinking her shoe beneath the water. She cleared the water, but her foot found a thick pocket of mud that instantly devoured her foot up to the ankle. She brought her other foot to the ground, trying to get leverage to free her first foot, but her second foot found a similar patch of mud, and she nearly toppled completely to the wet ground, only the deep, muddy capture of both her sunken feet keeping her upright.

The woman whispered a curse as she slowly freed her feet, careful not to lose her shoes, before taking the first steps up the bank in the direction of the house where she continued to find weak, damp earth beneath her feet. The wet heaviness of the mud and lake water seemed to pervade her shoes and cuffs, and she cursed again, louder this time, as she finally stood on solid ground kicking and shaking the loose strands of mud from her shoe.

The woman now turned toward the house, but she was disoriented from the gloom and her missteps out of the canoe, and in the darkness she could only vaguely see the structure in the distance. She could just barely make out the shapes of the orchard trees, which, judging by the smell, were almost directly in front of her. She reached a hand forward and touched a branch and then formed her hand around the pear that hung from it. She plucked the ripened fruit and held it to her nose, grimacing at the smell before dropping it at her feet.

The woman pulled the flashlight from the pocket of her robe and reluctantly switched it on, keeping the direction of the beam to the ground. She then began walking toward the Klahrs. The hunt was about to begin.

CHAPTER FOURTEEN

"GRETEL!" AMANDA KLAHR woke with a scream and raised her hands to her mouth to catch the last part of the gasping cry. It was the third time this week she'd awoken this way, and it was only Wednesday.

The dreams weren't new though; they'd started almost immediately after Gretel left for the Old World. They hadn't started off as debilitating—she had almost expected them to come—and at first they had done little more than leave her with a residue of disappointment in the morning when she awoke to the reality of Gretel's absence.

But gradually the dreams had grown more intense and detailed, and by around the sixth month of Gretel's absence, Amanda began to dread sleep.

"You okay, hon?" Georg's words were mechanical and barely above a whisper. He'd recently adapted to her outbursts and now mostly slept through them.

"Yes," Amanda replied absently. Even now, she felt the hint of embarrassment at her unconscious eruptions and had resigned herself to the belief that she'd likely never overcome them. "I thought I might have heard something outside."

Georg only cleared his throat and turned toward her, never opening his eyes.

Amanda climbed from the bed and walked to the bathroom, replaying the sound in her head, knowing full well the "something" she might have heard almost certainly had occurred in her dream. She used the toilet and then stood at the sink, staring in the mirror at her tired eyes.

The sound resonated again, outside the dream this time, somewhere in the distance.

Amanda's drooping eyelids shot open, and she jerked her head toward the window. Her mouth hung open as she looked toward the ceiling, listening.

The sound once again, this time fainter than the last.

Amanda walked slowly toward the window, barely lifting her feet from the floor. The last sound had been almost imperceptible, and even the patter of a slippered step would have drowned it out. She debated waking Georg but decided against it. She knew if she did, he would tell her that he was happy she'd done it, can't be too careful, but it wasn't fair to continue robbing him of his sleep because there was a fox in the orchard or a rat scavenging through one of the picking buckets.

Amanda arrived at the window that overlooked the orchard, but she could see only her reflection in the glass. She'd left the bathroom light on, and the glare made the night invisible from the room. She turned and began walking to the bathroom when she heard the noise again. A voice this time. She was sure of it.

She took the three or four remaining steps to the bathroom, this time as if she were escaping a fire, and toggled the light switch off. She rushed back to the window and pressed her face to the glass. And she saw it instantly, fifty yards or so in the distance, just in front of the lake. A light. No doubt the same one she'd seen coming from Gretel's house. And next to the light, hovering above like a phantom, was the black outline of a person. She was standing erect, staring at Amanda, a wide dirty smile just visible on her face. Amanda knew instantly who it was. There was no question at all in her mind.

"Georg!"

"Amanda." Georg Klahr sprang upright in his bed at a speed he'd probably not demonstrated in thirty years.

"Georg, I saw her! She's right outside!" Amanda squinted out the window now, cupping her eyes, trying to find the shape of the woman. The beacon of light was gone now, but she thought she could see movement somewhere in the orchard.

Georg had bypassed the slippers beneath his side of the bed and was now standing at his wife's side, pressing the sleep from his eyes with his fingertips.

Amanda looked over at him in disbelief, a new thought now lodged in her mind. "Oh my god, Georg," she said, her voice low and hoarse, "Petr was right. He was right all along. I can't believe it. I can't believe she's alive."

Georg was fully awake now and immersed in the moment. He had made his way to the armoire that faced their bed, reaching into the space between the wall and the wardrobe where the twelve-gauge shotgun patiently waited. "Are you sure it's her? I mean..." He shook his head, confused. "How can you be sure, Amanda?"

Amanda wanted to scream at her husband for doubting her, but she could hear the fear in his voice, and she wanted to bring them both back to a state of calm. They needed to be clear-headed right now. "It's her, Georg. And if it's not, then I don't—"

The unmistakable creak of the front door hinges rang through the house. The sound was deafening, as if amplified by the night and the tension.

"Stay here, Amanda," Georg commanded. He picked up the gun, holding it casually as he walked to the door of the bedroom.

"Georg!" Amanda replied in a whisper.

"It's okay."

Amanda saw the look of stillness in her husband's eyes and knew that he'd summoned something deep from within him. Whether it was true or not, Georg Klahr believed he was ready for whatever thing entered their home. She said a short, silent prayer that it was so.

From her position at the window, Amanda watched her husband cross through the bedroom doorway and stop at the landing. He was staring down the staircase into the blackness of the main floor. "What do you see, Georg?" she whispered.

Georg Klahr turned and looked at his wife for a beat and then turned his focus back to the stairs. He held up his index finger to Amanda, pausing her while he attempted to hear the noises coming from the level below. His mouth was open, anticipating, and he looked back at Amanda.

Amanda shook her head in confusion.

Georg shrugged at his wife; something was there, but he couldn't make out just what. Maybe they'd been wrong, after all. Maybe it was the wind.

But that wasn't right. She saw her. Smiling.

Amanda sighed and closed her eyes for just an instant, and in that moment—two seconds at most—the world filled with a sound so painful and unpleasant that Amanda's knees buckled under her, collapsing her to the floor. It was the sound of distress and agony. Georg's agony. She'd never heard a sound like it—from him or anyone. That sound would replace Gretel in her nightmares for the rest of Amanda's life.

"Georg." The words rattled from Amanda's mouth as if they'd been shot in the air on their way out. She got back to her feet and looked toward the top of the steps and then walked slowly to the threshold of the door. She wanted to rush to where he'd been, but her instincts took over and throttled back her pace, saving her from diving into her own disaster.

She couldn't see Georg anymore, but his screams continued below.

Amanda was crying now, covering her mouth to muffle her location; but the sound of her husband's pain, horrifying and tortuous, drowned her out completely, and seemed to be coming from every room of the main floor. Amanda fell to her knees again, distraught, and listened to the final dying sounds of her husband diminish into silence.

There was a pause, and then Amanda heard a final sound, a sustained wet, shredding sound that nearly caused her to vomit.

He was dead; Amanda did not allow hope for anything else. The tears streamed down her face in two equal rivers, one on each side.

"No. Not me. Not today."

Amanda backed away from the bedroom door and then felt her way back to the bathroom. Once inside, her instincts overpowered her grief and set her to work.

She kept the light off and locked herself in, positioning herself behind the door. It was no plan at all, really, but there wasn't much else to do at this point. If the woman forced herself inside, Amanda would fight. And likely die. She couldn't imagine much of a life without Georg anyway, so the prospect of death suddenly didn't trigger the fear that it had for most of Amanda's life. But she still had reasons to survive. Petr. Gretel.

The house was suddenly quiet again, and the locust-buzz of the night air had returned. And then, as if cued by the croak of a bullfrog, Amanda heard the click of shoes ascending the wooden staircase.

Amanda squeezed out the last of her tears and then frantically looked around the sink for something she could weaponize. Anything. She reached back behind the faucet and her fingers brushed against the bristles of a toothbrush that had dropped into the ceramic crevice between the faucet and backsplash and had stayed hidden there for what must have been weeks. It was an old wooden toothbrush, the kind that it seemed only she and Georg had used for far too long before finally switching to the more modern variety.

She pinched the neck of the toothbrush and fingered it up into her hand, bringing it up next to her face, gripping it so that the end of the handle faced outward like the blade of a knife. She stood motionless that way, holding her breath for what seemed like ten minutes but was probably only seconds, listening for the approach of footsteps to gauge the timing of her attack.

Like a bomb blast, the bedroom door slammed shut. The witch was now inside the bedroom, and with the door shut, escape would be nearly impossible. A fight was coming.

"Klahr woman?"

Amanda gagged at the sound of her name and at the dripping contempt in the woman's voice.

"I know you're here in this room. I can smell you. Like a piece of meat rotting in the sun."

The light of the bedroom flicked on; Amanda could see the strand of shining yellow under the door. Should she stay back from the door? Perhaps in the bathtub behind the curtain? Or should she position herself right in front, ready to attack the instant the door opened? She held her position for the moment, about halfway between the two options, not wanting to make any noise that would give proof of her presence.

"Your husband's spirit kept him from suffering. I hadn't suspected such fight from an old man. That wild axe play in the fields everyday paid off, it seems. He's dead, of course, that was never in question, but my plan had been to torture him first and then kill him. Sadly, he made that impossible. Too much resistance, you see. I can't take risks like that anymore." The woman paused, and her voice turned poisonous. "His body is at the foot of the stairs."

Amanda pulled open the door and rushed out toward the witch's voice. She held the toothbrush aloft and poised. The terror Amanda saw in the awful witch's eyes as she approached was inspiring, and it invigorated her muscles and reflexes to respond to the woman's fear.

The witch raised her hands to her face, protecting herself from the weapon that spiked down at her. Amanda realized the woman couldn't have known what she was holding in her fist. For the all old hag knew, Amanda was coming at her with an ice pick. The woman's psyche had sustained damage over the years, with Gretel and her mother playing no small part in the delivery of that emotional trauma.

Amanda swung the toothbrush down and caught the woman just above the eyebrow, digging it into her forehead before raising it again and giving one final vicious stab. The woman's skin was soft, and the feel of the wooden brush in her wrinkled flesh was primal and satisfying.

The woman growled at Amanda and backed away quickly, leaving Amanda off balance for just a moment. Amanda stumbled forward, and the witch grabbed her by the shoulders and spun her so that Amanda now faced the door. The witch collapsed upon her from behind like a leopard on an impala, chest to back, so that Amanda was pinned against the door. Amanda could feel the strength of the woman, a hardness in her muscles that Amanda had only known men to possess. She was helpless now. And with that feeling of helplessness came the knowledge that she would soon be dead.

"You have the spirit too, I see."

"Gretel will kill you next time." The words came from Amanda's mouth automatically, as if they weren't her words at all, a medium speaking the sentence of a soul long dead. She almost smiled at the sound of the witch gasping.

The witch opened her mouth to speak to rebut what Amanda had said, but the words didn't come.

"She's stronger than you. And you know that, don't you?"

The witch again said nothing.

"And what's more, she knows she's stronger than you. And that makes her even stronger." Amanda gave a defeated chuckle, as if she'd found the answer to a profound question but far too late for it to make any difference.

"Something tells me you may be right," the witch finally replied, her lips dusting the ears of Amanda with each word, the blood from the wound above her eye now spilling onto Amanda's cheek. "I've not had the pleasure of young Gretel's company for more than a few frantic moments at a time, but in those moments, my yes, she has shown a great strength. But, of course, she's an Aulwurm. We are strong on levels most in this world aren't even aware exist."

Amanda knew the name Aulwurm. Anika had mentioned it in the letter she delivered just before leaving for the Old World. It was the name of her ancestral family, the ones she and Gretel and Hansel sought.

"Were you not aware we were kin?"

Amanda was not aware of this part, but she didn't let on. "She'll kill you just the same. You Aulwurms don't seem to be a very close-knit family."

The witch brought her hand to Amanda's neck and gripped it just tight enough to allow her to breathe.

"Do it!" Amanda screamed.

The witch released the pressure just slightly and smiled. Amanda could feel the corners of her mouth turn up and the parting of her lips. "You won't die today, Amanda Klahr. I need you. You're going to tell me where Gretel and her mother have gone. And, if necessary, you'll take me to them."

Amanda laughed. "Is that what you think? That I know where they've gone?" Amanda laughed harder now. "I have no idea where they are. You might as well kill me here and now if you're expecting me to know that little bit of information."

The witch continued smiling, but Amanda could feel the stiffening tension in her body.

Amanda's voice was serious now, trying to avoid the tone of pleading. "She and Hansel never even said good-bye. They packed up and left in the night. Georg and I hardly even knew the mother. They wouldn't have told us where they were going. You're a fool if you think so."

The witch extended the nail of her right hand and brushed it down the side of Amanda's cheek, swirling the blood that had dripped there from the witch's eye wound. "You do know, Mrs. Klahr, I know you do." She paused and then stuck her nail into Amanda's cheek, piercing it all the way through until it came out on the inside of her mouth.

Amanda screamed, but the blood from the wound rushed to her throat and clogged the sound. She coughed it out and then screamed again.

"And for Petr's sake," the old woman continued, "you had better know."

CHAPTER FIFTEEN

"PETR, DON'T GO."

"I have to, Sofia. I haven't been home in two days."

Sofia Karlsson pouted and cocked her head. "Pleeease?"

If Petr had any hope of staying at the fishing hole for another hour or two, it was now wiped away entirely by Sofia's whining. He liked her just fine—she was very sweet and by far the prettiest of the girls in his group of friends—but her puerile tendencies were a turn off. He wanted her to not care what he did. It was the opposite though: when he brooded, she acted like a four-year-old, hoping it would convince him to see things her way. It hadn't worked yet; he had no idea why she kept trying.

Besides, he really did have to get home. It just felt wrong to be gone this long.

Since his meeting with Officer Dodd and Overseer Conway, Petr had kept quiet about the subject of the witch's missing body. He'd tripped a cord at the barracks, he was sure of it, certainly as far as Dodd was concerned anyway, and he now thought it wise to keep any further theories on the subject to himself for a while, especially since Georg had shown a mild interest in Petr's investigations lately. The last thing Petr wanted was to get Georg mixed up in his conspiracies.

So, Petr had asked Ben if he could stay at his house for a little while until the dust settled a bit. Ben's parents agreed after calling Amanda to get her approval, which she gave, though no doubt reluctantly, Petr had assumed. But it was just for a few days. No big deal.

But here it was only two days later and Petr wanted to go home—as much for the Klahrs as for himself.

"Ben told me you were staying with him. And Ben's not going anywhere. Are you Ben?"

Petr shuddered at the infantile lilt Sofia put on the question and immediately started walking back toward the pick-up truck.

"I was staying with Ben, but now I'm going home," he muttered, his back to the girl.

"Hey, you still haven't gotten your truck privileges back, young man," Ben Richter shouted from the pier. He didn't turn as he said it, focused instead on a taut fishing line and a potential bite in the water.

"It's fine, I'm walking," Petr shouted, his back still turned. "Thanks for the hospitality, Ben. I owe you one."

"One? Ha! Where did you learn to count?"

Petr smiled at this last dig and kept walking toward the road, his duffel across his back and his water jug in hand. His house was a little over three miles from the fishing hole; it was a walk he'd done a dozen times since moving in with the Klahrs.

"Hey, want some company?" Sofia tapped Petr on the opposite shoulder from where she'd run up on him, dragging her feet and kicking up dust as she arrived.

"Uh, well, sure. It's a little bit of a walk though. And if my...if Mr. Klahr isn't home, I won't be able to give you a ride back. At least not for a while anyway.

"I guess I'll have to hang out with you for the time being then." Sofia smiled at Petr, trying to get him to lock eyes with her, but Petr focused his attention on the road ahead.

The two teenagers walked in silence for a few moments, staring from the road to the woods that lined the pavement, pretending to be interested in the surrounding nature.

"I knew Gretel. Did you know that?"

Petr turned his head with a snap toward Sofia and stopped walking. Sofia stopped with him.

"Not well, but I knew her a little. She was always very nice to me. A little quiet, I guess, but nice. I can see why you would have liked her."

Petr forced a smile and nodded. This was the Sofia he liked, the sincere Sofia who had a knack for kind words. "Thank you for saying that, Sofia. I did...do like her."

Sofia smiled and raised her eyebrows. "Is she coming back?"

The two began their walk again, and Petr kept his gaze locked on his feet, pondering. "I think so, but..."

"What is it?"

"I had expected her back months ago. Certainly, by now. It's been a year. I honestly don't know if she's coming back. I hope so."

"Where did she go?"

Petr didn't respond.

"People say..." Sofia stopped and shook her head as if to strike the words.

Petr looked at her, his eyes wide with curiosity and defense. "What do they say?"

"That...that she's a witch, just like the one she killed. That—"

"That's not true!" Petr's words came out more like a growl than a yell, low and guttural.

"I don't believe it, Petr, of course not. I told you, I knew her and liked her, but some people have said that she was related to the witch in some way. A distant relative or something. I don't really know."

"I think I'd rather walk alone, actually." Petr stopped walking and faced Sofia, staring slightly up and past her eye line.

"Petr, I—"

"I would. Thank you," he interrupted. "I'll see you later. Please don't follow me."

Petr continued walking home, as fast as he could without running, listening to Sofia's footsteps as they faded in the opposite direction.

CHAPTER SIXTEEN

"YOU LIKE A DRINK, MADAM?" Oskar leaned back on the large stone boulder and closed his eyes in satisfaction, raising the iron mug to the sky as an offering. "It is, ah, how do you say it? Delicious!"

"Thank you, but I'm fine." Anika crouched in front of the fire, staring into the flames and rubbing her hands.

"It will keep you warm."

"The fire is plenty warm."

"Maybe you want Oskar to keep you warm." Oskar laughed at this, widening his eyes to show he was up for it if she was. He stared at Noah, who only looked away.

Anika's mouth opened slightly, and she shivered, instinctively hugging herself, tightening the perimeter of her body.

"I'm only for kidding, Anika. Relax. Have a drink!"

Anika stood from the fire and walked to a footprint of blankets and coats she had arranged as her bedding. "I'm going to try to sleep now. We'll leave at dawn."

Anika and her fellow travelers set off for the mountain home of her ancestors the day Hansel and Gretel boarded the *Schwebenberg*. There was no point in waiting, she decided; the one thing she knew for sure was that she wasn't going to get any better if she waited. And the sooner she got started on this desperate attempt to spare herself, to squeeze out a few more years in this living world, the sooner she'd know if there was any hope at all. Whether these people could help or not, only then would she be able to accept her fate and begin her journey back to the New Country to reunite with her children.

The Morgan family had all given each other their somber farewells that morning on the dock, surprisingly without any tears being shed. It had been hard for Anika to hold back the emotions she felt, and she imagined that was true for Gretel and Hansel as well; but for Anika, she had made the decision several days earlier that once she saw her children launch toward the New Country, she would get right to the work of healing. She wasn't going to spend critical moments worrying about them or what their lives without her would become. There was no reward in it, emotionally or otherwise. And once she began her trek up the Koudeheuvul Mountains, there would be no way to contact them anyway. She would just have to believe in the guidance of the universe and in her daughter's resolve. Anika didn't have the intuition of her Gretel, but she felt strongly in those two things.

And besides, with everything Hansel and Gretel had been through over the past two years, they would handle a sea crossing just fine. As for money, Anika had borrowed and saved enough to ensure they had plenty to get home, plus a little more for any trouble that arose along the way. The ten- or twelve-day voyage to the New Country would be through a smooth passage of sea, and they would have a relatively comfortable forward cabin, especially considering it was just the two of them taking up the space. The Schwebenberg would then dock about twenty minutes off the coast of the Urbanlands, where the children would take a tender to shore.

Once at port, they were to call the Klahrs.

Anika supposed the Klahrs were the wildcard in this whole plan. Would they even still be living in the orchard across the lake? How was their health? She couldn't have imagined them selling out and moving away, but their health concerned her. At a certain age, well-being was always a necessary consideration.

And then there was the question of forgiveness. What if they weren't willing to forgive them for vanishing and cutting off all communication with them?

But Anika dismissed this last notion almost immediately. Of course, they'd forgive. And even if they didn't forgive Anika—it was she, after all, who was to blame for their leaving and not staying in touch—they loved their Gretel. Anika saw it in their eyes when they spoke about her. They loved Gretel every bit as much as Anika did. And Gretel loved them with the same conviction. Yes, Hansel and Gretel would find their way home just fine.

Anika's journey, however, was a bit more involved.

"Noah? Hey Noah?" It was Oskar again, his drunkenness becoming more apparent with each syllable.

Noah gave only a dismissive grunt. He was lying away from the fire, shrouded in darkness, ostensibly trying to sleep.

"Noah, do you think she kind of likes me?" He erupted with laughter. It was the jovial, grog-impaired kind of laughter that always contained a dusting of sinisterness.

Anika pulled the wool blanket to her chin and listened, praying for just one or two more outbursts, followed by snoring. At the very least, though, Anika hoped Noah would chime in with a few subtle words of warning indicating he was ready for Oskar's foolishness to end. Noah was almost twice Oskar's size, and even if a drunken Oskar felt daring enough to defy his larger companion, if Noah truly wanted, he could bring Oskar to silence. But Noah was there as a guide, not a translator, and she now wondered if Noah even understood their conversations at all. He hadn't spoken since they set out.

Anika disliked Oskar from the day they met, but he was good with languages—as good as she could afford—and she needed someone who could translate complicated phrases and expressions, perhaps even some medical terminology that could make the difference between life and death.

But translations, she decided, would not come at the cost of her assault. She'd never live at the mercy of another person. Not ever again.

"I bet she does like me, right Noah? I mean, what is there not to like? I got my pretty face, my pretty teeth, a pretty big cock." He erupted with laughter again, this time almost choking on his ale. "Not as big as yours though, Noah! Ha ha! I never seen nobody's big as yours!"

Anika's expression became steely, and she lowered her hand to her shoe, keeping it hidden beneath the covering. She tapped the tip of the blade's handle with her middle finger and wrapped her hand around it before gliding it from her boot.

She raised her head a fraction and peeked over at Oskar, who had closed his eyes again and was leaning back against the rock. He was either asleep or almost there. Thank God, Anika thought, silently begging things wouldn't get messy now. Not yet. According to Noah—through Oskar's translation—they had another two days, which meant this camp night and then one more. She could make it. And once she got what she needed from the Aulwurm elders, whether that be a cure or a death sentence, Oskar could take his rotten liver to the summit of Mount Koude and jump. But for now, she still needed him.

"Anika, I'm feeling a little cold. This rock is so hard." Oskar's words were slurred but loud. He paused a beat and then shouted, "And so am I!"

Anika slithered her legs from the bedding and pushed the covers down with the soles of her feet. She rose in silence and stood on her bed quietly, knife in hand, eyes locked on the translator.

"I need something soft for my hard..."

The blade was microns from Oskar's Adam's apple before he could let out the last word of his vulgarity. Anika's hand was pressed against the back of the drunkard's neck as she placed her mouth next to the man's right ear, brushing it slightly with the chap of her lips. If the man swallowed, Anika would watch as he slit his own throat.

She turned the blade so it was now on its side, the flat cool steel against Oskar's neck, the blade pointing up toward his chin. "What do you think, translator? Is everyone going to make it through the next few days?"

Oskar was now fully awake and whimpering. "It was just some jokes, Anika. Nothing about real life."

Anika glanced over toward Noah's shadowy dwelling, examining the emptiness for any evidence that the larger guide was planning an attack to protect his imperiled companion. The two men had come as a package deal when the travel arrangements were made weeks ago, but Anika never got the impression they were at all acquainted. I guess she was about to find out.

"Jokes are funny, Oskar. So how could it be that you were telling jokes?"

"I am so sorry, okay. What you going to do? Kill me?"

Anika placed the edge of the blade on the fold of skin that bisected Oskar's chin and throat. "If you ever touch me, Oskar, or even take a step in my direction in a way that leads me to believe you're going to touch me, I will kill you, and with less thought than I'd give to smacking a mosquito that's landed on the back of my calf."

Oskar gave a nervous giggle and flashed a weak smile. "So then not that much thought, no?"

Anika smiled fully and relaxed the hand at the back of Oskar's neck. "You see, Oskar? That's a joke." She lowered the blade a half an inch and pulled the steel toward her, sliding the side of the knife against Oskar's stubbled skin, applying the slightest pressure as the metal drew against his windpipe. If the blade had been facing toward his throat, he would have been dead within seconds.

Oskar closed his eyes again and made a weeping sound.

"We leave at dawn then," Anika said flatly. "How does that sound to you, Noah?" Anika spoke up just slightly, directing her words to the empty space just outside the perimeter of the fire.

There was no answer at first and then she heard a response boom from the shadows. "Dawn."

AT DAWN, NO MENTION was made of the night before, and Anika wondered if Oskar remembered at all what had happened. It was the type of event, she thought, that people who live in the fog of intoxication must wonder about quite regularly. It was a strange way to exist, but there was something envious about it.

Anika's thoughts drifted back to her imprisonment at the cabin. The daily—sometimes twice daily—dosages of narcotics the despicable hag had administered to her, diluting the poison into her water and food, keeping her at once restrained and loquacious. Now, looking back on it with some distance, she appreciated the long-term barriers that had been erected by those drugs and the short-term memories that had been erased forever. There was so much horror she could remember; it was shocking to imagine what she had forgotten.

Noah stood at the foot of the path, appearing eager for the last full day's hike. He stood at least six foot five and had the girth of a sycamore. But he also had a kind face, the look of a person who'd been born to the wrong body, a man who had been judged on the surface because of his size but who would have enjoyed discussing literature and music and theatre. He was certainly quiet, but his quiet demeanor seemed to be more characteristic of introversion than unfriendliness or dimwittedness. Her trust in him was far from complete, but she thought the man emitted a good energy.

Oskar scuffled behind her, and Anika turned, ready to defend herself. But the translator's look and posture was anything but threatening. He teetered to one side, stumbling to keep balanced, looking pathetically around at the ground before scanning the wider campsite. He put his hands on his knees and breathed deeply and then began his search again, lifting the stray kindling and logs that were scattered about. He was hungover and miserable; his eyes were bloodshot and sagging, and his hair looked as if he'd been struck by lightning.

"Let's go, Oskar," Anika commanded. "It's past dawn. You do recall our agreement, yes?"

Oskar ignored her and kept searching, deepening Anika's suspicion that he didn't remember last night at all.

"We've got a full day to walk. Uphill most of the way."

Oskar groaned and then stopped suddenly, reaching his arm out in front of his body to stable himself before vomiting behind the large boulder he'd used as last night's support.

The reality of what lay ahead was suddenly too much for him, and Anika couldn't resist laughing. "Rough night?"

Oskar looked up at Anika and frowned, and then continued his disheveled search.

"What are you looking for?"

"I haven't one shoe. I can't go with the one shoe only."

"You've got two minutes, and then we're leaving."

"You don't go without me. You don't speak to the ancients with no me."

Anika pursed her lips and nodded, considering his point. "Maybe that's true. But only Noah knows exactly where we're going. And more importantly, he knows the way back. Do you know the way back Oskar? I'm guessing the decades of nightly grog and other less-than-healthy substances you've consumed over the years has made your memory, well, unreliable."

"Noah stays with me over you. He don't go without me."

"Is that true, Noah? Would you risk your reputation as a guide and your pay on this journey for Oskar?"

Oskar waved a hand at Anika as if dismissing her question. "He don't know what you say. He don't speak it this language. It's why you come with me."

It was true that Anika had barely heard an utterance from Noah since they set off—in any language. But he had responded to her last night. "Dawn" he had said, repeating the last word of the question she'd asked while also answering her question. The longer she considered it, Anika suspected Noah understood more than he let on.

"You go with only Noah, you don't speak to the ancients with no me."

"Yes, you said that already. And it's 'without me.' You say, 'without me,' not 'no me.'"

Oskar found his shoe beneath the unused pile of logs that had been stacked in reserve for last night's fire. The weather had suddenly turned unseasonably warm during the evening and the logs had been spared. Unfortunately, the forecast for the next few days was not so promising.

Oskar held his boot up for all to see. "Now you don't go without me."

Without looking back or saying a word, Noah began walking the path up the mountain. And Anika followed.

CHAPTER SEVENTEEN

TWO MORE DAYS ON THE *Schwebenberg* and then Gretel would finally reach the land of her birth. The New Country. The Southlands.

The Back Country.

The days at sea had gone by with brutal slowness. The endless circumference of water gave no indication of the ship's progress, and Gretel often felt like they'd somehow become stuck in this world of water, trapped in the horizon, anchored by nothingness.

She had spent most of her waking time talking and playing games with Hansel. There wasn't much in the way of entertainment, but they'd packed a deck of cards and a few puzzles, and Hansel enjoyed telling riddles and solving other word games. Gretel also did a lot of reading. Orphism took up a good share of her time, but it was a rule that she only read it at night in her cabin. During the day on the promenade deck, Gretel feared the huge black tome would draw too much attention; so, with little success, she attempted to pass the hours by losing herself in a handful of romance novels she'd brought along.

But her attention was usually shattered by her feelings of fear.

The instruction of Orphism over the past year had brought with it an intoxication. It was as if she'd shed the skin of a previous Gretel, releasing a new version of a girl who knew so much more about the world than the previous one.

But the magic of Orphism was not without a downside. Those lessons that had taught Gretel the techniques and exercises to grow her natural—supernatural—intuition, and how to distinguish between the invented fears of the mind and the more accurate senses in her body, also enhanced her worries. Her honed insights into the world now left her with perpetual feelings of both wisdom and dread.

And the closer she drifted toward the docks of the Urbanlands and the geography of the New Country, the stronger her feelings became. Her stomach had been in a regular state of discomfort for the past three days, and Gretel knew it had nothing to do with the motion of the boat. She was nearing her birthplace and the connection that increased the Orphic powers.

Suddenly Gretel wished she had come alone, without Hansel. She wasn't so worried about his safety—on some level she knew he would be safe upon their return—instead she thought of the maintenance, emotional and otherwise, that her brother required. She wouldn't have the time for it. She needed the freedom and mobility to search on a minute's notice, to pursue answers wherever they might be hiding. And perhaps to be a hero.

It was the Klahrs that now occupied most of her anxious thoughts, and she had no doubt her forebodings about them were accurate. The new Gretel had grown increasingly angry at her old self for not contacting her friends the instant they landed in the Old World. She loved her mother dearly and respected her even more, but the days of allowing her to make all the decisions should have ended the night they left the cannery.

Gretel was in charge of her life now. She had been for some time. She couldn't have said the exact day it happened—perhaps it was the day Mr. Klahr caught her stealing pears in the orchard—but that it had already happened was without dispute. She had crafted her own life during her mother's disappearance—the life of Odalinde and her immobile father and her work at the orchard. She didn't fault her mother for asserting her authority, she faulted herself for not leaning against that authority more heartily.

Gretel walked to the bow of the ship and draped her arms across the railing, folding her hands together. She looked down at the sapphire blue water for a few seconds and then lifted her head, staring out to the white sky in the distance. The wind had picked up in the last few minutes, signaling a storm was on the way.

"What are you looking at, Gretel?"

Gretel barely moved at the sound of her brother's voice. "Nothing. Everything."

"Are you okay?" Hansel's voice was timid, almost baby-like.

Gretel kept her back turned. "You'll have to be ready Hansel." Her voice was stern, formal. "When we get home, the second we step to the shore, even before I call for the Klahrs or speak to the port attendant, you have to be ready."

"I'm packing up tomorrow. I'll be ready to—"

"That's not what I'm talking about, Hansel." Gretel turned now and took an aggressive step toward her brother.

"You have to be ready to fight. To run. To hide or lie. To kill. Are you ready to kill?"

Hansel blinked innocently at his sister and swallowed, unsure of what to say, petrified by the person standing in front of him.

"The witch is alive, Hansel."

Hansel twitched, as if physically shaken by the words. He blinked again, quickly and repeatedly this time, fighting off the sting of tears. Instinctively, he began to shake his head, denying what he'd heard, or perhaps trying to wake from a nightmare. "No," he whispered.

"Yes, Han, she is. I wasn't sure at first, when mother mentioned the possibility back at—"

"Mother told you? How did she know? How could she? Why didn't she tell me?" Hansel looked down, embarrassed, and there was no need for Gretel to explain.

"Petr said something about the possibility to her before we left the Back Country. It seemed impossible but...but now...now that we're almost home, I know it's true. She is alive. And she's close. On the move."

"Gretel no! No! We can't go back then! Why would we go back?"

Gretel stood braced to the deck, committed to the lecture. "We are back, Hansel, and the day after tomorrow we'll be in our home. And you need to be ready. I can't do what I have to do and take care of you at the same time."

Hansel looked to the side, still processing Gretel's words from the minute before.

"Hansel! Do you hear me?"

"Yes! I heard you! I'll be ready!"

Gretel studied her brother, searching for a sign of truth in his words. She nodded as she walked past him and said, "Good. You had better be."

CHAPTER EIGHTEEN

AMANDA KLAHR SWALLOWED and felt the burn of cold iron beneath her chin, the chain resisting the downward movements of her throat as it squeezed against her trachea.

She was positioned on some type of metal stool, sitting rigid and tall against the seatback, blindfolded. She attempted to lift her hands up so she could release the chain that was squeezing against her neck, but her hands were tied down behind her at the wrists, low, the position of her arms pulling her body tight against the splat.

Her mouth was free, thank god, but with the chain nearly taut around her larynx, she could tell without attempting a whisper that any words she uttered would involve a struggle. The time would come when she had no choice but to speak, but that time was not now. Instead, Amanda concentrated on slowing her breathing and clearing her mind. The breathing part she managed relatively well; her thoughts, however, raced.

She squeezed her shrouded eyes tight, hoping to extract a memory from last night that would give her a clue as to where she was now. The last thing she remembered was the woman ranting incoherently and then shoving Amanda from the back, sending her reeling through the open passenger door of Georg's truck. Amanda shuddered now at the memory of the woman's strength and aggression.

Her mind now went to the moments just before then, when she descended the stairs with the witch's hot breath blasting on the back of her neck. The woman's grip on Amanda's throat was that of a strangler, and her fingers tightened at the tiniest hint of hesitation or resistance. Amanda had been screaming—she remembered that for certain—and she'd almost fallen face-forward several times. Only the iron-like grip of the witch had prevented that.

And then she saw Georg.

He was mangled, his body twisted as if he'd fallen from the top of a skyscraper. His right arm had been torn off at the shoulder, the tendons hanging like wires from an old transistor.

Amanda had tried to look away, hoping that if somehow, through the mercy of God, she survived this ordeal, she could hold on to some crumb of sanity. But she had not been shown grace. The witch had pushed Amanda's face until it was only inches from her dead husband's, nearly touching his nose to hers, forcing her to look upon the frozen expression of terror in Georg's eyes. But Amanda knew that fear wasn't for his own pain or death. His eyes shouted to her the horror and his sorrow in failing to protect his wife. His duty to keep abominations like the Northland witch from their home had gone unfulfilled. He could no longer defend her. Or Petr. Or Gretel.

She had known for some time of Georg's designs of revenge and his regret at having not acted quickly or bravely enough to save Gretel's nurse on the front drive of the Morgan property. She had watched her husband for months, tilling empty ares of land, smashing his pickaxe with ferocity and determination, his goal being nothing less than to make his aged body as strong as nature would allow. He had become infatuated with retribution against the woman.

He was dead now, but the failure wasn't his.

Amanda's thoughts careened now to Petr and his conspiracies. All of what he'd believed from the start was true. It was the System. Again. As infected with corruption and evil as ever. Even after the well-known exposure of Officer Stenson and the role he played in Gretel and her mother's nightmare, the insidious greed and addiction of the organization continued.

Thank god for Petr's curiosity, Amanda thought. And his wanderlust. Both had saved him last night—or maybe it was still the same night, she couldn't be sure. Had he been home during the invasion, the woman would have certainly gone for him first.

A sound came from somewhere behind her. It was muffled and low, as if it came from behind the closed door of another room. Amanda used the noise as a reference and began drawing a picture in her head. She was almost certainly in a house; the place didn't feel vast and open like a warehouse or barn. There was a stillness to the air and smells of domestication.

And then she thought of the cabin. Anika Morgan had been reticent to go into much detail with Amanda following the ordeal in the woman's cabin. After all, Amanda had never really been friends with Anika, and even though Amanda and Georg had grown close to Gretel, their relationship with her mother never had time to develop.

But Amanda knew the story well enough. She was at the infamous cabin. There was no doubt in her mind. Where else would the witch take her? This was her home. She had kidnapped Amanda, stolen her truck, and was now going to use her for the same purpose she intended for Anika.

"It may not be what you think," a voice from behind said, grating and hoarse.

It was the woman; Amanda knew it instantly. She wanted to respond but decided to keep quiet and listen for a moment, thinking that perhaps the words weren't meant for her and that she was hearing a conversation that had drifted into earshot.

But that didn't feel right. The voice was so close.

"You're probably thinking I'm going to use your parts for the elixir, yes?"

She was addressing Amanda—no doubt about that now. "I..." Amanda tried to speak and gagged. Her eyes blossomed wide with agony. The rings of the chain settled perfectly into the crevices of her windpipe, and she panicked as she struggled to force out a breath.

She managed to release just the slightest puff and then dragged in heavily, gasping for oxygen, but her lungs were still nearly full. Tears streaked down Amanda's face, and she could feel the heat of blood fill her face. Another thirty seconds, she thought, and she'd be dead. She thought of heaven now, and Georg, and she was suddenly terrified and eager about what lay beyond, wondering whether, in less than a minute, she would see the man she loved.

Amanda felt the slightest release from her neck, and her whole body lurched in exhalation. She took in another full breath and exhaled. And again. She now felt light-headed and tried to focus again on steadying her breathing, determined not to faint. She knew she was in terrible trouble, obviously, but it didn't keep her from wanting to stay alive for as long as possible, at least to know the woman's intentions.

"What elixir?" Amanda said finally, barely getting the words out in between breaths.

The woman cackled somewhere in the background. It was a hollow, liquid laugh that nauseated Amanda. If a monitor lizard could laugh, she thought, that was the sound it would make.

Amanda tried again to lift her hands, desperate this time, but the abrasive fibers binding her wrists held firm.

"Strange that you haven't heard the story," the woman continued, her tone mocking, "about a young mother held prisoner in a cabin in the woods of the Northlands. I would have believed that you, perhaps beyond just about anyone in the world, would have heard that story."

The cackling resumed, but for just a moment before the woman continued with her dialogue, more somber this time.

"Your body does me no good. Even before they were delivered to me, I'd have never spent a day's worth of light hunting you. Your old organs wouldn't keep me alive for a day."

"Lucky me," Amanda whispered.

"No, Mrs. Klahr, I assure you, you are quite unlucky. Though I've not brought you here for harvesting, nor have I brought you here to work my garden and iron my clothes."

Amanda tried to speak again, but the chain seemed to tighten. She felt panicky again and attempted to relax her muscles.

"Gretel, Mrs. Klahr. As I so pleasantly mentioned to you in your lovely bedroom, I will need you to tell me where I can find Gretel."

The silence that followed was a clear indicator that the old woman was giving her the space to spill the information quickly and to avoid any drawn-out threats of torture. To have it all end now.

Amanda opened her mouth as if to speak, but said nothing.

"Well, of course, Mrs. Klahr, I would never expect you to give such valuable secrets for nothing. Why would anyone do that? No, no, no. I will give you something first, and then you will tell me. That's fair, yes?"

"I don't...know...where." The words were tortuous squeaking from her throat.

"No?"

The woman approached the chair from the back; Amanda could hear the clicking of the soles of her shoes. The footsteps stopped, and Amanda felt the hot breath again, this time as a putrid wind in her ear canal.

"I'm not going to kill you yet, for no other reason than I think you do know where my Source and her family have gone. But make no mistake, you are going to die."

Amanda felt a merciful loosening of the chain at her throat and then felt it slither off her neck entirely. The relief felt like a bucket of water had been poured on her as she crawled from the desert. She swallowed in the air in long, slow inhalations. "We all die," she gasped, before sucking in another breath.

The woman cackled lightly, as if she was torn between fury and humor at the indignation but ultimately decided to go with humor. "That's true for most, Mrs. Klahr," the witch responded, stepping back slightly from the chair.

Amanda cringed at the "Klahr" sound, spoken as if it had become stuck in the woman's throat, freed only by the woman's breathy growl.

"I, as you know by now, am not most."

The sound of metal blades now replaced the woman's breath in Amanda's ear. Scissors. She was going to cut off an ear. With scissors.

"Is this your house? Your cabin?" Amanda panicked, speaking quickly, desperate for a delay. "They'll be looking for you. They know your body is missing. Obviously. You understand that, right? And I'm missing now. And they'll find Georg. Petr kno—" Amanda could feel the tears well behind the blindfold the instant she spoke Petr's name.

"Petr knows? Petr knows what?"

Amanda was quiet again, determined to stay that way.

She heard the scissors again and steeled herself for unimaginable pain.

And then the world filled with light. It was blinding and yellow and came pouring in through a small window near the ceiling. She had cut the blindfold.

Amanda squinted, trying to shield her eyes from all but a fraction of the rays. She couldn't tell just yet if she was right about this being the woman's home, but from the initial clues, the place appeared to be a cabin, rustic and small.

And as her pupils adjusted more fully, she became certain. The bed and the chain beside her was a dead giveaway. This was the witch's home.

"Petr Stenson, yes? He is your ward now. I know about it all, Mrs. Klahr. I've been watching your home for several days. The comings and goings of all of you. He is a rather naughty child, it would seem. Doesn't come home at night, hmm?"

"He's not our ward," Amanda lied. "He visits sometimes, but we...I...don't see him often. I don't even know where he's living right now. He moved out weeks ago. Staying with friends maybe."

The woman was still behind Amanda, so even with her eyes free, she couldn't look her in the face to judge her reaction. But Amanda could sense the hag was considering how much of what she was hearing was the truth.

"What does he know, Mrs. Klahr? 'Petr knows,' you were on the cusp of explaining."

There was no point lying here, Amanda realized. She'd revealed that Petr was on to something, and she wouldn't be able to back off from this entirely. She decided to go with the truth. "He knows you're alive. He's been looking for you. Or at least for the proof that you're alive. I don't really know what he does. He never told us very much, other than that he believed the System covered up your death...or at least they covered up the fact that they never found your body. He was convinced of it. You must have suspected this, right? I mean, you're not dead. They obviously didn't find your body."

"The System is corrupt. That is no news to anyone. We all know that as a matter of fact now. It's the reason young Petr no longer has a father."

The woman's words reminded Amanda again of Georg, and she forced herself to swallow back the tears that threatened to spill.

"But they're also lazy and foolish," the woman continued, a tinge of anger creeping into her voice. "I watched them trespass all over my land, walking over me time and again like blind giraffes. Stealing my possessions. Stealing my book."

"So where would they imagine your body went? If they never found you in the cannery, how could they think you were dead?"

Amanda heard the woman move behind her and then shuddered at the sight of her black cloaked body as it glided into her periphery. She came further into view, first her torso and then her head, hooded almost entirely by the heavy black cloak.

The woman stood tall in front of Amanda, staring down at her like some alien being examining its capture. She lowered the hood slowly, revealing a face so hideous it looked as if it had been designed and built in hell. During the battle in her bedroom, Amanda hadn't really seen the face she stabbed with the toothbrush, so fueled was she by fury and fear. But now, bound by the curse of captivity, the repugnancy of the woman's face was forced upon her.

Amanda screamed and looked away, now relishing the moments when she was blindfolded.

"This is what she has done to me, your cherished Gretel. This is her damage!" The woman was now in full-throated screams. "She and her cunt of a mother! I've lived in pain and starvation, unbearable heat and suffocating air, in hibernation, living in the ground like some kind of rodent!"

The woman paused, and Amanda looked toward the ground.

"Look at me, Klahr woman," the witch hissed.

Amanda forced herself to lift her head, struggling as if it were being weighed down by an anchor. She opened her eyes and stared at the woman's ruined face.

"This is why you'll tell me where to find her. This is what she owes to me."

"Why would I tell you that?" Amanda asked, genuinely confused. "Even if I knew, why would I tell you? You've already told me you'll kill me. Why would I also give Gretel to you?"

The woman smiled broadly. "Do you know about torture, Mrs. Klahr? Do you know about it intimately?"

Amanda stared hard into the shattered eye sockets of the woman standing before her, glaring. "If you think torturing me will give you Gretel's whereabouts, we're going to be in for some very long nights. I told you, I don't know where she is."

The woman's smile turned crooked now, her dulled incisors pointing down toward Amanda, threatening her. "Oh no, Mrs. Klahr, it's not you who will know about torture. It's young Petr, of course."

CHAPTER NINETEEN

DODD SCRUBBED THE LAST of the bloodstains from the grout of the kitchen tiles using one of the dozen washcloths he had found in the back of the Klahr's linen pantry. He ran the towel over the tiles a few more times for good measure and then stuffed the bloody rag into a large black trash bag along with about ten other towels that had been used for the same purpose. The scene was a massacre, and no matter how much water he poured and how furiously he mopped, he would never get all the blood out.

He decided that before he left, he would leave the water running and flood the place out. It wouldn't cover up all the forensic analysis, but it may fool the naked eye of Petr Stenson.

Dodd opened the sliding door to the back porch and checked on Georg Klahr's corpse. He had positioned the body in a sitting position with the one remaining arm draped impotently across the body, head bowing to the opposite side. He looked like a drunk who had put up his best fight against the night until finally passing out on a street corner.

Dodd closed the door and then ascended the stairs to the upper floor, urgent now, taking the steps two at a time. At the top of the staircase, he ducked left into the far bedroom for one last inspection of Petr's room. Petr was gone, obviously, but there was nothing to suggest he'd been killed or abducted. It wasn't impossible, but Dodd's professional detection concluded that the boy wasn't home when the witch stopped by and unleashed her wrath on the rest of his helpless family. There was no vehicle in the driveway. Dodd deduced that the boy had taken it.

But he would have to come home at some point, and it was Dodd's mission now to conceal as much of the evidence as possible.

The Klahr woman, on the other hand, was a mystery, and Dodd struggled to figure out where her body ended up.

He walked back to the main bedroom, which was, by all accounts, the primary arena of chaos, and one that had almost certainly involved Amanda Klahr. Dodd had cleaned the few puddles of blood from the floor and disposed of the toothbrush—no doubt Amanda Klahr's makeshift weapon. And one that had evidently hit its mark.

Dodd debated about whether he should clean the room entirely—to make the bed and arrange everything just so—or to just leave things as they were. He decided on the latter, figuring a scene of tidiness would be more suspicious to Petr, possibly indicating that a third party was at play. But the blood had to go. You could never leave the blood behind.

Of course, no matter the scene, Petr would be suspicious. His guardians were mysteriously gone, and the boy's first thought would obviously turn to the witch. He knew she was alive, he'd said as much, and now there would be no doubt in his mind.

But that was fine with Dodd. As long as he wasn't indicted, he didn't care too much about what the boy believed.

At first, Dodd considered leaving the entire house as it was, as if he had never been there at all. After all, why put himself at risk? Just leave all the blood and bodies behind and go hunt the witch down. It certainly would have saved him a lot of time and disgust.

But that simply wouldn't do. There was a dead body. And another one missing. And Petr, as intrepid and independent as he apparently was, would be forced to report the death. And an army of System agents would follow that report and scour the Klahr orchard. And the carnage at the scene combined with a missing person and Petr's months-long insistence that the woman was still alive would almost guarantee the re-opening of the case of the Witch of the North.

And then a lengthy inquiry about her missing corpse.

And that simply wouldn't do. There could be no more suspicion that she was alive. This was Dodd's secret, and he was determined to keep it his own. It was why he risked his reputation and career by covering up the crime scene, why he spent all those days and nights outside his patrol area, endlessly monitoring the cabin and its surroundings. This was his only chance to find the truth for himself, and he was determined to keep his chance at life-everlasting still intact.

Dodd glanced toward the upper-level of the house for the last time and then went back to the main level, stepping once more to the back porch. Disposing of the slumped body of Georg Klahr was going to be the trickiest part of this whole cleanup process.

There were two choices really: drag the body to the lake and dump it in the water or take it with him in the trunk of his cruiser to be disposed of later, possibly out near the witch's cabin. That was where he was headed next.

Dodd wasted little time on internal debate and decided to take the corpse with him, fearing that if the body were dumped in the lake, it would show up on the shore of some neighbor's beach in the next couple of days, the look of fear and regret fossilized on the man's face. And once that story broke, it would reignite his fear of indictment.

"Come on, old man," Dodd grunted, leaning down and ducking his shoulder under the torso of the body so that it fell across his back. He slipped his arm between the man's leg and the other arm behind his neck. With a lunge, Dodd lifted the body up and was now holding the corpse aloft in a kind of fireman's carry.

As quickly as he was able, Dodd made his way down the porch stairs to his cruiser. With a simultaneous duck and a heave, he plopped the body down from his shoulders, neck first, into the waiting trunk space, arranging the flailing limbs so they were tucked neatly inside. With a sigh and quick glance around, Dodd eased the trunk shut.

He considered taking a walk down to the shoreline to assess whether the woman could have gone back across to the Morgan property, but he'd decided that she wouldn't have made such a move. She was done here. There was nothing for her to gain by staying. She would go home now. She wouldn't be able to stay there forever though; the System would come eventually, forcing her to flee somewhere new.

But not just yet. There was still work for her to do.

Dodd fired up the cruiser and sped from the Klahr property, turning out toward the Interways to journey back to the Northlands.

He would never know just how well he'd spent his time, for twenty minutes later, Petr walked down the driveway and found his house empty.

CHAPTER TWENTY

GRETEL KNEW THE KLAHRS wouldn't answer the phone before she had dialed their number at the harbor station. She hung up before the third ring ended. The plan, as she and her mother had discussed, was to call the Klahrs when she and Hansel arrived at port. And Gretel had followed the plan, but her instincts told her there would be no celebratory pick up at the dock; she and Hansel would have to find their own way home.

She knew it was possible that Mrs. Klahr had just been out running errands—to the nursery perhaps or the post office—and that Mr. Klahr was working in the orchard. But it was late in the day when they'd arrived, well past six, and Mrs. Klahr ran her errands in the morning and should have been home preparing supper well before then. Gretel knew almost instantly that something much direr was at play.

And several hours later, as the taxi pulled in slowly to the driveway of her home, Gretel's feelings of doom had become almost unbearable.

"Thank you," Gretel said absently, suspiciously staring at her house as she handed the taxi driver the amount displayed on the fare monitor.

"It's customary to tip, young lady," the driver urged gently, unloading the bags from the trunk. "This was a long way from the harbor, you know."

"What?"

"A tip. Extra money for my efforts, you get it?"

"Oh, yes, I'm sorry." Gretel turned her focus from the house and began rifling in her personal bag as Hansel pulled the luggage toward the house.

"Are you okay here? Is there someone here to see you in?"

"Uh, yes, my mother will be home soon. And my, uh, grandparents live just across the lake. Thank you." Gretel shoved several bills toward the man, not quite sure of the proper amount.

"This will be fine," the man said, taking only two of the six or seven bills in front of him. "You have a good night, miss."

Gretel watched the taxi's taillights disappear as it turned east from the driveway. Normally the car would have been visible for several hundred more yards as it sped from sight, but their farm fields had grown over wildly since she'd last been home, and the once maintained landscape was now blanketed by gorse and fescue.

Gretel suddenly felt terrified and alone, incapable. If something terrible had happened to the Klahrs, it would be she who was responsible for everything that happened to her and Hansel going forward. There was no one else. Her decisions would determine their lives. She'd been here before, in this place where adulthood was foisted upon her, but during the worst days, with Odalinde acting the role of evil stepmother and her father incapacitated and useless, Gretel always believed there was someone out there who would help before things got mortally bad. The neighbors, perhaps, or Deda or even the System would whisk the children away before any real tragedy struck. This last thought—of the System—brought an icy shiver down the back of Gretel's neck, which she trapped by closing in the blades of her shoulders.

But the world was different now. Or maybe it was just that Gretel had learned the truth about the way things always were. If you were lucky, you had a handful of people who you could absolutely rely on for help and loyalty. For Gretel, besides her mother and Hansel, there was only the Klahrs. That was it.

Except for Petr. Maybe she had Petr.

"Gretel, it's open."

The sun was only a few minutes away from setting completely, and Gretel could barely see her brother standing at the front door of their house, his hand on the knob.

"Why is it open, Gretel?"

Gretel was still lost in her thoughts, which were careening toward panic.

"Gretel!"

"Yes, I'm here, Han, quiet down."

"I couldn't see you; it's dark. Did you hear me? The door is open."

"Yes, I heard you. What do you mean open? Open open, or unlocked?"

"Yeah, unlocked, I mean. Why is it unlocked?"

"I didn't get here before you, Han. So, I don't know." The last four words snapped from Gretel like a whip, and she regretted her tone instantly.

"Why are you yelling at me?"

Gretel resisted apologizing to her brother, and instead walked up to the door and stared at it with Hansel beside her, his hand still on the knob. "I think she was probably here. I think that's why it's unlocked. I don't have any way of knowing that, but I think when we go inside, we might find out for sure." She turned to her brother. "I wasn't kidding about what I said on the boat, Han. I wish you could have stayed with mother, I really do. But you're here with me, and I need you to be ready to act in whatever way is asked of you."

"I told you I'd be ready, and I will be."

Gretel nodded.

Hansel pushed the door, and before it was a quarter way open, the stench hit the children like a bomb blast.

"Oh god, Gretel." Hansel turned away, cupping his hands to his mouth and nose.

Gretel paused and turned away instinctively as well, but she pushed forward into the house.

"Gretel! What are you doing? What if she's here?" Hansel asked, his voice muffled.

Gretel ignored her brother and walked completely inside, leaving the door ajar to release some of the horrible odor. "Stay there. It's okay. I don't think she's here now. She may have been recently, but not now."

"I can't imagine the smell if she was here!"

Gretel smiled at her brother's joke, feeling somewhat buoyed by his ability to find humor in such a crisis. He may be helpful after all, or at least not the burden she originally feared.

Gretel walked through the kitchen to the sliding door of the screened porch and opened it, stepping out to the sealed off area before shutting the door behind her and breathing in the fresh air. By now, daylight was almost completely gone, so she scanned the porch quickly for any signs of intrusion. Finding no evidence that the witch had been to this area of the house, Gretel took another deep breath and went back inside to the kitchen, opening the first drawer beneath the counter and removing one of several flashlights her father had always kept there for their frequent power outages. She pressed the metal power button and strode back through the kitchen and out the front door to the porch. Hansel stood, eager for news.

"Where is she? Is it her?"

"I don't know. The smell is really bad, so I just checked the kitchen and had to get out to the back porch. It doesn't look—or smell—like anyone was out there. I grabbed a flashlight from the kitchen, and I'm going back in to check the rest of the rooms. Luckily, our house is so small I should be able to check them all in one breath. At least on this level. There's still the basement."

"What is the point of going back in there, Gret? What are you looking for?"

"I just need some kind of proof that the putrid smell isn't just the result of a family of raccoons who snuck into one of the air ducts and got stuck. Or even some vagrants who heard about the abandoned Morgan property and decided to make camp."

"Do you think that's possible?"

"Not really, but I have to be sure it's her. Wait here. I'll be right back."

Gretel took a gaping breath of air and pushed back through the front door, walking straight ahead to the living room and then left to the back bedrooms, which were only four or five steps farther. She was quick but thorough with her inspections and made sure to shine the beam of the flashlight on every bed and floor space and to open each of the closet doors. But there was nothing specific—other than the smell—to indicate the witch had been there.

Gretel came up for air again through the front door and revealed her assessment to Hansel.

And then she went back in to inspect the lower level.

As Gretel descended the open stairway leading to the basement, her suspicions were confirmed immediately, first by the increased putrid odor emanating up the staircase, and then by the dirty, brown nest of blankets and pillows that were piled up in a far corner of the L-shaped room. The rumpled mass of cloth was littered with bones and hair, and Gretel could only imagine what the brown stains puddled on the bedding and around the encampment consisted of. It was her turn to feel sick, and she dry heaved on the steps before turning back and running up the staircase and out the front door.

"Gretel, what's wrong?" Hansel shrieked. "Is she there?"

Gretel exhaled and began coughing before catching her wind. She shook her head, wide-eyed. "Not now. But she was. And she's mad, Hansel. Truly mad."

"She wasn't mad before?"

Gretel ignored her brother and tried desperately to shake the scene she'd just witnessed from her head. With her suspicions now confirmed, she had to decide what to do next. "We have to go to the Klahrs, Hansel. And I'm warning you now: things may be very bad over there."

"How bad?" Hansel choked out.

"I'm going back inside to get you a flashlight of your own, and then I'm going for the pistol under Papa's bed."

HANSEL AND GRETEL WALKED to the edge of the lake and scoured the shoreline with their flashlights, looking for signs of the canoe. The panic began building in Gretel once more; the missing boat implied several possibilities, most of which terrified her.

"Are you sure you left it behind the house, Gretel?" Hansel asked. "Maybe you left it down here and it drifted away while we were gone. You remember how high the water rose during storms."

"I left it where I always do. It didn't drift away."

"Well where is it then?"

"Where do you think I think it is, Han?" Gretel snapped.

Hansel pondered the question for a moment, genuinely mystified, and then it registered. "The witch? But...I thought she could fly or something. Why would she need a canoe?"

Gretel shook her head, trying to stay focused, annoyed at the childishness of her child brother. "It doesn't work like that," she mumbled, not interested in engaging with him.

"How are we going to get there? We don't have a car, and there's no way I'm walking the road to the Klahrs."

Hansel was panicking now, and Gretel was compelled to remind him of his promise. She steeled her voice, holding the flashlight up like a microphone and shining it on her face for effect. "You told me you could do this, Hansel, and I'm expecting you to uphold that agreement."

"I will, I just—"

"Hansel! That's enough! We don't have any space for excuses. It's you and I right now, so you will be ready for what is asked of you, and that's it. Do you understand?"

Hansel nodded.

Gretel was tempted to snap at him again, to insist he answer her verbally, but she decided to let it go. This wasn't the moment for breaking him completely; they still had to figure out how to get across to the orchard, and she would need him to be energized and united with her, if not confident. "Good," was all she said.

"Can we swim it?" Hansel asked, pouting slightly, but with a trace of pride in his voice.

"I thought of that, but it's deeper than you think, and it begins dropping off quickly just a few yards in. There's no place to bail out if one of us gets tired. If we go, we have to go all the way."

"I can make it," Hansel declared, a slight challenge in his tone.

Gretel smiled. "Okay, but we're obviously going to get wet too. And it's not like we can change our clothes when we get to the orchard. You're going to be uncomfortable."

"I've gotten wet before, Gretel. I think I can handle it."

Gretel considered the alternatives for another minute and then made the team decision that they would swim the width of the lake. The distance was barely ten rows of her oars in the canoe, but she'd never done the conversion to swimming. Neither she nor Hansel was going to win any competitions in the water, but she figured they were both decent enough to make it without a struggle. And, in fact, Gretel had to admit that between the two of them, Hansel was certainly the stronger swimmer.

"Let's go, then," Gretel said finally. "Leave your shoes on; it's going to make it a little heavy to kick, but we're going to need them on the other side. And we're going to stay together. This isn't a race, so don't go swimming off without me."

Gretel knew her backhanded compliment would bolster Hansel's confidence, but she meant it. If one of them got in trouble, the other could hopefully pull them both to shore.

Without any more discussion, Gretel led the way into the lake, wading in until she was waist high. "It's cold, but we can do this."

Hansel followed his sister until he was next to her, and they both continued walking, their feet on the bottom for two or three more steps before pushing off into the deeper water where they began their swim in earnest.

The flashlights and pistol weren't waterproof, Gretel was almost certain of that, so she doubted they'd have much light or protection when they reached the other side. But she made the attempt to keep the items salvageable and did her best to insulate them by putting the gun down her pants and the flashlights in Hansel's shirt, tied beneath his armpits. If they held, great; if not, it was only a prayer anyway.

As for their progress, they were doing fine, alternating between taking a few long exaggerated swimming strokes, and then easing up, pulling themselves gently toward the shore as they breast-stroked under the dark water, gliding their arms outward slowly, trying to use as little energy as possible. There is no rush, Gretel thought, not really, so let's just get there. Their shoes and clothes were weighing them both down a bit, but they were going to make it, and she was thankful they'd made the decision to swim.

"How you doing, Han?" Gretel finally asked, now confident that speaking wouldn't upset the balance of their journey.

"I'm fine. A little cold, but okay. How—?" Hansel paused. "Do you hear that?"

Gretel heard it the second the words left her brother's mouth. It was the familiar sound of steady oars chopping through water. She'd grown to love the sound over the months, when her life had deteriorated and rowing had become the only good thing in her life.

Now the sound was as ominous as an approaching tornado.

"Stay quiet, Han. Get your head down." Gretel sank her head so that her nose was just above the water line, though a lot of good that would do if the boat came within ten yards or so of them. At that point, they'd be seen and escape would be impossible.

The slap of the oars was visible, and Gretel watched in horror at the shadow of the canoe as it made a slight turn and came directly toward them.

CHAPTER TWENTY-ONE

THE SCENE JUST BEYOND the clearing was nothing short of spectacular, and it was nothing at all what Anika had expected.

The moment when Noah pushed through the last of the lush foliage and announced to his benefactor that they had arrived, Anika's first thought was that there had been a terrible mistake, that she had not properly communicated the details of where she needed to go or whom she needed to find.

For several moments, the three travelers stood silently, watching from atop the bluff, Anika in wonderment, believing that her guide had not led her to the ancient land of her ancestors but instead to some other magnificent civilization. It felt as if they had stumbled upon an entirely new land, a previously undiscovered territory where all the benefits of the modern and the beauty of the primitive had converged into one community.

As she looked down upon the bustling crowds of people, Anika's first assessment of the surreal society was that there were simply too many people. She couldn't possibly be in the right place. It wasn't the size of the Urbanlands, of course, not even close—there weren't cars and paved streets and such—but this mountain society was nothing short of a town. Perhaps even a city.

Anika's expectations were based loosely on tales from people who basked in hyperbole and were largely uninformed—that when she reached this place, she would barely notice a society at all, and that quite a bit of effort would be required to even to find a person with whom to speak. But here they were, people by the dozens, in the throes of their days, crowding the busy streets. And there were presumably more people in the surrounding homes.

But she was shocked by more than just the crowds; it was the modernity of this place. From what she could see, they all seemed to wear clothes that were far too modern for this place, this isolated territory that had been shrouded in the hills of the Old Country for centuries. Perhaps millennia. Modernity had reached across the seas, of course, but not to the ancients—at least not according to Anika's father, who had told the wild story of her mother during his demented confession in the warehouse all those months ago.

But as she looked down upon these people, she saw modernity thriving.

"I don't think this is the right place, Noah," she said to the translator as they stood at the top of the clearing, the panic in her voice clearly audible.

But Noah had only nodded and said "Here. Aulwurms."

It was the right name, and as Anika would soon learn, it was indeed the right place.

With Noah at the front, the three travelers descended the hill of the gradual bluff with confidence, and once they made their first contact with a woman selling some type of cauliflower, Anika's journey toward her cure began.

It only took a few questions and a short conversation with the woman and some remedial directions from the man buying the cauliflower before Oskar learned the names relevant to Anika's quest. Within the hour, Anika stood in the home of one of the village elders—a tall, dark-skinned woman with large, friendly eyes.

From what Anika could decipher of Oskar's initial conversations with the woman, other than their names, the translator hadn't revealed much information to the host regarding where they had come from or why they were there.

Whatever he had said, though, had been enough to warrant a warm home in which to rest and a meal consisting of a meatless cuisine that left Anika feeling refreshed and almost euphoric. Anika hadn't been sure which meal she was eating; with daylight hours that seemingly never ended, and Anika's sleep limited to little more than two or three hours a night, she had lost all track of time.

Anika, Oskar, and Noah sat in a circle around a stone table that had been prepared just for them, and as Anika finished the last crumbs of what must have been the sixth course of the meal, she was eager to get on with the business of their company.

"This was wonderful, thank you. You're very generous."

Anika moved to clear some dishes away, for which she was shooed back to her seat.

"Very well. Thank you again. And if you have a few moments, perhaps when you're done in the kitchen, I would like to talk to you. I would like to explain why I'm here. Why we've come." Anika had stared at the woman anxiously while Oskar translated.

The woman bowed slightly and muttered a few words, which Oskar had translated as, "We speak another day. To now you go snore."

The translation was rough, but Anika got the idea, and despite her temptation to press the issue, after cleaning up for the night, she allowed the woman to walk her to her shelter, a solidly built, wooden structure just east of the woman's home. The woman unlocked and opened the door, holding out a welcoming hand and encouraging Anika to enter, the way a gentleman might hold the door for a lady entering a shop. Oskar and Noah had been shown to other quarters.

The next morning, Anika awoke to a box of food and a pitcher of water, as well as a bedpan, delivered to her door. She spotted the small covered opening at the baseboard of the structure through which the items had been passed.

The previous evening, when the woman had offered the dwelling with a soft, inviting gesture, Anika felt welcomed and thankful. After all, it was unlikely this community got many visitors, and she and her companions could just have easily been met by some warring, savage tribe, one familiar with the Orphic ways and eager for outside organs to blend. That was not an impossible scenario; in fact, it was probably far more likely than the one they'd encountered.

But the innate fears that had blossomed within Anika at the time had been subdued by food and exhaustion. And once she'd entered the room and climbed atop the soft bed enticing her from the corner, Anika had fallen asleep within minutes and hadn't stirred for almost half a day.

But she was awake now, clear-minded, and she lay staring wide-eyed at the door. She was trembling at the memories of her imprisonment at the hands of the witch, paralleling them with the situation in which she found herself now. What if it's locked? she thought. What if this is all happening again?

Anika swallowed hard and swung her feet to the floor. She had slept in her clothes—shoes and all—and she walked briskly to the door of the cabin, ready to begin her crazed escape if it didn't open immediately. But what she felt wasn't quite fear, at least not the fear of malice and pain that had occupied most of her thoughts during her time at the witch's cabin. This fear was steeped in impatience. She didn't have time for sleep and relaxation—or captivity, if that's what this was. She was dying, drifting farther from her children. This place was her last hope, and she was ready either to begin the steps of healing or of learning her mortal fate.

As Anika's hand cupped the knob of the door, she heard and felt a knock on the other side, followed by the sound of a man's voice. She couldn't make out the words.

Anika removed her hand and backed away, spooked by the coincidence. She waited, silent.

"Anika, bosomari?"

The voice sounded childish and friendly, as if reluctant to disturb her, and Anika walked back to the door and pulled it toward her, swinging it fully open.

A man as small as any she'd ever seen was standing at the base of the steps that led from the cabin. Oskar and Noah stood beside him.

"Bosomari," the man squeaked again, this time more persistent in his tone.

Oskar translated. "He says it's your time, just now. Time for talk."

Anika was mesmerized by the dwarf's size, and she had to force herself to look away. She imagined he was used to the stares by this point in his life—he must have been sixty years old—but then again, he was isolated from most of the world, and his fellow villagers probably never even gave his diminutive stature a thought anymore.

Anika gave a serious nod to the man, locking on his eyes, and then stepped out to the cool morning air, the sun's brightness making her raise her forearm over her head and snap her gaze to the ground like some movie vampire.

"Is more bright up here," Oskar explained. "You high here."

"Where are we going?"

"I tell them you come to speak for some medicine. They bring you to speak for doctor."

Anika stopped walking. "I never told anyone my reason for coming here. Why do you think I'm here for medicine? How would you know that?"

"Why else someone like you come here?" Oskar called back over his shoulder as he walked on. "Plus, I see you..."

Anika hadn't seen herself in days—weeks maybe—but, based on Oskar's observation, the disease was apparently taking hold. She felt fine enough, especially considering her journey thus far, but the journey could be the reason for her continued good health. The exercise and mountain air. And determination.

Maybe, however, she didn't have quite the time she had calculated.

Anika started to protest, to tell him he'd read her wrong, that she had other, very different reasons for trekking to this vast, nearly uncharted territory of the Old World. But Oskar had walked too far ahead now, and shouting after him required a level of feigned indignation that she was not capable of expressing right now. So, she stayed silent and followed him. Besides, what difference did it make? He would know the truth soon enough.

Anika, Noah, and Oskar walked single file behind the dwarf, heading toward the home of the woman who had fed them the night before. It was she, Anika assumed, who would act as the liaison between Anika and this village doctor. As they reached the house, however, and then continued walking, Anika realized this was not to be the plan at all.

The small man walked past the house and continued for several blocks until they were outside the most populated areas of the village. These outskirt areas were as quiet as the village center was bustling, and Anika observed only one old man sitting like a sculpture on a stool and a few stray chickens bobbing and pecking in the street. From the outskirts, they continued walking until, within only a few minutes, they were beyond the boundaries of the village altogether.

It was amazing, Anika thought, how only a few steps beyond the outer roads of the village and suddenly there was no sign that a village existed anywhere at all. There were no indicators—no signs or outposts—that could have directed anyone traveling nearby in the proper direction. There was just dense forest and wilderness. It was no wonder these people went unnoticed by most of the world; it was as if the village had spontaneously sprouted up in the middle of nowhere.

The dwarf was manic as he led them through the overgrowth, saying almost nothing along the way other than a few one- or two-word exchanges with Oskar. The man was small, but his movements were quick and sharp, and he knew exactly where to turn within the woods, despite the lack of any real path or significant landmarks from what Anika could tell.

"Where are we going?" Anika finally spoke up. "Oskar, ask him."

"I ask. He just say, 'Bosomari.' Time to talk."

"Yes, I got that part. I asked where we're going."

Oskar just shrugged.

"Noah, do you know where we are?" Anika asked, remembering the language barrier just as the words came out.

"Oskar, translate please." But Oskar was too far ahead now and had followed the path around a thicket of trees. Anika grumped.

"I don't know where we are now. I only know the way to the village."

Noah's voice was clear, articulate, almost scholarly, Anika thought.

"Noah! How can you...? This whole time...? Why haven't you been speaking to me?"

"I'm here as your guide; that's all."

"You communicate better than Oskar! I could have left him behind and maybe gotten a few more hours of sleep at night. *And* saved some money!"

Noah smiled. "I can speak your language, Ms. Morgan. I cannot speak whatever language these people speak. I assure you, we'd not be on the path we're on currently if not for Oskar."

"I'm not so sure that would be a minus."

Anika settled into the revelation of Noah's language quite easily, having always suspected there was more to him than he was letting on. She'd always felt comfortable around him, despite his distance, and she wouldn't be surprised to find there was more about him yet that she didn't know.

"I don't understand where we could be headed. The village—with all those people—how can that not be the right place?"

Noah just shrugged.

Anika had lost sight of Oskar and their tiny leader, and broke into a half jog to catch up. As she made her way around a bend of trees that nearly looped back on itself, she came within inches of barreling over the miniature pathfinder and toppling them both to the ground. He and Oskar were standing in front of a wall covered with ivy. There was a narrow opening through which Anika could see a group of men standing. They looked calm, peaceful, almost disinterested in the presence of the strangers who'd come upon them.

"Hal bosomari," the man said. "Chime tup."

"It's time for talk," Oskar relayed once again. "They wait for us."

Anika looked at Noah—her newfound comfort in this place of foreign things and people—but he only stared ahead, drifting back into his role of silent guide.

"Okay then," she said. "Let's not keep them waiting."

CHAPTER TWENTY-TWO

GRETEL INSTINCTIVELY reached for her crotch, wrapping her hand around the pistol that nested there.

"Who is that, Gretel?" Hansel whispered. "Is that her? It has to be, right?"

"I don't know. Stay quiet."

Gretel slipped the gun past her waistband and raised it above the water line, trying to shake it dry with slow motion flicks of her wrist, as if doing so would repair any water damage that had been sustained over the past several minutes.

The canoe approached rapidly and was now less than thirty yards from Gretel. She swam in front of Hansel protectively and reached back with her free hand to feel him, to make sure he was still with her.

She wanted to shout at the boat, to threaten the intruder with her gun, but her instincts told her there wasn't much benefit in that. If the assailant hadn't seen them, then Gretel's hollering would only give away their position, and if it was the witch, informing her that she had a weapon would take away that advantage as well.

The canoe was almost upon them now, and Gretel pulled back the hammer of the pistol slowly as she aimed the gun straight ahead, holding it with both hands, using all the strength left in her thighs to tread water with her feet alone.

"Gretel?" The voice sounded frightened, distant. It wasn't the witch. The voice was male.

"Who is that?" Gretel released the hammer and lowered her hands and the gun back into the water.

"Gretel? Gretel, it's Petr!"

"Petr? Petr! What are you doing out here?"

Petr pulled the arms of the oars toward him and shut down the canoe directly in front of Gretel, instinctively reaching for her hand. "Hansel? What are you two doing out here? When did you get back?"

"Just a few hours ago. We called from the docks. We called your house and no one answered."

Petr lifted Gretel under her arm until she was far enough up the side of the canoe to pull herself forward, and then they both helped Hansel inside.

"What's wrong, Petr?" Gretel asked, ruffling the water from her hair. "You just came from there, right? I know something is wrong."

"I just got back here less than an hour ago. I've been away for a few days. I've been away a lot lately. I just got home and they were gone." Peter sounded on the verge of panic now, like a worried parent. "I can't remember the last time Georg and Amanda were both gone this late at night. I don't think there's ever been a time, not when I wasn't with them."

"Has she been there?" Hansel asked, his voice elevating and cracking on the last word.

Petr knew who 'she' was, and there was a silent recognition amongst the three children: the Witch of the North was alive, and they all knew it.

"I don't know for sure. But someone was there. The water was running and flooding over the sink onto the floor."

"She was there, Petr. Of course she was."

"How do you know?"

"Because you're in my canoe. How else would the canoe have gotten to the Klahrs? They're in trouble, Petr. We have to find them."

Petr was silent for a moment, as if considering where that plan would begin. "Where is your mother?"

"She didn't come home with us. She's..." Gretel paused, having to work to keep her eyes off Hansel. "She had some things to tie up. With our family. It's a long story. But she'll be coming home soon. Later this month, I think."

"Did you find what you were looking for? About the book or whatever?"

"There's a lot to discuss, Petr. I couldn't start it now. But yes, we found out a lot. We should go back to the house now. To the Klahr's. We'll talk about everything later."

"Of course, I just—"

"I know. I want to talk too, but let's find out what happened here first."

The canoe glided into the muddied bank of the Klahr orchard, and Petr and Gretel hopped out and pulled it up just past the waterline, as if they were a team that had practiced the move a thousand times. Gretel couldn't help flashing a grin.

"Okay, let's not pretend anymore. We know she was here, so we have to look more specifically for some type of clue. Or something."

"Like what?" Hansel asked. His voice teetered on whiny, and Gretel ignored him.

"What if she killed them, Gretel? What if Georg and Mrs. Klahr are dead?" It was Petr this time.

Gretel didn't follow up with Petr calling Mr. Klahr 'Georg.' "I don't know, Petr. But...if they're dead, then where are their bodies? You said you were inside, right? You would have seen them if she had...hurt them." Gretel, even more than Petr, she believed, couldn't imagine the thought of losing the Klahrs. Especially Amanda.

Petr nodded and then gave a knowing look toward Gretel before averting his eyes toward the direction of the house.

"What is it, Petr? What do you know?"

Petr shook his head quickly, dismissing any encouragement Gretel may have seen burgeoning. "I don't know anything, except that if she is alive—and it looks like she is—then she'll want to find you. And your mother. Don't you think so? To get her revenge, for sure, but also to finish making her..." Petr didn't need to finish the sentence.

"Of course, but what does that have to do with the Klahrs?"

"She—the witch—knows you'll come for them. If you suspect that she has them, then she thinks you'll come for them."

"She's right about that. But I don't know where they've gone. How could I come for them?"

Petr thought about it. "I don't know."

The three entered the house through the basement door and then took the steps up to the main level. Gretel sloshed through the water that coated the kitchen floor and walked up to the sink, inspecting the counters. She opened cupboards and drawers, feeling nostalgia for this place, even under these circumstances, as she thought of her time in this kitchen, cooking and cleaning, following Mrs. Klahr in from the workers' lunch table after setting out the midday meal. Those were the wonderful days, Gretel now realized, when her hours were filled with work and routine and rowing sessions on the lake. She didn't have her mother then, so each day was stained with at least some residue of sadness, but it was during those days when she had discovered her true self.

"Gretel look at this." Petr commanded, snatching Gretel from her reverie. "I think this is blood."

Gretel walked to the bannister where Petr stood and examined the long purple streak that began on the top of the finial and draped down in a frozen cascade to the base of the stair board. Gretel considered sliding her finger through it, to test if it was indeed blood, but she thought better of it, not knowing exactly what she would do with the substance once her finger was caked with it.

"It's blood, right? Don't you think?" Petr seemed fairly certain, but he wanted Gretel's endorsement.

Gretel nodded. "Yes."

"What should we do?"

"We have to find her. Find them."

"Where?"

"I don't know, Petr!" It was Gretel's turn to panic now. Tears stung her eyes at the thought of Amanda and Georg Klahr tortured and killed by the monster she thought she had killed only months ago. The blame she would carry due to her inability to follow through and verify the hag's death began creeping into her thoughts.

"Is your truck here?" Hansel asked. His voice was calm, measured.

"What?"

"Your truck. Mr. Klahr's truck. Is it here?"

"No, I told you, they weren't here. They went out. Or they were already out. Or..." Petr was slowly unraveling Hansel's point. "She took the truck? Do you think she took the truck?"

"Well, if she didn't, then where is she? Where are the Klahrs?" Hansel's questions were rhetorical. "Someone took it."

"Oh my god," Gretel whispered.

"What is it, Gretel?" Petr whipped his head around, now overwhelmed by the information coming at him.

"I know it now. I can feel it. They went to the cabin. And you're right Petr, she wants me to follow them there. She's starting the nightmare again."

CHAPTER TWENTY-THREE

THE OLD WOMAN SMELLED the System officer before he stepped out of the cruiser.

She'd been kneeling on the floor, steeped in prayer, sending her gratitude and loyalty to this Life that had been provided to her, to the universe that had unfolded all of the riches of her being. Her existence had been a struggle over the past few years—a nearly mortal one at times—but she'd ultimately persevered, and now felt compelled to give thanks for those challenges. And it was Life that deserved all the credit.

A tear streaked from the corner of the woman's eye and wedged its way into her mouth, the salty water coating her large incisor. She spat it out and snarled, giving a wicked look toward the window through which the smell of the intruder had wafted. She'd come too far; she wasn't ready to give up on her journey yet. Maybe she would never be ready.

The woman had known all along the System would come—of course they would—but she hadn't expected them this quickly. She and the Klahr woman had left the Back Country less than eight hours ago. By her own primitive calculations, she figured she'd have at least a few days alone with the woman before Petr Stenson came calling. Perhaps even more if the boy didn't come home for several days, which, the woman had observed, wasn't completely out of the question.

But, apparently, he had come home and wasted no time alerting the authorities to the absence of his guardians.

But why would he have scrambled so quickly to contact the System? She never would have imagined the boy would turn to them with such haste. This wasn't part of her strategy. She was depending on the boy's cynicism, his wariness that the corrupt police force would see him as the main suspect in whatever crime was declared. The woman was almost certain he would hold back, at least for a few days, especially considering Officer Stenson's well-documented fall from the good graces of the System. She always believed the boy himself would come to rescue his adoptive keepers, and from there, the woman would begin her torture.

The witch tilted an eye through the curtain crack and watched the officer open the door and put his foot to the gravel. He stood and looked toward the house. He was tall and burly, with wide shoulders and a stiff jaw. But most alarming to the woman was that he projected a confidence that hadn't quite existed in Stenson. Stenson was far from milquetoast, but this officer projected something more dangerous.

The woman took note of the man's demeanor and then quickly walked to the back room where Amanda Klahr lay semi-conscious, a loop of black iron clasped to her ankle. The chain was unnecessary at this stage, since the effects of the solution had rendered her helpless, but there was no reason for carelessness.

"Who's here?" Amanda grumbled. "Is that Petr?" The words came out in a sleepy panic, as if she were having a nightmare, speaking in protest to her own imagination.

"No one is here," the old woman said, disinterested, attempting to stay composed.

"Petr! Stay away!" Her drugged whimper fell well short of the shout for which she was aiming.

"Shut up! It's not Petr!" the woman hissed.

Amanda Klahr tried to rise, and feeling the tug of at her ankle, slapped at it as if a mosquito had landed near her foot. She moaned in despair and collapsed back to the bed.

"Petr," she said once more and then took a heavy breath before sliding into another bout of sleep.

The woman glared at Amanda Klahr for several seconds, gauging the depth of her slumber, and then hurried back to the front room, carrying with her the wooden chair to which her prisoner had been strapped only hours earlier.

The witch placed the chair beside her dining table and then sat with her back facing the front door of the cabin. She pulled up the oversized hood of her cloak and sighed, and then focused on calling forth the strength in her cells. She'd been sloppy again and had been caught off guard; there was nothing to do now but turn completely to the problem at hand.

The first set of knocks was jarring, authoritative; three sharp wraps followed by a "Hello!"

The woman stayed silent. She listened for the turn of the knob, followed by the sound of boot steps entering the cabin. As she waited, she did rudimentary calculations in her mind, measuring how many paces she would allow the man to take before unfurling her attack. Six seemed like the right number, maybe five if he started to get jumpy.

Another set of knocks, followed by the painful creak of rusted door hinges.

The woman breathed deeply and swallowed, eager now, waiting for the steps to begin. She'd positioned herself tall and narrow in the chair, and slightly off-center from the view of the doorway so that only her shoulder, perhaps only an arm, could be seen by someone entering. It was an enticement for the officer to come closer, as far as necessary to get a good look at the figure sitting in silence.

The woman sensed the apprehension, the officer's leeriness as he stalled at the threshold, treating the scene like the minefield it was. She was working hard at restraint, wanting nothing more than to spin and leap toward the arrestor, the pirate who had come to steal her life.

"Hello?" the officer asked again, curious, perhaps not realizing she was sitting only a few feet away. She waited, her muscles tense, eyeball bulging, shifted left in its socket as if trying to look behind her without turning her neck.

"I can see you there, so I know you can hear me. Are you going to answer me?"

This wasn't going at all as the woman expected, but she managed her composure and kept calm. She stayed seated, her head tilted slightly forward, demurring. "Yes?" she said finally. It was a breathy, sleepy noise, as if she'd just been drawn from a trance. Another layer to her trap.

"Is that your truck parked outside?"

Without pause the witch said, "No, it's not."

The officer said nothing for a beat, letting silence fill the gap of the obvious follow-up question. "Well, whose truck is it?" The officer remained on the porch, at a safe distance to avoid an attack.

"I think you know whose truck it is. It's why you're here, yes?"

And with that, the witch had said too much to turn back. Her words weren't quite a confession, but they teetered on the edge, and the officer would certainly continue pushing her until she careened over it. She had to move now; if she waited another ten seconds, she may have the barrel of a revolver pointed between her shoulder blades.

The woman was still confident in her speed and quickness, but the truth was, at the distance she was currently from the door, she wouldn't beat the squeeze of a System officer's trigger finger. She had to go before he drew his gun. She had to attack now.

And then another smell drifted in through the open door, one that she recognized instantly.

She lifted her chin and pushed her nose forward, chasing the odor as it floated above her. She smiled, reconfiguring her attack plan. "Oh yes, yes you do. You certainly know whose truck that is. I can smell it on you. Perhaps I smell it beyond that?"

The woman could almost hear the drop of the officer's jaw. "It's true, isn't it?" he asked.

The woman was not entirely sure as to which truth the man was referring, but she sensed the scene was trending in her favor. "What is your name, System officer?"

There was a pause. "Dodd. Officer Carl Dodd. But I'm far more interested in your name, ma'am. We never quite figured out that information in our investigation. And I'm rather sure it's not the Witch of the North."

Her name.

She hadn't thought of her forename in decades, and she hadn't the remotest idea when it was that someone last called it out. Fifty years, maybe? Was that possible?

Her throat constricted. The pressure she hadn't felt from the presence of the System officer, she now experienced with the challenge of recollecting her name. She still possessed it inside of her. It was in her mind, buried deeply in the folds perhaps, but still retrievable, like a tool left in the forest for years which gradually gets enveloped by leaves and limbs. There was some digging to do, but it was there, able to be extracted.

"You don't know your name?"

The woman shook her head once, as if jiggling away the distraction. She needed to think. Martha? No, that wasn't quite it, but it was close. The M was correct though. She squeezed her one functioning eye closed tight, pressing her brain to work. She found Tanja first, her mother's name, and then just beneath it, floating alone in her ancient intellect, she found her own.

Marlene.

"Marlene. My name is Marlene." The words sounded glorious in her ears, like some type of audible medicine had been applied to her eardrums.

"Marlene. That's actually quite pretty." The words were more surprise than flattery. "Is it true, Marlene? What I've heard about your...abilities, I suppose you would call them?"

Marlene stood now and slowly turned toward Dodd, careful not to make any sudden movements. Being a System officer, he would have known as well as anyone what she was capable of, about the details surrounding the attack from the Morgan women. He would be aware of her strength, and he wouldn't allow himself to be caught off guard the way Officer Stenson did.

"Easy, Marlene. I'm not here to hurt you." Dodd's hand slipped to his waist; his pinky finger brushed the handle of his sidearm.

"But you wish to take me away, yes? I'm afraid I can't allow that to happen."

"I'm not here to do that either. I understand why you would think that, obviously, but I'm not." Dodd paused again and then looked the woman squarely in the eyes. "What I'm here to do is help you. To help us, really. If what I've heard about you is true, I think we can help each other quite a bit."

"I couldn't say what is true and what is not, since I don't know what's been said." This was no longer just banter; Marlene was intrigued by this news of her infamy. She gave the officer a narrow look of suspicion. "What have you heard? And from whom?"

Dodd exhaled a chuckle. "Everyone knows the story of Anika and Gretel Morgan, Marlene. It's a local fairy tale by now. The details are so fantastic that it's already grown past this region of the New Country. It may even reach the shores of the Old World someday. Perhaps become a cautionary tale throughout the world, a chronicle parents tell their children to curb their naughty behavior. Of course, I'm a bit ahead of things here; it hasn't quite reached that point yet. Besides, it would be a bit too soon to tell kids such a gruesome tale. Wouldn't you agree?"

Marlene felt the sting of an insult at this last part. There was a tone suggesting the officer viewed her as some kind of monster. "What do you want, Mr. Dodd? If you're here to help me—and to help yourself—why don't you tell me how we would go about making those things happen."

"Okay, I'll get right to it then. In her official statement to the System, Anika Morgan spoke repeatedly of a potion. She described it as some type of putrid soup or something." A pop of recognition appeared on the officer's face. "Pies. That was it. She said the potion was put into pies."

Dodd paused, and Marlene could see him searching her face for a tell, some blink of familiarity to validate the story. Her expression didn't waver.

"She recounted to us how, for several months, she was being used—or, more specifically, that you were using her—to make some ancient concoction. A witch's brew, if you will. She said you took her blood and ... other things."

Marlene delighted in the officer's words and silently waited for the full dissertation of the events surrounding the Morgan woman. Dodd, however, left the tale there.

"I see," she said without expression.

"It was madness of course, this story, at least to those closest to the investigation. And it was even more widely dismissed by everyone in the barracks. At least everyone I talked to. As I've heard, the whole narrative has become a bit of legend across the full span of the System."

"But not to you. You thought it was more than legend." Marlene instinctively knew the rest of Dodd's story, but she let him finish the broad strokes of it.

"I wasn't so convinced." He paused. "Do you know who Officer Stenson is?"

Marlene took an involuntary step back, her body preparing itself for defense.

"So, I guess you do." Dodd put his hands up, palms facing flat toward Marlene. "But I'm not here to relive his demise. I don't care. He made his choices. I only mention him as a reference for you."

Marlene exhaled quietly but kept her distance.

"I'm the one who found him in this cabin. He was torn to shreds. My partner and the rest of the investigators assumed he'd been killed by an animal. They figured you kept crazed dogs or wild pigs or something and that you'd released them on him when he came to question you about Anika Morgan."

This time Marlene couldn't help the slight curl of a smile, though she doubted it was detectable by the officer.

"But that isn't what happened, is it? You did that. Somehow you did that to his body."

Marlene could again sense Dodd waited for some reciprocation from her, some dialogue so they could devise their plan to "help each other." She still gave him nothing.

"But I don't blame you, Marlene."

The woman closed her eyes and basked in the sound of her own name.

"He was coming to hurt you, wasn't he?"

"Yes," she whispered, her eyes still closed, her head tilted back slightly.

"I knew him well enough to see the change in him. I sensed his corruption for months. His behavior became erratic. I didn't know if it was something in his personal life or beyond, but it was real. You aren't to blame, Marlene. Officer Stenson was using you, wasn't he? He was using you for your powers, and then he was going to steal it all away from you. Isn't that right?"

"Yes!" the woman screamed. Her mouth hung gaping, like an opera singer, holding the short-E sound as if ending an aria. She felt the cool air on her exposed fangs.

Dodd stayed composed, expressionless.

"They're always coming to steal from me, you and your kind. They don't have the talent to do what I do, so they take it from me, compelling me. The tools they used to use were rape and torture, now it's the threat of my freedom and the thievery of my secrets."

Marlene thought of her book. Somewhere in the recesses of her mind she registered that this officer standing outside on her porch was the first to come here following the escape of Anika Morgan.

"I think I preferred it before, when what the men stole from me took only a few minutes to obtain. Now they want not just me but my life's work. My possessions. But no more. I've found the secret. What I've been searching for as far back as my memory goes. I don't fear you anymore. And I don't need you."

"As I said, Marlene, I'm not here to force you or coerce you to do anything. You say you don't need me, but you will. We can help each other."

"It's too late for you to stop them, Officer Dodd. They'll be coming for me. I've already made sure of that." Marlene again readied herself for attack, waiting for Dodd to lower his defenses for just a moment.

"I know about Georg Klahr. The neighbor. The one who lived across the lake."

Marlene had smelled the man on the officer seconds after he appeared at the door; what she didn't know was that he'd been to the house already. That he had already discovered everything.

"It was the boy then. He put his trust in your detestable organization after all. I hadn't expected that."

"No, it wasn't Petr. There's been no call from Petr Stenson to The System."

"Then how?"

"I'll tell you, but first I'd like to come inside. To talk. We can keep this same distance from each other if you like, but I'd rather be off the porch."

Marlene unconsciously glanced toward the bedroom.

Officer Dodd picked up on the movement. "She is here then. I assumed so. Is she dead?"

Marlene shook her head, like a child who'd just confessed to attempting some dangerous stunt and had been asked if she was hurt.

"Okay, that's good. There can't be any more of that. Not yet. May I come in?"

Marlene nodded, and Dodd walked inside, closing the door gently behind him. He walked to the kitchen, keeping the proper radius, his eyes fixed on the woman as he moved behind the counter, a natural barrier of protection should the need arise.

"Why don't you sit down, Marlene. We have some things to figure out. Very serious things. You've created quite a bit of damage over these past few weeks. And I'm not just speaking of the Klahrs. Those boys who disappeared? I assume that was you? Am I right to assume that?"

Marlene was confused at first; she hadn't thought of the boys since she'd buried the second one at the edge of her property. "They've been found." It was a statement.

"No, they haven't, but that is only because of me. The younger brother of one of the missing boys gave a rather convincing account about the day they were last seen. Please, sit down."

Marlene followed the order to sit and now recalled how the boy's escape had seemed problematic at the time, a future worry to contend with. Yet it didn't appear as if any detectives or System officers had come to her home since that day.

As if reading her mind, Dodd said, "I can make a lot of things go away, as you can see. If it wasn't for me, there would be a large-scale manhunt underway right now. But I can't make problems go away forever, Marlene. People are beginning to get suspicious again. The myth of the Northlands Witch and the possibility that she might be alive and roaming the New Country looking for victims is starting to make its way out of the school yards and into the barracks. And that's not where you want those stories to be."

Marlene gave a knowing nod, keeping her eyes locked on the officer, waiting to hear about her contribution to their deal.

"I always believed you were alive," Dodd continued. "I'm not going to get into the whole story about why I believed that, because it's not important, but just know that I've done quite a bit of work to keep everyone else believing you were dead. And one of the biggest problems I've had to work out has been the Stenson boy, Petr. He's made things quite difficult over the last year. He's been busy with his own investigations, raising questions about the disappearance of your body and why no one at the System has been able to give him a straight answer. He's formulated some pretty accurate theories that some people are starting to consider. And now, with his normally stable guardians suddenly disappearing and two boys vanishing from your property, along with a witness who heard screams, well, those people who were only lightly considering Petr's theories before are going to start considering them very seriously now."

"What do you want, Officer Dodd?"

Dodd smiled and nodded, pleased that the woman understood that negotiations had begun. He looked at the walls and ceiling of the cabin, as if just noticing them for the first time, and then took a cursory scan of the one large room that made up the bulk of the cabin. "Do you enjoy living here, Marlene? Living like this?"

Marlene frowned and shook her head, confused. "Enjoy living here?"

"Yes. Do you enjoy your life? This life?"

Marlene's expression flattened, and she shook her head slowly, now realizing what the officer asked. "I enjoy almost nothing, Officer Dodd. Joy is fleeting, like the memory of a dream. When you've lived as I have there is little about life you can truly enjoy. Enjoyment is for children. At a very young age, it transitions into struggle. For most, life is struggle. It has always been the way. Struggle is what your ancestors did for millions of years to bring you into existence."

"Then why? If not for the joy, why do you keep doing it? Why do you try so hard to stay alive? Why do you want to keep struggling?"

Marlene rose from her chair and took a step forward, staring the officer in his eyes, imparting the magnitude of what she was about to say. "Because life is no longer about struggle for me, Officer Dodd. I've moved to the next phase. Beyond joy. Beyond struggle. I crave, Officer Dodd. I keep chasing this life because I crave it."

Dodd was mesmerized by the woman, but his instincts kept his hand at his waist.

"When you crave, there is nothing to consider. No reason for doing. Do you want to crave, Officer Dodd? Is that what we're doing here? Are you making this deal to keep the intruders away in exchange for this life?"

Dodd nodded. "Yes," he whispered.

Marlene nodded slowly. "Then we need the Morgan women."

"Let's find them."

Marlene smiled. "No need, Officer Dodd. They'll come to us."

CHAPTER TWENTY-FOUR

ANIKA SAT ON THE GROUND directly across from
the four men, cross-legged, like a schoolgirl listening to her
teacher at story time. The ground of this new land was dusty
and barren, grassless, a stark contrast to the lush jungle-like
terrain from where she had come only minutes before. This
new region reminded Anika of ruined cropland, or perhaps
a field that had been cleared and leveled for construction.

In between Anika and the men was a meticulously
straight row of large stones, each of which was approximately
the size of a pumpkin.

The four men, who sat as Anika did, were thin and frail,
and judging by the gray of their beards and the sun-scorched
lines of their faces, the youngest among them couldn't have
been a year less than seventy. The distance they'd walked
from the village couldn't have been much farther than three
or four miles, yet these men seemed as if they belonged to
a race as different as the natives of the New Country. They
didn't appear to be savages though—the naked headhunter
types she'd read of in picture books as a child—yet they also
didn't resemble the relatively sophisticated people she'd seen
throughout the marketplace back at the village. It wasn't just
their gauntness; their unshaven faces and matted hair along
with their tattered, dirty clothes gave these men the appear-

ance of lowly monks or street beggars. Anika saw no one back in the village with such characteristics.

Oskar stood just over Anika's left shoulder, hands folded, positioned to translate. Noah stood back near the entrance to the clearing, guarding them. The tiny guide who had led them to this place left them at the gate, never entering through the opening. Anika assumed he was waiting on the opposite side of the ivy wall to guide them back but knew the possibility that he had abandoned them was real.

Anika remained still on the ground, having been given no other instruction than the motion of an outstretched hand guiding her to sit. She'd obeyed and kept her eyes on the men as they took their own sitting positions.

She discreetly scanned the grounds, trying to find where the perimeter of the place ended, but it seemed to stretch on forever. She noted some rather primitive structures, huts and things, scattered about the landscape, and the few people she'd spotted when she'd first entered through the passageway—other than the men who now sat before her—had since dispersed.

"Do you speak their language, Oskar?" Anika asked, keeping her eyes straight ahead on the men.

"I not heard them. Couldn't say."

"But our little Bosomari man could talk to them? And you can communicate with him, so you should be able to do this, right? I need you to be able to do this Oskar."

Oskar shrugged, giving no promises.

Anika decided to begin the dialogue. She pointed the tips of her fingers toward her chest, tapping herself. "Anika," she said.

None of the men moved.

Anika pointed at the first man seated to her left. "You? Who are you? What is your name? Me. I'm Anika. Anika."

She repeated the chest-tapping motions once more, repeating her name again until the man to the far right of the line, opposite the man Anika had pointed to originally, put an outstretched finger to his closed mouth, giving the ever-expanding universal signal of quiet. He smiled and nodded with his finger held in place. Anika felt slightly offended and further diminished to the childish role she'd already assumed, but there was nothing threatening in the motion, so she followed the order.

Almost in unison, the four men closed their eyes and held their hands up, chest high, with their palms facing out toward Anika. They held their mime-like pose in silence for what was maybe twenty seconds. There was no chanting or humming, just stillness, and Anika soon became fidgety, unsure if she was supposed to follow their action.

Finally, the man who had shushed her spoke. "Donti," he said, lowering his hands. The rest of the men followed.

Anika wanted to look back at Oskar, to see if he had the translation, but she decided to stay still and wait it out a little longer.

The man second from the left held out his hands again, but this time they were lower, and his palms faced up. He looked Anika in the eyes and gave a short, encouraging nod. She took the bait and held her hands out to the man, who grabbed her by the wrists. He studied her palms for a few seconds and then turned her hands over and placed them flat on one of the rocks in the row. Despite the heavy heat that had been pressing down on Anika since she woke that morning, the stone felt cold. It felt refreshing, almost thirst-quenching.

The same man then wrapped his own fingers on the stone next to Anika's, and the man next to him placed his hands on his own rock. Anika's hands were now in the middle of the two pairs of hands. The two men closed their eyes again, and this time Anika did the same.

At first Anika felt nothing, but then the rock warmed slightly, until it reached a temperature which was almost unbearable. The first man, the man who'd placed Anika's hands there, lifted his own from the rock and looked over at the man to the far left, frowning. He shook his head. "Omale. Omale."

"Ti Omale?" the far-left man replied, this time looking at the other man whose hands were still on the rock.

"Bi," the other man said. "Omale."

Anika had enough of the language barrier, and she turned back toward Oskar. "What are they saying, Oskar? Do you know?"

"Omale. That mean dead." Oskar sounded subdued. "They both say dead."

"Me? I'm dead? Is that what they're saying?"

Oskar shrugged again.

"Well ask them!"

Oskar rattled off a sentence that was about fourteen words longer than Anika would have thought necessary to convey her request, and the first man replied with an equally long response. She heard the name Aulwurm in the reply.

"They say you are from their tribe; your blood comes from their tribe. They feel the vibrations or something. I don't get it all, but most."

Anika's eyes teared, not from fear or sadness, but from the reality that she had reached this point. All of this was true, these people, this magic. Orphism. And now that she was here, she wasn't sure how she should proceed. This was it. This is what she had come for. This was the reason she had risked spending the remaining days of her life with these strange men in the broad ranges of the Old World. If this band of remote hermits couldn't give her the answers she needed, then that would be the end.

"But you got the sickness," Oskar continued. "They say you got the sickness."

She was sick, but she wasn't prepared to die. "I have cancer, Oskar. It's why I'm here. Tell them I've come for their help. I'm not dead yet. Tell them I believe they have medicine that can help me." Anika paused. "Is that true? Can they help me?"

Oskar translated to the rapt audience of the four men, each of whom was studying him intensely, unblinking, perfectly concentrated on the words that were coming at them in what was almost certainly broken syntax.

Oskar waited, equally rapt for their response, and then began the translation. "You don't have the cancer. That's what they say. But true you are sick."

"But I've been to the doctors. They say I do have cancer." Anika wasn't arguing, just laying out the facts so that these men had a complete picture of her situation.

Oskar did his shrug again. "I not sure what that means. They just say you have poison. You have too much poison."

"That's the cancer. Right? The cancer is the poison? That must be what they mean."

Oskar shook her off. "No cancer. Poison. They make the difference." Anika knew he meant distinction.

Anika now looked straight ahead at the men in front of her, confused and focused. "What poison?"

The second man in the row listened to Oskar and then made a motion with his hands as if he was drinking soup, shaping both hands wide and lifting them to his mouth.

Anika shook her head, not understanding the charade.

The man then made another motion, and this time Anika's eyes flooded with tears. He turned one of his soup-sipping hands into the shape of a claw, keeping the other soup hand in place, and then started pretending to shovel food into his mouth. Anika knew instantly what he showed her. It was the perfect pantomime of someone eating pie with his hands. If anyone could see it, she could; Anika had made the motion dozens of times during her captivity in the cabin. She still sometimes saw herself eating pie that way in her dreams.

"The pie."

The man smiled. "Pie," he said, nodding eagerly.

"I was poisoned by the pie? The witch's pie? That's why I'm dying? Ask them, Oskar!"

Oskar translated and waited for a response, which he conveyed affirmatively to Anika. "Yes. The pie. Sometime it could be soup, but sometime the pie. They say it's too much for you that you eat. Too much to live."

Anika thought back on those horrendous days of pies and potions, when she would lay frozen, constantly raising her head to stare toward the door, dreading the turn of the knob and the entry of the evil woman carrying that black, wrought iron tray of food. So delicious that first day, so vile virtually every day after.

"But they can save me, right? They have the medicine here that can cure this? An antidote?"

Oskar converted the questions again, and this time the response from the group of men was lengthy, with each person taking a share of the time. Anika listened to them as if she understood, watching their mouths and mannerisms, hoping to pick up any clue as to how the verdict would fall.

Oskar looked down at Anika and frowned. "It's too late, they say. You have too late."

Anika was bemused, and she stood defiantly. "Too late? That's it? That's all they said? They must have told you more than that. All they said just now was that it was too late?"

"They say other things too. 'They sorry for you.' 'They want but can't help you.' Like that."

"What did they say Oskar?" Anika screamed at him, looking back and forth between Oskar and the four men, whose expressions were now serious and concerned.

"They said something else." The sound of Noah's voice boomed from behind the cluster of Anika, Oskar, and the four men, instantly freezing them, as if he were the director of a stage play who had seen enough of a miserable rehearsal and was now bringing it to an end.

Oskar turned toward his companion, an expression close to terror on his face.

"They said much more."

Anika stared at Noah, disbelieving, studying him as if he were an ancient mythical statue, uncovered after a thousand years. She was awed not only by this new ability to understand the language of the tribesmen, but also, again, by his incredible articulation of her own. She was beginning to suspect Noah was a person far more substantive than even she had originally suspected.

Whatever else there was, though, would have to wait. "What more did they say, Noah?"

"Noah," Oskar whimpered, "How you—"

"Quiet, Oskar." Anika's face was stone, her eyes dispassionate, reptilian in their coldness. "What else did they say, Noah?"

"Oskar was telling the truth about the poison, but he didn't tell you all of it." Noah walked up to the group and stood beside Oskar, a look of measured distrust in his eyes. He turned now and looked toward Anika. "You will die because of the pies, that much is true. But they said there is hope for you. A chance for you to live."

Anika glowered at Oskar.

"It isn't true, these things," Oskar pleaded. "I no want you to waste your hope. Waste your time."

"What did they say, Noah? What are my options?"

"They spoke of a book. A book of magic or spells or something. The word they used doesn't translate exactly, but it's the—"

"I know about the book. My daughter has it. A copy of it. It was my father's."

Noah's face scrunched in confusion. "The book they spoke of, they say it belonged to a woman. "Tanja's book" I think was the name they said...I think they were speaking of the witch you spoke of. I don't know this language like Oskar, but I know it. It's a different language than that of the villagers. It's the tongue of my grandmother, but I haven't used it in many years. I didn't get all of what they said, but I'm almost sure it was her book—that witch's book they were speaking of."

Anika paused, swallowing slowly. "Yes, she had the book too."

"Was your daughter's book the same as this woman's? Exactly the same?"

Anika had always assumed the two books were the same, but she had never explored the possibility that they were different. "I don't know. Ask them. Ask them if all the books are the same. Orphism. The title of the book is Orphism."

Noah spoke in the native language, stumbling through some of the words, but gradually easing into a flow. Oskar discreetly slinked back toward the doorway. Anika followed him, prepared to admonish him for his dereliction of duty.

"You no have to pay me, I know that," he sulked. "And they no say 'Tanja's book.'" They call it the daughter of Tanja's book. I not know what it mean. But there no cure for you. This is for robbing people. How you say? A con, yes? You can't believe in the witchcraft. Is for fools."

Anika felt no need to recount to Oskar the things she'd seen or the magic that she knew existed in the world. Or that he was in no position to judge people's foolishness. "Oskar, what else did they say? Tell me. I am going to pay you; you've done more than I ever expected to this point, so I need you to keep doing your job. And there's no point hiding it now. Noah will tell me in a minute anyway."

Oskar looked down and frowned at the overgrowth of buffalo grass sprouting up the border wall. "They say there is cure, but it is in one book only. Only the book of Tanja's daughter. This other book, of your daughter, they say that one no have it."

Noah had arrived behind Anika and listened to Oskar. "This would seem to be true. The men told me that all the books contain the recipe, but not the cure. The anti-recipe. But again, that's not the exact translation of the word he used; I think it's close though, close to the same meaning. He said this anti-recipe can undo the sickness. But it is contained in the one book only."

"Do you believe them, Noah? Do you think there is a chance any of it is true? I already know Oskar's opinion."

"I would believe it worth trying. You came this far. And what are you losing by trying? They may not have been able to heal you, not directly, but they gave you hope—information—maybe it's all the information you need. Why would you not try?"

"Because you waste your time," Oskar barked. "Tell her, Noah. Tell what she have to do. You can no read the book Anika. You no can make this recipe. How you will do it?"

Noah stared directly at Anika, his eyes earnest and hypnotic. "If you choose to do this, choose to try to heal yourself, they said to bring it to them. To translate it. You won't be able to understand it."

Anika closed her eyes and took in a deep breath, beginning to weigh all that would be required to bring this task to fruition. Just finding the book would be formidable, returning here, to this secret village in the middle of the Old World, would be nearly impossible, especially considering the small measure of time she presumably had left. "You can do it, Noah. Or you, Oskar. One of you can decipher it, right?"

Noah shook his head. "Not me, Anika, and I don't think Oskar either. They say this language of the book goes back beyond them. There is only one here who can translate it. And she cannot travel due to her age and her physical debilitation."

"How then? How can this be done? Ask them, Noah." Anika nearly whispered now, as if she were communicating with the dead. "Ask them how this can be done."

Anika, Noah, and Oskar walked back to the group of men. They had remained virtually unmoved in their seated positions, the expressions on their faces calm and caring. Anika sat down in the spot where she'd been diagnosed just moments before and reversed the actions, holding out her hands now, beckoning the closest man to reach out to her. The second man in the row gave his hands to her, smiling.

"I want you to translate, Oskar." Anika looked up at her interpreter, eyebrows high. "I'm paying you to do this, and I need you to do your job. I need the translation to be precise."

Oskar nodded.

Anika looked at the man seated before her and squeezed his hands gently, gaining his attention. "I'm dying, that's what you said." Anika paused, waiting for the interpretation.

"You've also told me what I have to do to live, yes? Get the book—Orphism—and bring it back here. But that will take time." Anika paused again, piercing the man's eyes, waiting for Oskar's foreign words to finish.

The man nodded, affirming the reiteration of the day's events.

"How long do I have to do this? I live very far from here." Anika made what she believed was the universal signal for far—large, forward-raking motions of her arms above her head. "Can you help me?"

The man waited for Oskar to finish and then looked at Anika, the first real sign of sympathy showing on his face. He blinked twice and then stood and turned his back to Anika. He cupped his hands to his mouth and gave an animal-like call to the sky.

There was a delay of a few seconds, and then a slight woman walked out from between two of the small huts lining the edges of the common area. As she came closer, Anika noticed the woman carried a duffel no larger than a grapefruit down by her thigh. The woman approached and walked past the group of men, placing the bag on one of the stones forming the divide.

The cloth sack was loosely tied at the top by some type of vine or grass. As she stood to leave, the woman pulled the vine with her in one motion, and the cloth sack unfolded, falling flat, opening like a cloth napkin. In the middle of the fabric sat a berry so orange that it looked as if it had been painted.

"What is it?" Anika asked.

"I don't know." Noah said, sounding rapt.

"Oskar?"

"Thunta?" Oskar asked, translating for her.

The man spoke two or three sentences, and Oskar relayed the rendition to Anika. "You take this. It makes you sick, but it will give you time. Slow the sickness. But no cure. The cure is in the book only. And maybe no time for to come back here. You sick, Anika. They say you not have so much time. Even with berry."

"What?" Anika was dismayed, and tears welled in her eyes.

Oskar just shrugged and looked away, and Anika thought she saw the glint of water in his eyes too.

Anika reached for the berry, and the man immediately placed his hand over it, blocking her. He peered up at Oskar with a look that signaled he wanted Anika to be sure she knew what she was signing up for.

"You going to get sick," Oskar warned again.

Anika shifted her eyes from the man and then back to Oskar. "How sick?"

"People die from it. They have died. But when you don't die, you get more time. Makes the sickness weak. Not for so long, but more time. He can't know how long."

Anika looked at Noah, who nodded, having nothing further to offer in the translation.

Anika signaled her awareness to the old tribesman with a head dip and a long blink, and the man removed the canopy of his hand; the bright berry winked at Anika, its color as potent as its rumored effects. Anika assumed his warning of sickness and death was a formality, a necessary advisory to any who indulged, just in the off-chance some terrible side-effect occurred. And anyway, what difference did it make now?

Anika grabbed the berry and, just as she was to toss it past her lips, the tribesmen grunted in unison. Anika looked up and saw one of the men making a chewing motion with his mouth while simultaneously waving his hands and shaking his head. Swallow it whole, he was saying. She got the message.

The berry entered her throat and belly and, at first entry, rested benignly in her stomach.

By nightfall, the poison was flowing through Anika fully, and the fever inside her was a raging storm.

CHAPTER TWENTY-FIVE

HANSEL, GRETEL, AND Petr stood on Ben Richter's porch. The sun had risen less than an hour earlier, which meant, based on Gretel's calculations, they each had gotten about four and half hours of sleep. Not much, but considering the circumstances, it wasn't too bad. Time was critical, of course, but if the woman was waiting for them, luring them as Gretel suspected, maybe things weren't quite as urgent as she had originally thought.

And besides, they had to sleep.

Petr gave a quiet rap on his friend's front door, and seconds later, a boy about the same age as Petr peeked through the foyer window, holding up one finger and making a signal of someone shaking a keychain.

"Why won't he let you just borrow it?" Gretel asked Petr, her tone indicating that they may have to consider another option if his friend insisted on going with them. The sleep had stabilized Gretel's emotions, and she was thankful for the time they had before the impending confrontation with the witch. But additional players in the game felt like added weight of responsibility on her shoulders.

"I may have burned a few bridges as it pertains to Ben Richter's truck. He's a nice guy, but—"

"Are you all ready?" Ben joined the children on the porch, keys jangling.

"Ben, I know I always say this, but I need to go alone this time. This is important." Petr was somber, curt with his syntax.

"Alone? So you're going without these two then?" Ben smiled at the siblings. "Hi, I'm Ben. Ben Richter. Petr has never been great with introductions."

"Hi," Gretel said, "I'm—"

"Oh, I guessed who you were the second I saw you. Petr spent a good deal of conversation on the great Gretel Morgan."

Gretel blushed and recognized the same color in Petr's cheeks.

"And anyway, you're somewhat of a celebrity in these parts, Gretel." Ben looked at Hansel. "And you, I presume, are the brother. Hansel, eh?"

"Yes, hi," Hansel said.

Gretel interrupted the charm before it got out of hand. "Petr's right, Ben, you shouldn't come with us. It could be dangerous."

"That's right," Hansel chimed. "It's probably best you stay. Like Gretel says, it could be dangerous."

Gretel couldn't help but grin, proud of her brother's assertion.

"Well now I'm definitely going. As far as I'm concerned, there's nothing more dangerous than missing out on danger. Also, we have a stop to make on the way to wherever it is we're going."

"No!" Petr yelped. "Ben, no, this is real. We need your help, we need your truck, so you can call it the way it is. But we need to go now. Quickly."

Ben nodded, dropping the playfulness from his expression. "Fine, but I told her I'd get her."

"Who?"

"Sofia. She needs a lift. She asked me a week ago. And I don't like to let people down. You know that about me, Petr." Ben looked at each member of the group. "But if it's out of the way from where we're going, I'll leave her."

"You promise me, Ben. If it's out of the way."

"Of course. It's a promise. You're in a hurry though, right? So let's get off this porch."

The four kids walked to Ben's truck and hopped inside, with Ben and Petr flanking Gretel in the middle of the bench seat. Hansel sat alone on a fold-down seat just behind the driver's seat.

"Sofia?" Gretel asked. She looked over at Petr, an eyebrow raised.

"Do you know her?" Petr sounded surprised.

"If it's Sofia Karlsson, then of course. Everybody knows Sofia Karlsson. That is who you mean, right?"

"Yes."

"She was the most popular girl in school from the moment she moved here. Moving up to the big time, I see."

"And she's quite smitten with Mr. Stenson," Ben added.

"All right, that's enough. And it's not true."

Gretel smiled and looked at Ben for the truth. Ben smiled back, wrinkled his nose and nodded, affirming the rumor.

"So where are we going, Petr? What's the emergency?"

"The Northlands."

Ben looked wide-eyed at his friend; there was nothing else to say. "I had a feeling you were going to say that. But you know what that means, right?"

"Yeah, I get it."

Gretel's smile faded. "Does that mean Sofia is coming with us?"

"No," Petr corrected, "it means she's getting a ride to her stop on the way. She's not coming with us."

"Yes, right, that's what I meant." Gretel turned and stared through the windshield at the road unfolding before them, and within a few minutes was sound asleep, dreaming of how she would kill the witch for good.

"HI, SOFIA."

Gretel awoke to the sound of Ben's delightful voice greeting Sofia.

Sofia. The name had a lovely timbre, and it roused Gretel as if she were tickled by a feather.

"You remember Gretel, right? And this is her brother, Hansel."

Gretel shook her head clear and forced a thin smile.

"Of course. Hi, Gretel, how are you?" Sofia's intonation was laced with sympathy and paternalism. "And you're Hansel. Hi."

Petr jumped down and pulled the seat forward, allowing Sofia to take the position opposite Hansel in the back seat.

"Hi, Sofia, it's nice to see you again. You look great as always," Gretel replied, the civility and compliments painful in their delivery.

"Thanks. Where are you all off to so early? It was such a surprise when Ben called and told me you were on his porch. I almost didn't believe him."

Gretel looked back at Hansel, a glean of warning in her eyes. "Uh, my grandfather's house. There are some things there that still need to be cleaned out from his basement. Petr's helping me. Us."

"That's very sweet of you, Petr."

Petr barely nodded, keeping his gaze forward.

"When did you get back in town?" Sofia asked, and Gretel detected just a hint of suspicion in the girl's voice.

"Yesterday. Late."

"Wow! You're all very ambitious. Getting right to work then. How is your mother?"

Gretel started getting the itch of irritation, as if she were being interrogated. "We're all fine, Sofia. How have you been? Still the queen of the school?"

"Gretel, come on." Petr said, trying to calm the tension.

"I'm teasing, Petr, so you come on. Sofia knows I'm kidding her."

"I've been fine, thanks."

As coincidence would have it, Sofia was headed to a park only an hour from where the witch's cabin stood, and thus the truck ride was long and awkward and mostly silent. When they came to Sofia's exit, the one that would take them at least a half an hour out of the way, Sofia decided to speak bluntly. "Are you going to her cabin?"

"What?" Petr blurted, just a beat too quickly in Gretel's estimation. "Why did you ask that?"

"Are you? Hansel?"

Cheap shot, Gretel thought to herself. The pretty, teenage girl extracting the truth from a boy Hansel's age. Gretel saw in the rearview mirror the blush blossoming on his face.

"Sofia, what are you doing?" Ben said, taking charge of the conversation in his truck.

"Nothing. I just think you guys are up to something. And I want to go."

"No!" Petr barked.

"So you are going."

Gretel stared over at Petr, frowning, as if to ask, how did you just fall for that?

"Yes, we are. But you're not."

"Why? Is she there? Is she alive? Were you right this whole time, Petr? Oh my god, you were."

No one answered Sofia, giving her all the answers she needed.

"Listen," she continued, "if you go straight to her cabin you'll save forty-five minutes. At least. Once you take this exit, it's another twenty miles. And then twenty back to the Interways. Just keep going, Ben. Go straight there and save the time."

"Don't you have to be somewhere, Sofia? Isn't that the whole point of why you're here in the first place?" Petr was stammering now, as if he was helpless to stop where this train was headed.

"Yes, but it doesn't really matter. It's a family thing that no one thought I was coming to anyway. Ben was able to give me a ride at the last minute, so I decided to go."

"I thought you arranged this a week ago?"

Sofia ignored Petr. "I was going to surprise some people. Just show up. But no one will miss me. It's settled. I'm going with you guys."

"Sofia, listen—"

"Fine," Gretel interrupted, the command in her voice resonating through the truck like a timpani.

"Gretel, no! I'm not going to put her at risk. You know more than anyone what that woman will do. What she has done to people."

"So does Sofia. Don't you? You know my story by now." Gretel gave a half-look over her shoulder. Sofia nodded, and Gretel thought she detected a grin from the girl. "And besides, she's right, it will save time. If she wants to come, it's up to her. She knows the risk. And who knows? Maybe she can help us."

"Yes, Gretel!" Sofia was giddy, clapping like she'd just been selected to come to the stage to be the volunteer in a magic show.

"I don't agree with this, Gretel. For the record, I don't agree. I would never have agreed to this." Petr was sulking now, a look of betrayal on his face.

"It's Mrs. Klahr, Petr."

"I know who it is! I'm the one who stayed here! I'm the one that had to listen to her cry every night for the first month. You were the one who left. You left us behind!"

Gretel held Petr's stare, allowing him to finish unloading on her whatever resentment he still held, bubbling beneath the coolness that he presented to her and the rest of the world most of the time. His breathing was heavy now, as if ready to begin another verbal outpouring, but he said nothing else.

"I don't have to go," Sofia offered quietly. "I didn't mean to start this trouble."

Gretel turned toward Sofia and studied her peer's face like a scientist. Sofia blinked meekly and demur, evading Gretel's examination. "I would like you to come," Gretel said. "I don't want to put you at any risk—this isn't your fight—but the truth is we could probably use your help. This isn't an adventure though, Sofia. There won't be any fun involved. You need to know that going in. Petr is right about the danger. If anything, he's underplayed it."

Sofia nodded, giving Gretel's words real consideration. "I understand. I want to help Petr. And you."

Gretel looked from Sofia and then to Petr, silently regrouping everyone, making sure there was a tacit understanding that everyone knew what they were getting into. She straightened her back and looked coldly toward the front of the truck, watching the road. "Ben, do you know where you're going?"

"No. Not really."

"I'm sure Petr can tell you then. I have a feeling he's been where we're going more than a few times over the past year."

CHAPTER TWENTY-SIX

"DO YOU KNOW WHO I AM?"

Carl Dodd lurched at the sound of the female voice; it was groggy and indistinct, as if seeping through the walls.

"Excuse me?" Dodd's voice squeaked. He was irritated at the lack of resonance in his speech. He cleared his throat and hastily stood from his seat. It had been a long night, and he needed more sleep, but it was vital that he remain composed. Going forward, there would be no room for weakness.

"Do you know me?" the woman asked again. "She's done this. Please help me."

Dodd walked a few paces until he was standing next to the bed where Amanda Klahr had propped herself up slightly on the bed's lone pillow. He leaned forward and was now face-to-face with the prisoner, studying her dilated pupils and drooping eyelids, an indication that she'd been heavily drugged. He'd seen the look many times in his line of work. "Just rest, Amanda," he said, "You'll be okay."

"You do know me." The woman's eyes fluttered and then fell shut. A second later, her head flopped back down toward her chest.

Dodd walked out toward the kitchen area, stopping just at the threshold of the stone floor where a thin strip of wood partitioned off the two areas. He stood just out of sight and watched Marlene, who was staring out the window at the front of the cabin. Her eyes were eager, paranoid, like a dog staring at a closed door when it's heard the growl of an animal on the front porch. For the first time since arriving at the cabin, Dodd began doubting his decisions. "You don't plan to kill her, do you?"

Marlene closed her eyes and dropped the hem of the curtain, slowly turning toward the System officer. She opened her eyes and smiled. "I don't make plans like that, Officer Dodd. I simply do what is necessary. Nothing more or less. If the death of Anika Morgan's neighbor brings me closer to my Source, then I most certainly will kill her. It makes no difference to me. Does the fly you swat on your kitchen counter weigh upon your mind?"

Dodd stayed quiet, understanding the rhetorical nature of the question.

"When did you know, Officer Dodd?"

"When did I know what?" Dodd was sure he knew what Marlene referred to, but he asked anyway.

"When did you know I was alive?"

Dodd paused, as if considering the question for the first time. "Honestly, I guess I didn't know until only a few hours ago. But I suspected long before. Of course, it was obvious to me that you didn't die in the cannery that night. That was always impossible to me. Your body went missing almost instantly. And the nonsense rumor that you'd been dragged away by a mass of wild animals was absurd. Only a bear, maybe a pack of strong wolves, could have taken your carcass in that amount of time. And no one has seen a predator of that size in these parts for a hundred years."

Marlene was rapt with the tale, and Dodd relished the power of his words over this timeless being.

"Most of us thought you somehow survived the attack and then staggered out of the cannery, delirious and critically wounded before finally collapsing at the shore of the lake where the water took you under. It was possible that you even made it to the deep woods, a place somewhere isolated and dense before you eventually collapsed there to be consumed by smaller, less ferocious woodland beasts than the ones that tend to find their way into such fantastic stories as yours." Dodd paused. "But my mind was changed within a few minutes of walking onto this property. I knew there was another story that was quite possible."

Dodd paused again for effect, sensing the witch's enchantment.

"I saw the hole, Marlene. I saw your ditch."

Marlene caught her breath.

"But I wasn't alone here, of course." Dodd's words were fast now, racing. "So I had to be discreet. I lifted the canopy—a brilliantly designed construct, by the way, just amazing—and I saw your body there. It was surreal. Whether you were dead or alive, I didn't know at first, but you were there. Crumpled and destroyed, an iron hammer jutting from your forehead. But you had made it back somehow, and quickly enough that you arrived back here before the System even knew the story of Anika Morgan."

"So why then? Why didn't you take me away when you had the chance? I never even sensed that you were there. I was as vulnerable as I've ever been. Will ever be again. So why did you leave me there?

"Because, Marlene, by the time I found you, I had heard Anika's story. And I had just seen the body of Stenson."

Dodd could see that this wasn't a good enough answer for Marlene. She needed the whole truth.

"I had seen the change in Stenson over the course of several months, the secrecy and withdrawal in him. We all saw it. And then there he was, his dead body, here at this cabin, at the place where a lowly farm woman had just escaped before telling perhaps the most incredible story anyone had ever heard. A story of immortality. As I said before, I didn't believe any of it at first. But...the things that had been done to him..."

Dodd frowned and dropped the woman's gaze.

"After I found your...grave, I suppose I'd call it, I wasn't quite sure why I didn't have the whole System descend on this place to arrest you or kill you, why I didn't have them dig up your entire property for any more bodies that may have gone missing from this area over the years. But I know now. I know now why none of that happened. Because I believed in the story. I believed in the accounts of Anika and Gretel Morgan. And I knew you had come back here for recovery, rejuvenation. It all made sense to me. In an instant. Stenson knew the story too, and he had seen or heard enough to believe in this magic. I knew then the myths were true. Just looking at you lying in that ditch, I knew I could never have the trampling boots of System clods ending that magic forever."

"They're thieves," Marlene spat, her teeth bared wide and sinister.

Dodd smiled. "Yes, very often they are. But not me, Marlene."

Dodd realized this wasn't quite true as he thought of the stark black book resting high on the shelf in his office. He walked to the front door and opened it casually, staring out toward the tree line.

"So I waited very patiently—for just about a year—for some sign that you were awake, that you had emerged."

"Get from the door. They'll see you."

In the isolation of the cabin, Dodd could have heard a car coming from ten miles away, but he didn't want to set the witch off, so he closed the door gently and looked back at her. "And then I heard it, the manifestation, crackling over the radio, surfacing like lava from a volcano. The report of two boys who had gone missing from your property. I was patrolling here—right here—the moment the call came! It was a miracle."

Marlene narrowed her gaze, a sign that suspicion had snuck back into play for her.

Dodd chuckled. "It doesn't matter to me. I don't care about the disappearance of a pair of adolescent criminals, Marlene. I just wanted you to come back. I just wanted to learn from you. To become like you."

Marlene walked confidently from the window toward the front door and stood next to Officer Dodd. At this distance, he could have taken her by force, and there was little she could have done.

"You may want my life span, Officer Dodd, but you don't want to become like me. It's the 'becoming' part that is so onerous. Even with the methods known to them, most could never withstand the process. It's a long life of misery before you ever get to where I am."

"I don't care about the work. About the pain. It's nothing compared to death. Death has to be worse."

Marlene's eyes widened while the rest of her face was stone, and then she belted out a horrible laughter that must have certainly awoken Amanda Klahr from her intoxicated sleep in the back bedroom. She composed herself and said, "I could name a hundred things worse than death, Officer Dodd."

"But you're here. You pushed through it. Whatever pain you endured was worth it to you."

"I'm from another place and time, Officer Dodd. And that makes a difference. The life you must lead to stay alive this long is not one most would agree to. They're unable to forego the luxuries of modernity. And I don't mean conditioned air and powerful driving machines, Officer Dodd. I mean sleep. Palatable food. Warmth."

"I don't—"

Dodd's argument was interrupted by a scream from the back bedroom. Mrs. Klahr.

Dodd noticed Marlene hadn't flinched at the scream. "What's wrong with her?"

"The pharma. It's subsiding."

"Is she in pain?"

"Probably not physical pain. They're usually screams of terror. Of realizing where they are and what's been done to ones they love."

"Give her more of the drugs then."

Marlene smirked. "Officer Dodd, is that sympathy I smell on you?"

"I just don't want anyone to suffer unnecessarily. Who wants that?"

"This is what I mean, Officer Dodd. Modernity. To live this life, suffering is almost always necessary."

Dodd said nothing.

"But she'll soon have her rescuers arriving. I can feel them. The boy will come first. And then, Life willing, the Morgan women will follow. So you will get your wish, Officer Dodd. We will indeed give her more of the pharma, but only to keep her disgusting mouth shut. That is another necessity of this life: you must always think of yourself. Only yourself. There is no place for sympathy or consideration. And there is certainly no place for love."

Dodd swallowed and gave an understanding nod. He followed Marlene, who had begun her walk to the back bedroom. Amanda Klahr sat straight up in bed. Dodd could see the clarity and recognition in the prisoner's eyes, and he dropped his own, embarrassed by his criminality.

"Who are you?" Amanda asked, her voice quick, staccato, and laced with fear. "Is that a System uniform? You're from the System?"

Dodd forgot about his uniform. System uniforms were purposely designed to be plain and unrecognizable, the idea being that officers would have more success pursuing suspects on foot, particularly in the Urbanlands, if they didn't stand out with flashy badges and clothes. But laws still required officers be identifiable by uniform, and discerning citizens usually noticed them. It was no surprise that Amanda

Klahr was one of those citizens, given the recent tribulations of her adopted son.

"Petr was right. Of course, he was. That boy is always right. Some people see the good in everyone, and Petr does too. But he also sees the evil."

Dodd could feel the burn of shame on his face. He wanted this part to be finished already. He wanted the potion and the longevity, not the ignominy.

"I should test this theory of yours when he arrives," Marlene finally said, clearly sharing none of Officer Dodd's chagrin. "Certainly a boy as smart as your Petr would have figured out by now where you've disappeared to? Would you agree with that, Mrs. Klahr? Bright little Petr Stenson. Perhaps he'll bring his girlfriend with him."

Amanda let the woman's words set in and then let out a gregarious laugh that sounded genuine to Dodd. "Gretel? Are you talking about Gretel? Is that who you think is coming?" She laughed heartier now, making a show of it, and Marlene couldn't help but scowl. "You are quite the violent fool, aren't you? Gretel left for the Old World ages ago. I don't know how long it's been now, but...ah yes...I remember. It was only a few weeks after she smashed your head in."

Marlene instinctively reached for the spot on her head where the hammer had been lodged. Dodd suspected this was a recent habit, and one she would maintain for decades.

"I haven't heard from her in over a year. She's not coming for me. She or her mother."

Dodd looked at Marlene sheepishly. He sensed a bubbling in the woman and felt this could be news that would send her into some wild convulsion of fury, a portion of which, he imagined, would almost certainly be directed toward him.

His fingertips once again brushed the handle of his pistol. He had known about the Morgans' flight days after they left for the Old World. It was part of the job to keep up with the whereabouts of witnesses, after all, and there was no doubt Marlene would come to this realization too.

He spoke preemptively. "She's right. Gretel and her mother left a week or so after...but from the rumors, it sounded as if they'd be gone for only a month or two. Three at the most. But they never came back. I don't really know why. It's strange. I've asked around, and no one at the barracks has any word on them."

Marlene looked to the ground, considering this news. "The Old World is like that; it entices. Mysteries live there that can only be discovered by standing on that soil. But she'll come. She'll come soon. Orphism has this power too. It will be the draw of love that brings her back. Her love of this wretched woman and Petr will bring her back."

Dodd gave Marlene's words space, just to let her know he had fully heard her, and then said, "That's all very philosophical, Marlene, and I'm sure you'd very much like to believe it's all true, but how can you know that? If Anika and Gretel haven't even been in communication, how can she know anything has happened? How can she know to come?"

Marlene walked slowly toward Dodd, her arms clasped behind her back like a professor sauntering his classroom while discussing some ambiguous phrase in a timeless piece of literature. "Because that's how it works, Officer Dodd. There is more to eternal life than the long years you so yearn for. There is the learning of flow, the recognition of the un-seeable. You come to understand the movements of the universe and, most importantly, how to draw toward you those things that are essential. The girl Gretel is ripe with this understanding. It will simultaneously be her divining rod and her downfall."

"She may come." Amanda Klahr now sat forward, propped on her knees, her back straight, eyes as wide as bicycle tires. "But she'll come on her own terms. She's smarter than you. Smarter than both of you. And with Petr's courage and determination, they'll find the way to kill you for good. They've been through too much to let you win."

Marlene smiled at Amanda Klahr; it was the ironic, cocky grin of the person who owns the high ground. But it wasn't sustained, and Dodd sensed an apprehension in the look, a sudden unease at being in the presence of the Klahr woman. "We shall see," is all she said before leaving the room.

Dodd began to follow when Amanda spoke again, nearly causing the officer to trip mid stride. "You thought you would be the one, is that it? The one to capture the secret of immortality?" Mrs. Klahr didn't wait for a reply. "Look at her. When you walk out of this room, really look at her again. Is that what you want to become?"

Dodd turned toward the prisoner now, his eyes and mouth flat and expressionless.

"She's alone, miserable, and she lives here," Mrs. Klahr glanced around the room, "in this tumbledown slaughter-house in the middle of an out-of-the-way forest in the Northlands."

"That won't be how I choose to live," Dodd replied too quickly.

"Choose? Do you think she chose this? Do you think she ever thought she would end up this way? Ask her. Ask her what her plans were a thousand years ago or whenever it was."

"Everyone's life is different. People who live normal life spans don't all live the same way. Some are happy or poor or lonely. Why should it be any different for the immortal?"

"Because this life, the life of this ancient woman, is one of addiction. Can't you see it? If you go through with this, you may indeed make different choices. Your background is very different than hers, so your paths will be different. That's true. But you will always be an addict. Addicted to death. And you will end up like some variation of that monster out there."

Dodd closed his eyes now, trying not to absorb the words, to wish away the guilt he felt.

"And if you have a maker, Officer Dodd, what will He have to say of this when your time finally comes? Maybe you don't believe in a god, but what if?"

"I don't know!" Dodd's eyes were open now, and his guilt descended into rage. From her knees, Amanda Klahr slowly backed toward the headboard. "I just know it's what I've decided to do, and I've come too far now."

"You haven't though. I'll never say anything about any—"

"I've come too far." Dodd was calm now, his voice fresh with resignation. "I don't want to hurt you, ma'am. I have no interest in hurting anyone. But if that is what I must do to stave off my death, then I will. You. Gretel. Petr. It doesn't matter who."

This time Amanda was quiet. Fear returned to her eyes.

"And I've thought of what God will think. And you're right. I suppose I am damned. If such a maker lives in heaven, then I'll be damned for all hereafter."

Behind Dodd, the click of heels quickly erupted into the room, and suddenly Marlene moved past him toward the bed. A shallow stone cup was visible in Marlene's grasp.

"Drink this willingly, or I'll cut open the veins of your arms and pour it into your blood. Either way, you're going to sleep."

Amanda took the cup without protest and drank the demitasse dry. She stared at Officer Dodd the entire time.

CHAPTER TWENTY-SEVEN

THE SOUNDS OF CLICK-clacking on wood entered Anika's dream randomly, and the serenity of the family reunion in which she was adrift was interrupted by her recurring nightmare—the crescendo of a woman's feet strutting down a long, dark hallway.

Anika jolted awake and saw that the source of the sound was a stray chicken that had entered her quarters and was searching the room for stray feed. She got to her feet and scanned the room, instantly recognizing it as the hut in the sophisticated mountain village that she had slept in the previous night.

The taste of vomit was strong on Anika's palate, and she was desperate for water. She opened the door and walked out into what she assumed was dawn, but with the cloud cover thick on the low sky, it could have been dusk.

"Anika."

Anika turned to see Oskar, groggy and concerned, a thin blanket pulled up to his chin. "What are you doing, Oskar? I...I can't remember much. How did I end up back here?"

"I watch for you to wake. Noah just leave from the night watch."

Anika could sense the disquiet in Oskar's vigil, and she suspected there was an equal anxiety on Noah's shift. There was no need to follow up on her second question; they had gotten her here safely, and Anika felt touched by their efforts. "How long have I...how long have we been back?"

"We been two days back. Noah carry you here."

Anika thought back to the route they'd taken to get to the isolated village. It wasn't the arduous mountain climb they'd made to this place, but it was no stroll to the village market either. She struggled to conceive of how Noah had hauled her from there. "Carried me?"

"Well, you no walk in your sleep!" Oskar broke out in a wild laughter that was reminiscent of the vulgar, drunken personality that was so prevalent during the early days of their journey.

"I guess not." Anika's voice turned solemn. "Was I close to...did I almost die?"

Oskar looked serious. "I think so. You so sick." He smiled now. "But now you are better."

"Better for a while, Oskar. The pill bought me some time. But now we have to go. I must get back. I must find the book and...and I don't even know where to look." Anika sighed, and suddenly, at once, the thought of her daughter and the magnitude of all the efforts that lay ahead collapsed upon her. "I can never bring it back here." She gave Oskar a bemused smile. "How can I do this, Oskar?"

"We can do. We get going now. Down the mountain much faster. You be back home in no time. You get the book first, then you worry who can read it."

"But I don't even know the sailing schedule. What if nothing is available to the New Country for weeks?" Anika's voice cracked, the first signs of panic, and the thought of traveling even to the edge of the village was overwhelming, let alone to the other side of the world.

"Boats leave every day for the New Country." Noah's voice explained from behind the open door. "I navigated the seas for many years before I finally settled on becoming a ground guide. I know men at the docks who can get us to the far shores in just over a week."

"Don't you need to sleep, Noah?" Anika asked with true concern. "And thank you. Thank you both, but this isn't part of your fee. You've done far too much already."

Anika started down the wooden steps to get on equal ground with her companions, but by the second step, her knees buckled beneath her and she fell forward into the arms of both men, Oskar rising just before she lurched, as if recognizing the danger before it happened.

"You're not ready, Ms. Anika. Getting you here from the village of the tribesmen was one thing; I can't carry you down a mountain."

"Of course not, Noah, but I have to go." Anika's challenge was hazy and sounded as if it came during a sleepwalk, the mild rebuttal of an eager lover in a dream perhaps.

"How, Ms. Anika?" It was Oskar this time, desperate for an answer that didn't seem to exist.

"We can help you."

Anika heard the voice as if it had rained down from a cloud far off in the distance, and she doubted the reality of it. It was calm, pleasant, sounding much like the dark woman with the pleasant face who had welcomed them upon their arrival.

"We know of your plight, Anika, and the toil you face. And of the honor you two have shown."

Anika smiled weakly, hovering just above sleep. She imagined the bashful look spreading quickly across Oskar's face.

"And you are correct: you cannot wait. The Medicine People are truthful men and women, and they know of the Book and its secrets in a way that few else on this planet do. But they are imprecise. They have helped many but have been quite wrong in their estimates before. You may not have as much time as they promised. But it may last longer."

"What help?" Anika gasped out. Her eyes were only half slits, but they were alive, and her attention full.

"Our horses are fast and durable, bred over two thousand years to gallop easily through these mountains. Our dragoons can get you to the shores in a little over two moons. You can leave on the next ship the following morning."

"I don't..." Anika began to cough, the feeling of nausea coming on strong.

"Don't speak, Anika. I will arrange this. You have come to us for help in a brave manner, and we shall reciprocate that bravery with the help we are able to supply."

CHAPTER TWENTY-EIGHT

"THE HOUSE IS LESS THAN a mile through these woods. The first time I came here was the day after you left." Petr kept his eyes forward through the windshield of Ben's truck. "I didn't want to go. I was as scared as I'd ever been in my life, but I forced myself. I had to be sure I was in the right place. And I was. It's there. I've been back at least ten times since."

Petr swallowed heavily, and Gretel could almost see the memories of his father brewing inside him.

No one spoke for several seconds before Sofia finally broke the tension. "Do you think she's there, Petr? Your guardian, I mean? Do you think she's being held prisoner or something? Is that what this is?"

Gretel thought the girl sounded too eager to be there, like she was excited for a fantastic story to tell the glee girls once school started.

Petr shook off the trance and answered directly. "Yes, I do. But you sound to me as if you think you'll be going with me, and you're not. I'm going alone."

Gretel paused a moment and then burst out laughing. "Is that so?"

Petr started to answer, but Gretel cut him off before the first word crossed his lips.

"No, you're not going alone. That might be the most absurd thing I've ever heard anyone say. I know her in a way that you don't, Petr. I've seen the real evil inside of her. She's cruel, Petr, and I know what she's capable of. And believe me, it's a lot."

"I was there too, Gretel. I didn't see the things you saw in the cannery. I wasn't the hero of the story like you, but I saw enough."

"That isn't fair, Petr, and how dare you throw what I went through back at me like that."

"I'm not throwing anything—"

"Kids, listen," Ben interrupted, "it sounds like you two still have some things to work out, but it's all kind of a moot issue, because if you think I'm staying behind, you clearly don't know Ben Richter very well."

Gretel *didn't* know Ben very well, but she got the impression that nothing either of them said was going to keep him from coming along.

"Let's just all go," Sofia said, with a slightly superior tone in her voice. "Wasn't that what we kind of agreed to before we left? Safety in numbers and such. Besides, I'm not staying in this truck alone."

"You won't be alone. Hansel will be here." Gretel said the words matter-of-factly, hoping she would slip a little psychology into her brother's intentions, hypnotizing him into staying behind.

"I'm going, Gretel," Hansel said quickly before reaching across Ben and pulling the latch of the truck door. He squeezed between the seat and the cab and stepped out on the dirt road. Gretel thought he looked like a weasel squeezing into a gap between two floorboards.

"Being the first one out doesn't mean anything, Hansel."

"You know we're all going, Petr," Ben said. "Let's just all acknowledge that now so that we can start moving in that direction."

They were the last words spoken in the truck before they made the tacit agreement and quietly exited the vehicle to join Hansel on the road.

The day was cloudy and cool, and the cold breeze triggered an absent thought in Gretel's mind, which soon grew like an ocean wave. They were astonishingly unprepared for this endeavor, especially because what lay ahead probably would last longer than the afternoon.

They hadn't brought any food or extra clothing, and though it was likely that Ben kept some emergency supplies in his truck—most who grew up in the Back Country did—it certainly wouldn't be enough for any serious injury or long-term exposure.

What were they thinking? What was she thinking?

Petr, Ben, Hansel, and Sofia walked in unison toward the tree line, and Gretel followed unconsciously, silently categorizing all the provisions they lacked. She had the gun, that was true, but what else? The clothes on her back. Petr had a past with the witch, and vengeance provided him with motivation. But Ben and Sofia? Why had she led them here? They had no idea what they were walking into. And Gretel now admitted to herself that she led Sofia into this dangerous den because of some unconscious, petty jealousy over Petr.

This was all a mistake.

"We can't do this." Gretel's voice hit everyone like steel, stopping them mid stride.

Petr stopped but didn't turn around to face Gretel; she couldn't see his face, but she sensed a wave of relief wash over him. "We are doing this Gretel," he said finally, the words themselves far more convincing than the tone with which they were spoken.

"No, Petr. You know we can't do this. This is suicide. We aren't prepared. We can't just walk up to her cabin, the five of us, like some band of gunfighters. Especially since we have but one gun between us. And no plan. We do this, and we'll die this way. All of us."

"Gretel, we have to, it's—"

"I know it's Mrs. Klahr, Petr. I know. I love her as much as I love anyone in this world, but if she was here right now, she would scream for us to stay away."

"That's what anybody would do. It doesn't mean they're right."

"No, Petr, Mrs. Klahr would want us to help her, just not like this. She's waiting for us, Petr. The witch is there, and she knows we're coming. We're doing exactly what she knew we would. We're making it easy for her."

Gretel looked at Sofia. "And you shouldn't be here at all, Sofia. The woman in that cabin is no woman at all. She's a monster. If ever such a thing existed in the world, she is one. Her mouth is full of teeth like sawblades, and her strength is that of a musk ox. She'll rip your head from your body. And you're young; she'll want your liver and spinal fluid for her soup. But first she'll torture you."

Sofia started crying, looking like she would vomit. Gretel was purposely brutal in her description, but not without cause.

"That's enough, Gretel." Petr didn't yell, and Gretel knew it was mainly for fear of being heard, but the sternness in his voice was unmistakable.

"She needs to know these things, Petr. And you do too, Ben. Neither of you should have anything to do with this battle."

Ben stayed calm and stared back at her. Gretel sensed awe in him.

"Okay, Gretel, I've only known you for a few hours, but I trust you. Everything you've said makes sense. And I agree: this plan of ours suddenly sounds like a very bad idea. But then what do we do? And you should know that before you answer my question, whatever it is, I intend to be included. Petr is my friend, and the three of you seem like you could use the help. And plus, you'll need a truck."

Ben flashed a smile that Gretel couldn't help but return. She imagined he'd captured many a young girl's heart with a very similar grin.

Gretel sighed. "I haven't figured it all out yet, but we need to reverse this scenario. Turn the whole thing around."

"What does that mean?" Petr asked.

"We have to let her come to us."

"What?" Sofia asked. Her question was followed by a sniffle, the last remnants of her weeping.

"She knows we're coming—or she thinks she knows—and now, when we don't show up, when we don't simply walk into her trap like she planned, she'll sense something has gone wrong."

"But what about Mrs. Klahr, Gretel?" Petr's tone was pleading now, and his protests sounded more defeated with every iteration. "We can't just leave her here."

"She won't hurt Mrs. Klahr. Not kill her anyway. Not yet. Mrs. Klahr is her leverage. She doesn't want or need Mrs. Klahr other than to get to me. The witch needs me. And my mother."

"But how can she know we were coming?" Sofia asked, all her earlier playfulness absent from her pitch.

"My sister is magic," Hansel stated flatly. "She knows about things before they happen. The same way the witch does. It's in their blood, passed down by our ancestors."

There was a pause before the clue settled in to Sofia's understanding. "That woman? She passed it down to you? She's your...what? Grandmother?"

Gretel snorted a beleaguered laugh. "She's far too old for that. I'll likely never be able to trace exactly what our relationship is. But Hansel's right, we are her kin."

"She got the magic, and I didn't."

Sofia ignored Hansel's bait at pity. "Then doesn't she know we're here? Wouldn't she know we're out here right now? What are we doing here at all? We need to call someone. The System." Sofia backed toward the truck, a detectable terror in her tone. She turned now and ran the remaining steps to Ben's truck, assuming her place in the rear.

"I guess she believes you now," Ben said sardonically.

"She's right," Gretel said. "We are in danger here. We need to leave. But you need to make sure she keeps quiet,

Ben. She can't tell anyone. Especially as far as the System is concerned. I wouldn't be surprised if they're still a part of this."

"You have to be kidding me."

"Just keep her quiet, Ben. She can't start talking about this."

"Okay, okay. I'll tell her. She's really scared, so I don't think keeping her quiet will be a problem."

"It's settled then. We're leaving. And we're going back to my house. We need to prepare for her. She'll be coming eventually."

Hansel groaned.

"We'll clean up the basement, Hansel. And air the house out. It will be fine, I promise. If we have to, we can go to the Klahrs for tonight, but I want to be at our home when she finally comes. I feel like this has to happen on our land." Gretel looked to the ground and wrinkled her forehead. "Whatever this is."

"Okay, Gretel." Hansel's voice was stable, mature, and accepting of her decision.

"But how are we going to get her to come to your house Gretel?" It was Petr this time, still a bit unsure of the strategy.

Gretel thought for a moment and then said, "We're going to have to lure her; I just don't know how."

Petr's eyes flashed, and a smiled trailed across his face. "I do."

CHAPTER TWENTY-NINE

"THEY'RE NOT COMING."

Marlene had been standing at the window for hours now, staring at the unmoving thicket of trees that shrouded her cabin. Her eyes were still alert, and her posture was statuesque.

"Whatever feelings you had must have been wrong."

Marlene turned to the voice now, as if recognizing the sound for the first time. "What did you say?"

Dodd held his hands up defensively. "I just don't think anyone is coming. For the record, I never thought anyone would. Not yet. This...event just happened. The Klahr woman is here, I cleaned up the mess you made with the old man. No one would know that anything has happened yet. Maybe the Stenson boy hasn't even come home."

"I felt someone, Mr. Dodd. I don't know who it was, but they were close. And now...well, I said they were coming. I told you that. Did I not tell you that?"

"Yes, you did. That's why I said your feelings must have been wrong. No one is here."

At any other time in Marlene's new life, Officer Dodd would have been dead before the last word left his mouth, and soon after, his innards would have been preserved as neatly as possible for future blending.

But the times were different now. Things had changed for her. Beyond all the lessons she'd learned over the last year, the most important, perhaps, was restraint. Impulsivity was a curse that she'd battled her entire life, and it had cost her dearly at times. Marlene didn't have the energy for another crisis right now.

And besides, there was more to Dodd than he was revealing. He had something she needed beyond what he'd offered already. She felt a connection to him that she couldn't quite identify.

"My feelings are rarely wrong, Officer Dodd. I've told you, the girl has these kinds of feelings too. She's powerful in this way. Perhaps my only error was an underestimation of Gretel's own understanding of herself."

"I don't really understand what that means, Marlene, but it sounds to me like you think the Morgans are back from the New Country. How can that be? It would have taken at least a week for them to get here from the New Country, and this thing with the Klahrs just happened. What you're saying is impossible."

"I don't know what is, Officer Dodd, only what I feel. And through the centuries, what is and what I feel have usually coincided. And I've used up all the energy I plan to trying to convince you about the truth of this."

Dodd said nothing else, and Marlene felt the reverence in his gaze as she walked from the window and then back to the bedroom where Amanda Klahr lay chained.

Marlene opened the door and then eased it back into the jamb quietly, turning toward the bed as she did. As she looked up, she was startled by the wide smiling eyes piercing into her. Amanda looked spry and healthy despite the time of day and the consistent dose of drugs. "You thought Petr would come that easily? I heard you, waiting for them. You don't know him. You don't know either of them."

Marlene was close to exasperated, past the point where she'd normally have disposed of any of these complicated distractions like an old useless woman, someone who was incapable of providing anything of source. But she focused on her restraint again, seeing the larger prize on the horizon. "You think it was Petr? You think he was the reason I've not provided you his company in this prison of a room?"

Amanda maintained her stare, but Marlene saw the slightest wrinkle of questioning between her eyes. "Gretel?"

"Why did they leave, Klahr woman? Why did the Morgans leave with such haste? What did they seek?"

"I don't know what you're talking about."

"They fled to the Old World, but where?"

"I told you I don't know."

"Yes, you have told me that, but now I believe you even less than I did before. She's coming back. I can feel her. But where did they go, Amanda Klahr?"

"Wherever it was, hopefully they're bringing back a can of gasoline and a match." Amanda rose tall on her knees and screamed, "To burn this fucking place to the ground!"

Marlene was largely unmoved by the volume and intensity of her captor, and she simply turned away until the prisoner finished. "That is amusing, Mrs. Klahr. But I've run out of time for amusement. I'm afraid I'll need the answer now."

Marlene opened the door behind her. "Officer Dodd," she called, "could you be of some assistance?"

Officer Dodd appeared seconds later. "What was the screaming for?"

Marlene ignored the question and directed her conspirator to the far bedpost, while she positioned herself on the opposite side. "I've placed a large band of rubber beside the bed, Officer Dodd, please use it to tie Mrs. Klahr's hand to the post of the bed. Her foot on that side is shackled, so only her hand is necessary on your side."

"What is this Marlene? What are you doing?"

Marlene ignored this question as well and stayed focused on tightening the strap on Mrs. Klahr's left hand to the post on her side of the bed. She then moved down to her free ankle, using the remaining band to secure it to the foot post.

Marlene then crossed over to Officer Dodd's side and took the band from him, which he gave without a struggle, and finished the tie job on Mrs. Klahr's limbs. Mrs. Klahr was now recumbent, her limbs wide, making her appear as a human X on the bed. Only her right leg was slightly bent due to the slack in the chain.

"I'm disappointed in you, Officer Dodd. I thought we made an agreement to help each other. Wasn't that the deal?"

"We can help each other without torturing people, Marlene. That was not part of the deal. That isn't who I am. I'm a System officer."

Marlene stared at Officer Dodd for a moment and then erupted in a cackle. "Of course, Officer Dodd, the System's honor and purity would never allow such atrocities."

Officer Dodd looked down and away in humiliation.

"Get out, Officer Dodd. And if you decide this life is not for you after all, you had better decide now. When I ask you to do something again and you decline, that will be the end of any treaty between us." And then, for added effect, she added, "And at that point, who knows what will happen."

Dodd stood motionless for a moment and then nodded before walking out of the bedroom. He didn't make any more eye contact with Marlene.

She didn't watch him go but instead kept her eyes fixed on Mrs. Klahr as she walked to the foot of the bed, allowing herself to be in full view of her prisoner.

"What are you doing?" Mrs. Klahr asked with a defiant snivel. "What are you going to do to me?"

Marlene walked from the bedroom for a moment and then returned with a small saucepan and something that resembled a large baby rattle, only it was metal and had small openings on the bulb.

"What is that?"

"Which?"

"That metal thing in your hand."

"Ah, this. This is called a lead sprinkler."

"What is it for?"

Marlene wrinkled her face in bemusement. "It's for torture, Mrs. Klahr."

Marlene removed a small clasp in the middle of the bulb and folded the top half back on its tiny hinges. She then picked up the saucepan and poured two or three tablespoons of boiling oil into the bottom portion of the bulb before folding the top half shut and re-clasping the whole thing tightly. The smell of the burning oil on the lead brought Marlene back to her childhood, though the memory was without place or context.

"I told you, I don't know!" Mrs. Klahr screamed. "I don't know where they went!"

"We shall see, won't we?"

Marlene held the lead sprinkler up and out slightly as she walked next to the side of the bed, stopping near Mrs. Klahr's midsection. She might have been a magician, she thought to herself, holding the magic wand above her assistant in preparation for the ensuing trick.

The screams that detonated from Mrs. Klahr as the oil dribbled from the holes at the top of the sprinkler on to her naked abdomen and breasts were slightly muffled by Marlene's wailing laughter as she was overcome with the joy of her life. Whether she got the answers she wanted was secondary right now. She was happy again.

OFFICER DODD SQUEEZED his palms to his ears, praying the dueling horror of the two sounds in the back room would come to an end. This is madness, he thought. I am mad for believing that I could ever deal with this demon. She was insane, that was without question now, but he supposed he knew that the instant he saw her through the doorway, sitting as quiet and still as a mannequin.

But Dodd had also hoped she would be malleable, or at least reasonable, and that he would be able to shepherd this arrangement, to work toward a common goal in a way that would suit his conscience. An old woman like that should have been easy to maneuver in the direction he wanted her to go.

He could leave now. Forget the deal. Forget his dream of immortality.

But he couldn't. He understood now the lure that had captured Stenson. Once it was known, this potential, once it was unquestionably real, there was no rejecting it.

The screaming, though, had to stop. He couldn't listen to the screams any longer.

Dodd ran to the bedroom and swung open the door, automatically preparing himself for an attack; it was an instinct he'd acquired over his years in the System whenever he entered a strange building or room.

Marlene stood hunched over the poor Klahr woman, releasing tiny droplets of acid or perhaps boiling water onto her torso, licking her lips each time a tiny bead hit skin, sizzling.

"Stop it, Marlene!" he commanded. "That's enough."

She continued, as if unaware of Dodd's presence in the room.

"I've got something of yours, Marlene."

Marlene cocked her head faintly to one side and held the metal torture device upright, holding back whatever evil remained inside.

"I told you I was one of the first officers here after hearing Anika Morgan's story. And I found something that day. On the counter, there in the kitchen."

"*Orphism*," she said. The voice sounded like it had been released in a gas, like the whisper of a ghost.

"Yes. *Orphism*."

Marlene turned and faced Dodd, and he knew she was weighing the consequences of an attack. This was another instinct he'd developed as a System officer.

"I don't have it with me, Marlene, but I can get it. Just stop hurting her. Please."

Marlene smiled. "Certainly, Officer Dodd. I think I've already gotten what I wanted."

"What is that?"

"There's a letter apparently. At her home. It apparently has details about the Morgans' trip."

"She told you that?"

Marlene laughed. "Of course. You've never felt the lead sprinkler, I take it. It is quite effective. I only use the hot oil in this one. The molten lead sprinkler is the true test, however."

Dodd paused, attempting to imagine the pain of molten lead on his stomach. "Why?"

"Why what?"

"Why were you still torturing her when I came in? Why did you keep torturing her after she told you what you wanted?"

In a flash, Marlene's smile turned to a snarl. "Because I enjoy the sound of it." She paused. "Now I'll need that book from you, Officer Dodd. That will be necessary for our deal to come to fruition. And I will need the letter as well."

"The letter? How can I get that? You said it's at her home. I can't go back there. I've risked too much already."

"Did we not agree that you would do as I said, lest the treaty be broken?"

"I won't go to prison for it."

Marlene frowned, and Dodd could see he'd won this round.

"Perhaps it's not fair that you do both tasks. Perhaps a compromise is in order. You just get the book then. And you bring it back here. We'll figure about the letter later."

"Why do you even need this letter? You said they were on their way here. If that's true, why do you care where they went?"

"It could be interesting, Officer Dodd, that's all. They may have gone somewhere that was once very important in my life."

CHAPTER THIRTY

GRETEL, PETR, AND HANSEL said their goodbyes to Ben and made their way up the porch steps to Gretel's house. When they were on the road, outside the perimeter of the witch's cabin, Gretel had suggested they could stay at the Klahrs for the night. But after some discussion and a quick assessment of their own house, Hansel and Gretel decided the screened porch would work fine. The night was unseasonably warm, and the porch was well-stocked with blankets and pillows. They hadn't done so in years, but when Gretel and Hansel were younger, they would sleep out on the porch quite often. Gretel had always loved the warm air and the buzz of insects; it made her feel like she was on another planet.

But those days of fantasy were far behind her now. In the morning, she and Hansel would begin the awful task of cleaning the basement.

And then prepare for the coming storm.

Ben had dropped off a stunned Sofia, who had said she understood the importance of keeping quiet about the things she knew, though she hadn't quite promised to do so. But Ben seemed confident there were enough gestures and nods from the girl to imply she'd keep their secret safe. It didn't, however, seem likely that she would accompany them to this battle, despite her earlier show of intrigue.

Ben was still in though, and Gretel was pleased with this. He seemed inherently strong-willed—and physically strong as well—both attributes they needed.

The next morning, Gretel woke just as the sun rose over the trees, and she immediately went to work on the basement. She wrapped a large dish towel around her neck, which she would use to cover her nose and mouth, and dressed from head to toe in a layer of old clothes she'd taken from the shelf of her bedroom.

She was surprised how the cabin no longer felt like her home; they would leave this place for good once this ordeal ended, though she had no idea where they would go. There was so much still in question, including whether she would ever see her mother again. As strong as her intuition was—and it was getting stronger every day, it seemed—she couldn't imagine where her mother was right now. Or if she was even alive.

Ben had picked up Petr early to leave for the Urbanlands. If everything went as planned, by mid-morning, the first morsel of bait would have been laid. Gretel still wasn't entirely sold on the strategy, but she trusted Petr. He was skeptical of most things, so if he thought this had a chance to work, then so did she.

Gretel descended the steps and immediately saw Hansel in the basement, toiling. He looked like he'd been up for hours, a lather of sweat coating the back of his neck. The back door was slid wide, and he tossed things by the armload into the yard. Apparently, he had had the same idea as she of using a towel around his mouth and nose.

Gretel motioned to him and they both walked out to the backyard and into the freedom of the open air.

"I see you're copying my new fashion," Gretel joked.

"I did it first, so you're copying me."

"What time did you get up today? It looks pretty good down here. I mean, considering."

"Early. Before Petr left with Ben. I barely slept last night. Knowing what was down here. It was like our house was toxic. Stained with hate or something. I couldn't stand it."

Gretel reached out and placed her hand on her brother's shoulder. "I'm proud of you, Han. I really am. This would be so much harder if I had come alone. I'm glad you're here."

Hansel smiled wide and rumpled his glistening eyes. "Of course you are, otherwise you'd be cleaning the house alone."

Gretel laughed. "Dummy."

"I think if we get to it and work through the day, we can probably finish cleaning by tonight. It will probably need another full day of airing out though before we can live here again. Maybe two."

"That's fine. We'll do what we can during the day and keep to the porch at night. At least it isn't winter. Tomorrow I need to get back to the Klahrs."

"But they'll know by then, Gretel. Right? If Petr is right about the System, they'll know soon that we're back. She could be coming by then." There was no fear in Hansel's voice, just making sure his sister understood the situation.

Gretel nodded and gave a look of deep thought. "We'll just have to see. Let's see what Petr thinks when he gets back. For now, you can keep copying my new style so we can get to work."

"SO WHO IS THE GUY WE'RE looking for again? What is his name? The one you trust?"

Ben was filled with questions, most of which Petr had already answered three times or more. The two boys sat in the truck outside the System station, and Petr walked through the names again as he revisited the details of the plan. It wasn't complicated, but there was no harm in making sure they were on the same page.

"His name is Conway. He's the overseer of the case. But it shouldn't matter to you. I'll do the talking. They know who I am here; they know I have a special interest in this case. It's been my obsession for the last eleven months, as you already know. You, however, they do not know, so I think it best for that part of this story to remain the same."

"The overseer? That means he's the boss, right?"

"The boss of this case, yes. You know, the more I think about it, the more I think it might be best if you stayed in the truck, Ben. No point risking any mistakes."

Ben laughed, opened the door, and stepped to the pavement. "Thanks, overseer. I think I'll come along though. I've never seen the inside of one of these places. And I didn't come along just as someone for you to talk to on the way. I'll be an extra pair of ears and eyes. Sometimes you miss things when you're so close to it."

Petr had expected nothing less. "Just let me do the talking."

Ben saluted, and the two boys walked toward the front of the barracks. The plan, as Petr first explained on the truck ride back from the Northlands, was to inform the case overseer that Gretel had finally returned from the Old World. Petr would explain that he wanted to make sure the System had all the up-to-date information they needed. He was committed to assisting them in any way he could. The Case of the Missing Witch, as they knew, was somewhat of a project of his.

Petr never thought Conway was involved; on the contrary, in his brief meeting with the officer, he seemed to Petr like a man of integrity. But Petr also knew the System a bit by now, and he knew that Conway, at some point, during lunch or on a coffee break perhaps, would casually let fly the news of the Morgan girl returning to the Back Country.

And then it would be set. If Petr was right, the woman would come to them.

The scoundrels on the inside who had covered up the witch's missing body, who had doctored the reports with myths and outlandish theories of bears devouring the corpse or wolves dragging it to some mysterious den, would begin to blossom like rotten mushrooms. And in Petr's estimation, there was only one reason why anyone in the System would have gone to such lengths to hide the truth, and it was the same reason Petr's father had. They were seeking the potion. They were assisting the witch for the promise of immortality.

Petr didn't have any proof about who any of the players were in this deranged show, but he was fairly certain he knew at least one of them.

Petr and Ben hadn't been in the station more than thirty seconds when he heard his name spoken from behind him. "Petr Stenson, right?"

Petr turned to see a large man approaching him, his eyes curious but kind. "Yes," Petr said, his voice crackling.

"It's Officer Conway. Do you remember me?"

"You're the overseer!" It was Ben, apparently excited to be able to put a face to the name.

Conway gave a puzzled smile. "That's right. And you are?"

Petr gritted his teeth, wanting to punch Ben. "This is Ben. He's my transportation here today. I have some important news about the case that I want to deliver."

"Not the Case of the Disappearing Witch, I hope. Because, as I told you the last time you were here, that one isn't at the top of the docket anymore."

"She didn't disappear. She never died. I told you." Petr felt himself flush with anger but reined it back, remembering that showing his conviction was not the point of this confrontation.

"What can I do for you, Petr? I don't have a lot of time for more theories, if that's all you've come for. I'm on my way out."

"No sir, Officer Conway. It is to do with my father's case, but not about the...body. I just thought you should know, in case you had any more follow-up questions for the Morgans, that Gretel Morgan is back from the New Country. She came home yesterday."

"Is that so? Well that's not that interesting, but okay, Petr, I appreciate your meticulousness as this case is concerned. And should I have any more questions, I'll be sure to contact her."

Petr had planted the seed, but he didn't like Conway's manner. He seemed distracted, disinterested. This plan only worked if word spread throughout the System, if it reached the right ears, and Conway wasn't acting like he was champing at the bit to spill some dirt.

To this point in his quest, Petr's instincts had been close to spot on, so he made the decision to pile his eggs high into one lone basket. "Overseer Conway?"

Conway stopped and turned at the threshold of the exit door, an eyebrow cocked.

"I know this isn't a high priority for the System right now, but I was hoping you could do one more thing for me."

"What's that?"

"Will you make sure Officer Dodd gets the news I just told you? The last time I was here he said he wanted to stay on top of things."

"I can do you one better kid. Dodd's in his office now. Go tell him yourself."

CHAPTER THIRTY-ONE

"YOU HAVE TO GO TO YOUR feet, Ms. Anika. They not let you board if you no walking. Ms. Anika!"

"What?" Anika woke with a jolt; her senses were blurry but quickly beginning to tingle back to life. "What are we doing? Where are we?"

"They think you drunk if you no stand, Anika. You can't go drunk."

Anika recognized the voice of Oskar and the urgency in his tenor. Without another word, she forced herself to sit up in the carriage.

Her memory of the journey from the mountain village consisted of no more than a few minutes of the commencing dash of the quartet of huge stallions pulling from the village to the shore. After those first moments, she didn't remember anything

Before they left, the tall woman had given them provisions and made them as comfortable as possible in the covered carriage, which, for Oskar and Noah wasn't very comfortable at all. Anika had watched them in a fog as they sat scrunched together beside the driver in the box seat, while she lay alone, blanketed in the back. She had tried to protest, to tell them she would sleep sitting and that they could ride in the back with her, but as she now recalled, the words may not have even been spoken outside of her fevered mind.

"It's not unusual," she had heard the host woman tell Oskar before they left. "The fever will break in a day or two. The pill is forcing her body to fight the sickness. It's a good thing. She will be okay. Just keep her warm. Weather is approaching."

They were the last words she heard until Oskar's voice encouraged her to stand.

Anika looked to her left and saw Noah standing next to the carriage with an outstretched hand. She grabbed it and stood, and then stepped down gingerly to the wooden planks layering the ground below. The smell of this place is familiar, she thought, and she looked up quickly, instinctively, and immediately recognized the terminal. It was the port where she'd left Gretel and Hansel only a couple of weeks earlier.

"How are you feeling?" Noah asked.

Anika looked at Noah, stunned. "How is this possible? How can we be here already?"

Noah laughed. "Yes, already. Well, I can only say that you should be happy for your ability to slumber as you did along the way. It was quite a ride! There have never been horses as those in this country. I will assure you of that."

"What time of day is it?"

"It's just before dawn. We made it here in less than eighteen hours. It was like nothing I've ever experienced. The driver pushed the horses through. It seems you made an impression back at the village."

"Where is he now? His carriage is here, but where are the horses? They obviously couldn't have gone back. I want to thank him."

"He's taken the horses for feed and gone to look for lodging. He insisted we tell you that thanks were not necessary."

Anika accepted this news with a nod and asked, "When does the ship arrive? When are we leaving?"

Oskar and Noah shifted their eyes toward each other and then back to Anika.

"You go alone, Ms. Anika," Oskar said. "But we wait for you here. When you come back here."

"What? You have to come...I...you just have to."

"Our home is here, Anika," Noah said, "but Oskar is right. When you come back, we'll be here if you still need us."

Anika sighed and nodded again. "I understand." She paused and looked to the ground. "But I'm not coming back."

"Anika...but you have to." It was Noah this time, concerned.

"Not soon anyway. Not for this...cure."

"But why?"

"I've been away from my children for too long. There is a very real chance they may be in danger. I can't leave them again."

"Bring them back with you. Of course."

"I don't think so, Noah. Gretel and Hansel aside, returning here never made sense to me. Not to those mountains. It's hard to explain but...I trust the men of the village, the medicine men or whatever they are, and I believe them when they say the cure to my sickness is in the book. But I don't think they're too concerned about helping me. I think they just want the book. I think they gave me the pill to keep me alive long enough to find the book and bring it to them.

"But if they're the only ones who can read it, what difference does it make why they want it? They will help you, even if they ultimately just want the book."

"But that's just it, Noah, I don't think they're the only ones who can help me. I think they told me that so I'd come back immediately."

"But what if you're wrong, Anika? You'll die."

Anika gave a tired smile. "I don't know, Noah. But I don't plan to die. Something tells me there's still hope. At home. I need to be home."

"I will come, Anika. With you." Oskar's eyes were desperate.

"I know you will, Oskar. You've come a long way in your personality since the first few days of our time together. I'd say you are a different man."

"I sorry about—"

"Oskar, stop it. You've nothing to apologize for. The payment for both of you is at the travel office. I wish I had more to give you."

Noah seemed to have resigned himself to the decisions that were being made before him, and Anika could see him struggling with his own emotion. "Your ship is scheduled to arrive in less than an hour," he said finally. "Everything has been taken care of."

"Noah, thank you. Thank you for everything. I'll send you money for my ticket the instant I arrive. To what address should it go?"

Noah shook his head and grinned. "Anika, I've known the captain of your vessel since the times I was still in school. The list of favors he owes to me would take a lifetime for me to document. It is my pleasure to have at least one of them repaid in your honor."

Anika slipped her palms into Noah's and took one long stride toward him. "Thank you again," she said, and then placed a soft kiss on his mouth. She could feel the heat of blush on his cheeks.

Noah blinked several times and then cleared his throat. "Uh, I know you must have things here, yes? Belongings to be sent? Would you like me to see about those things?"

Anika giggled. "Thank you, Noah, that was all pre-arranged in case...in the event I didn't return from the mountains. Thankfully, what I envisioned didn't come to pass, but it all works out the same, I suppose."

Anika grabbed her duffel from the back of the carriage and slung it across her shoulder and then walked silently to the edge of the dock to wait for her vessel.

CHAPTER THIRTY-TWO

AMANDA KLAHR'S EYES sprung to life at the sound of the hollow bouncing sound invading her sleep. She held her breath and lay board still, her eyes searching the room, trying to place the sound and wondering if it only existed in her dream.

Thoom! Thoom! Thoom! The sound again. It came from the bedroom window.

Amanda turned her body slowly toward the noise; it was an exaggerated motion that she imagined would have looked almost comical to an outside observer, like a bad actor who'd been cast in a low-budget monster movie.

Amanda had to swallow a shriek caused by the face she met at the window.

The face was young and beautiful, that of a teenager, and the expression appeared locked with fright.

Amanda's first thought was that it was Petr, but as her focus cleared through the outside glare, she saw it was the face of a girl. Amanda met her eyes, casting back a frightened look of her own, an expression she imagined was very similar to the girl's.

The mystery girl now turned her body away from the window, always keeping her face to the glass, and made a waving gesture to her right, beckoning with her hands to come to her. Within seconds, another face appeared beside the girl's. This face was slightly older, male; Amanda guessed he was barely in his twenties. She had never seen either of them before.

The two people just stood there for several moments, staring at Amanda through the glass, mesmerized, as if Amanda was some new species of animal that had been recently captured and exhibited at the city zoo.

Amanda's immediate impulse was to scream at them to help her, to tell them she was being held prisoner and that they needed to act quickly or they would all die. But the truth was she didn't know who they were or why they were there, and the possibility remained that they were there as some kind of trap.

Amanda stayed calm, and with eyes wide, she finally shrugged up her shoulders and held her palms up with fingers out, hands high near her head. What are you going to do? her signal asked.

The girl did nothing and continued staring at Amanda with the same locked expression. But the young man finally moved, looking down for a few beats before holding up a piece of paper. Amanda read the words: WE'RE GOING TO HELP YOU.

Amanda felt an impulse to laugh, and a new energy surged through her muscles. She got to her knees and leaned forward as far as possible toward the window. She couldn't get very close with the shackle on her leg, so there wasn't much use in the move, but it felt to her like the right position. Amanda breathed heavily now, a combination of hope and fear. A thin smile began to form on her face.

And then she watched in terror as the boy lifted a small rod of thick metal—it looked to Amanda like an iron stake—and began to measure the down stroke he would make to the window pane.

Amanda began shaking her head and waving furiously toward the window, her arms crisscrossing, silently pleading for the man to stop.

His focus on the impending blow appeared sharp, and Amanda suddenly envisioned the torture and death that would come to them all in a matter of seconds. The window would shatter, and then the witch would appear in the room seconds later. She supposed the kids could get away, which Amanda would pray for, but the chain around her ankle would prevent any chance of her own escape.

Why wasn't the girl saying something to her companion? She obviously could see Amanda gesturing like a mad person; instead, the girl just stood staring like a lobotomized fool.

There's nothing to lose at this point, Amanda thought, so she desperately barked out a grunt, cupping her mouth in an attempt to project her voice toward the window, hoping the loud, low-pitched sound would land in those young ears outside the cabin while avoiding the old ones of the woman who was, ostensibly, still somewhere inside.

As he was on the final reel of what was certain to be the impact swing, the man heard Amanda's animal-like noise and looked up, the shock in his eyes matching that of the girl. Amanda took a heavy breath at her victory, though the second part of the plan, the part about the witch not hearing her, remained to be seen.

Amanda held up her hands now with her palms out, signaling the man to hold off on his plan. She then pointed toward the kitchen and mouthed, "She's there." Amanda then sat back against the wall and held up her ankle as high as possible to show the clasp of the metal chain resting on her foot and the chain snaking off it.

For the final piece of the charade, Amanda made the gruesome motion of a throat being slit. It was a dramatic move, she realized, but it was a necessary payoff to the equation.

The sound of the breaking window plus the witch plus the chain around Amanda's ankle equaled death.

The man nodded immediately in understanding and then held up a finger for her to wait. Seconds later he held up a pistol to the window, a mammoth of a gun that almost certainly did not belong to him. The gun helps, Amanda thought, but she didn't necessarily trust the man's acumen with it. She would rather they left immediately and brought back help. Perhaps a group of men, preferably who had begun shaving. The young man and the simple girl with him were no match for the woman of this house.

As for the System officer, Amanda couldn't be entirely sure where he was, but she thought she heard the cruiser pulling away this morning. And that would have made perfect sense, she now realized. What was his alternative, really? To hole up in this place until Petr and Gretel and Anika miraculously appeared on the stoop? Unless that happened today, that plan wouldn't work at all. A System officer was a very serious position, and he would have to keep his patrol. It would raise a considerable number of eyebrows if a System

officer suddenly didn't show up for his shift. The disappearance of a System officer was not something that was ignored
for long, particularly considering the not-so-distant scandal
of Officer Oliver Stenson.

But even if the System officer was gone and the witch
was alone, Amanda didn't like the setup of the scenario. The
man outside appeared prepared to fight, in theory, but not in
experience. And the girl seemed fated to prove a liability.

How did they know she was there though? And it was
clear they knew. Nobody without plaid gear and a hunting
rifle would slog through this part of the Northlands forest.
And these two weren't hunters. The man had an iron stake
and a pistol.

No, they knew she was here, or at least they had heard
she was here, and they were now investigating the rumor for
themselves.

Whether they had thought through this entire rescue
seemed another thing entirely.

"Go for help," Amanda mouthed, waving her hands outward as if directing a driver who was trying to back his truck
from a tight space. "Go."

The man flashed the gun again, as if she hadn't quite understood he had it, but Amanda shook him off, continuing
to wave them off.

The girl was now nodding furiously, apparently liking
this suggestion and in complete agreement with Amanda's
strategy.

The young man, who Amanda had now concluded was
the girl's brother, still wavered, not quite sure this was the
best course of action. He turned and said something to the

girl, who replied instantly, never stopping the up and down head-bobbing of assent.

The conversation finally ended and the two faces looked back toward the window. The girl smiled now, tears in her eyes, and then lifted her hand to give Amanda a half-wave. The man looked more solemn as he nodded while mouthing the letters "OK."

Amanda smiled weakly at them both, and then watched surreally as the young hero's lips peeled back, stuck in an exaggerated mouthing of the letter K. From behind his head, the blade of a knife appeared and slid quietly across his throat. A river of blood appeared just under the man's chin and then quickly cascaded in a sheet down to the bottom of his neck and chest. His tongue convulsed for a moment, lingering in the air like a cobra before falling limply to the side of his mouth, and his eyes scrunched tightly in what Amanda could only assume was unimaginable, gruesome pain.

The scene played out in eerie silence and irony; the girl sat waving to Amanda while her brother choked on his last breaths of life. Amanda unconsciously thought of the signal of murder she had made just moments ago, and she closed her eyes in guilt and despair.

After a few seconds, the young girl's screams broke the silence. She suddenly realized the horror that was happening beside her. Amanda thought she would have rather heard the choking man than those dull screams from the girl.

Her howls lasted only a moment, and then Amanda saw the knuckles of a gnarled hand bury into the top of the girl's head and then snatch it from sight.

And then there was silence.

Amanda sat back against the headboard, pressing back on it as if trying to roll an impossibly large boulder off the edge of a cliff. She was crying now, hysterical, shaking her head in a useless attempt to get those images from her mind.

"No!' she screamed. "Noooo!"

Amanda closed her eyes and tilted her head to the ceiling, feeling as if she were on the verge of hyperventilating. She tried to slow her breathing, holding her position, quietly mouthing a prayer.

After a minute, when she felt her composure had returned, Amanda looked back to the window, and there, as repulsive as any ogre she'd ever imagined in a fairy tale, was the smiling face of the witch. She stared at Amanda, her eyes crazed like those of the rabid dogs Amanda's father had made her put down when she was a young farm girl growing up in the Back Country.

Amanda stayed quiet, waiting, anticipating. Finally, the woman lifted her arm slowly, smiling wider as she did so, and then displayed the dangling head of the boy who had come to save her. His tongue hung like a thick glob of meat from his mouth; his eyes shined with terror.

The woman started laughing, and Amanda screamed again.

CHAPTER THIRTY-THREE

"WHAT ARE YOU GOING to do, Pete?"

Petr and Ben stood in the lobby of the System station and watched as Overseer Conway drove his cruiser from the lot, unaware of the position he'd put Petr in with the news that Dodd was at the station. The decision Petr made next could cost him and his friends everything.

"I don't think we have much of a choice, Ben. If we leave now without seeing him, he'll find out we were here. Conway will say something to him about it. About speaking with me. That's almost a certainty."

"So what if he does?"

"He'll be suspicious. Probably assume I was up to something. Especially since I asked Conway to let Dodd know about Gretel's return. If I knew he was here, which I do because Conway just told me, why would I then leave without telling him myself?"

"Good. I like the logic, Petr. Decision made. Let's go talk to this Officer Dodd."

"I need you to wait for me here, Ben."

Ben rolled his eyes. "Are we doing this again?"

"Listen, Ben, please. I need to have this conversation one-on-one."

Ben looked at the floor, still not convinced.

"Come with me to his office then. But I need you to wait outside. Please."

"Fine, but if he tries to snatch you up or something, I'm coming in guns blazing."

Petr laughed. "You don't have a gun with you, and nothing like that is going to happen. I'm not here to make trouble. This wasn't in the original plan, so I'm going to say as little as possible and then get out of there. We just came to plant the seed, so I'm going to plant it and then we're leaving. I want to get back and help Hansel and Gretel clean up a little." Petr paused, and his face turned grim. "And then prepare for her."

The two boys turned into the hallway and walked toward Dodd's office, Petr feeling a strange sense of power in his stride despite the butterflies in his belly. As they approached the frosted door of Detective Dodd, Petr noticed it was ajar by about six inches. He walked up slowly to the crack and dropped his arm in front of Ben, holding up a hand in the gesture to hold tight.

Petr glanced around the station to see if anyone was noticing them, but the few people who were mulling about either had a head buried in a folder or were engaged in some important conversation. He put his eye up close to the gap in the door, Ben behind him now, and peered through, maneuvering his body to get a line of sight on the desk.

Dodd was seated there, hunched, hands by his side, staring at a large black book that lay sprawled across the middle of the desk.

Petr stood frozen for a moment, narrowing his eyes, trying to focus in on the book, but unable to note anything other than its size, which was massive. He'd seen this book before; it was the one high on Dodd's bookshelf when he was there a few weeks back.

Petr stepped back quietly from the door and motioned for Ben to join him, and they walked away several feet past the office.

"The plans are changing again, Ben. I do need your help. But you could get into trouble, so I understand if you say no. I can figure something else out."

"Still, Petr? Still with the doubt?"

"I don't doubt you, Ben, I just want you to understand that there is a risk."

"I've got it. Now what do you need me to do?"

"There's a book in Dodd's office, he's reading it now; I want to see what it is."

"Okay, easy enough."

"Well, I don't know about that, but I have a plan."

"Fine, but before I hear it, can I ask you something?"

Petr nodded. "Of course."

"Do you think Gretel likes me? Because I kind of think she does."

Petr rolled his eyes and shook his head. "I don't know, Ben. You can ask her yourself when all of this is over. Right now, I need you to listen to me."

DODD PICKED UP THE phone on the first ring, his mind snatched away from the hypnotic symbols and scribbles of the mysterious book. He looked at the clock as he answered and saw that he'd been staring at the same page for over twenty minutes. "This is Dodd."

"Officer Dodd there's someone to see you. I tried to send him back to your office but he insisted you come to the front desk. He said it has to do with one of the cases you worked on, the one about the Witch of the North."

The mention of Marlene stopped Dodd's breathing. "I'll be right there."

Dodd rose from his chair and left the book in place, slipping out the door in a rush, too focused on the front lobby to see Petr Stenson standing just a foot away, shielded by the open door.

Dodd saw the boy sitting in a chair in the lobby area. He walked to him slowly, not wanting to appear too eager. He reasoned now that he should have given it a few minutes before leaving his office. "Son, are you the person that wanted to speak with me?"

"Yes, hello, are you Officer Dodd?"

A simpleton, this one, Dodd thought. "Yes, son, the receptionist said you have some news about one of the cases I worked. Is that right?"

"Yes, I'm a friend of Petr Stenson. Do you know him?"

The name brought a lump to Dodd's throat. "What is your name?"

"My name is Ben. Richter. As I said, I'm a friend of Petr's."

"All right Ben Richter, friend of Petr Stenson, what is this news you have for me?"

"She's come home. Gretel Morgan. And her mother is on the way soon. Petr thought it important to tell you."

Dodd could feel the first bead of sweat form on his temple, and he had to fight back a smile. Marlene. She was right all along. Not exactly right, of course, because they hadn't come to the cabin as she predicted, but she was right about Gretel. She was back. Home. It couldn't have been a coincidence.

"Mr. Dodd?"

Officer Dodd shook off his visions of magic and fantasies, of living for another two or three centuries like a god. "Yes, thank you Ben, I heard you. I was just wondering, though, this is a long way to come to tell me this. Why not just call us?"

Ben looked away, ashamed, and then stared back at Dodd with a pleading look of innocence. "He said he didn't trust the System. Except for you and the overseer. He didn't want to risk leaving a message with someone else. He still thinks the witch is alive, which is crazy, I know, but he does, so he asked me to relay the message to you."

"Ben, what are you saying?" The voice came from behind Dodd, and he turned to see Petr Stenson walking quickly toward him.

"Petr?"

Petr stayed focused on Ben, staring daggers at him.

"What is going on, Petr? Ben?"

Petr sighed and slumped his shoulders in defeat. "Did he tell you? Did he tell you about Gretel?"

Dodd nodded slowly and said nothing, staring at both boys with a look of obvious suspicion.

Petr gave another malicious look in the direction of his friend and then turned back to Dodd. "I came to tell you. That's why we're here. But..."

Petr paused, and Dodd thought he saw a tear form in the boy's eye.

Petr sniffled and took a deep breath. "But I had second thoughts after I saw Overseer Conway leaving and told him about Gretel. My distrust in the System flared. I felt like I'd betrayed her or something, even though I'm just trying to find the... Anyway, Ben told me it was too late and that I needed to personally tell you that she was back. That I'd told you I would and had to honor that promise. And we were here and I'd already told Conway, and if we left then it would seem suspicious or something."

Petr was racing now, the words coming like the confession of a child.

"I didn't care. I told him we were leaving."

Petr shook his head and rolled his eyes in disgust.

"He said he needed to use the restroom before we left, so I waited in the car."

Dodd's suspicious look flattened a bit, and he just stared at the boys for a moment, waiting to see if there was any crack in the expressions or story.

"And then I saw him talking to you." Petr looked to Ben. "How did you even know who he was?"

"It doesn't matter, Petr." Dodd intercepted the bickering. "I'm glad you told me about Gretel. And I don't blame you for your apprehension. I would feel the same way."

"Please don't let her know I told you. She doesn't know I'm here. I just..."

"You didn't tell me, Petr, your friend Ben here did. Remember?"

"Right. I guess I'm off the hook on a technicality."

"In this business, Petr, technicalities are everything."

Petr smiled, and Officer Dodd reciprocated.

"And your friend Ben also told me some other interesting news about the Morgans."

Petr's mouth opened and he looked at his friend, his face of anger now drawn into one of dread and betrayal. "What was that?"

"He tells me Anika Morgan is coming home soon as well. As you know, she was the main witness in this case, so I'd like to talk with her as well. Any ideas when exactly she'll be arriving in the New Country?"

Petr's eyes narrowed now, and he looked coldly at Dodd.

Dodd felt a shiver at the base of his skull, and he dropped the boy's gaze, looking back at Ben to see if he had anything to offer.

Petr smiled now, a glimmer of life returning to his eyes. "In a week or so, I believe. I'll let them know that you still have a few questions. Just to give them notice that you may be stopping by at some point. Certainly, you'll allow several months though. They need to get back to their lives here."

Dodd knew there would be no grace period for the Morgans. Not even a day. Once he returned the book to Marlene and brought the news these boys had just delivered, she would wait only until she believed Anika had returned. Another week. Maybe less. And then his life would begin again. Forever would begin.

"Of course, Petr. We will give them all the time they need."

DODD CHASED HIS CRUISER up the driveway, almost clipping the boardwalk below the porch as his tires skidded on the soft dirt. His news was urgent; it was what they'd been waiting for. She was here—Gretel—and the other one was on the way.

He ran in through the cabin door, expecting the woman would be either sitting in her chair in still meditation or toiling around in her kitchen as she often did, baking her little flour and syrup cakes that she seemed to subsist on almost exclusively. Upon Marlene's insistence, Dodd had eaten one of the cakes just yesterday and was surprised at how delicious it tasted.

Marlene was not in the main room of the cabin, so Dodd headed to the back bedroom, dreading his entry, fearing the Klahr woman would be conscious and eager to torment him. She had rarely been fully cognizant since he had arrived, but on the few occasions he'd been alone with her when she was awake, the guilt she foisted upon him was prodigious.

Dodd cracked the door a couple of inches and peered through. The prisoner was asleep, bedpan full, and her body turned so that her head was at the footboard. Her face was contorted in a way that made her tongue hang loosely against the side of her open mouth. She must have had a double dose, he thought.

Dodd opened the door fully now, remaining outside the threshold.

Marlene wasn't inside.

Dodd tried to remember a time over the past few days when the woman hadn't been at the cabin at all, but he couldn't think of one. He went back down the front porch steps and then around the side of the house to check if the Klahr's truck was still there. He couldn't have imagined the woman taking the risk of driving a missing truck on the main road in the middle of the day, but he supposed it was a possibility. She was deranged, after all. He had to continue reminding himself of that.

Dodd had insisted on pulling the Klahr truck to the back of the house, where it now sat covered by an old tarp. It was probably a pointless precaution, he knew, especially considering that if anyone from the System came to investigate the cabin, they would have found it easily after only a few minutes. But Dodd had insisted anyway, and he had driven the vehicle to the back edge of the yard himself before covering it with the large gray canvas.

He now took soft, quiet steps as he walked along the short length of the house, eventually reaching the corner where the back and side walls met. The shape of the truck under the tarp appeared first to his senses, followed by a slurping, crunching sound that drifted violently into his ears.

Dodd looked to his left and saw a woman kneeling—Marlene he presumed—her back turned to him; the foxtail weeds that surrounded the woman nearly reached her shoulders, obscuring his vision of her.

Dodd moved in closer and knew immediately by the black cloak and the crusty locks of hair, that it was Marlene. Who else would it be? he thought. "Marlene," he called, invoking his System officer voice that was designed and honed to freeze the citizenry.

The woman paused.

Was she eating?

"Marlene. What are you doing back here?"

Marlene stood slowly and turned toward Dodd, her face almost black with blood and dirt. A string of rubbery flesh hung from her mouth, another from her forehead. *She looks like a toddler with a plate of spaghetti*, Dodd thought.

"Good god," Dodd whispered. "Who is that?"

"Shall I wait for Him to answer, Officer Dodd—God I mean—or would you prefer it if I did?"

The woman's mouth opened in full with every word she spoke, as if exaggerating her enunciation for someone who was deaf or less than fluent in the language. But there was no irony in the way she spoke, Dodd noticed, it was automatic, animal, a side-effect of whatever transformation she'd evidently gone through since he'd been away.

And her teeth. With every word, they seemed to point at him saying, *you're next if you have a problem*.

"Is that...?"

"The Klahr woman?" Marlene interrupted, her eyes wide, almost infant-like and playful.

The piece of flesh that had clung to Marlene's hair finally released its grip, and she watched it as it fell. It was the way a satiated bear might watch a salmon jump from a stream.

"I know it isn't her, I saw her in the room. She looks almost dead."

"You meant Gretel then?" Marlene asked, ignoring Dodd's observation about Amanda Klahr. "I'm not a fool, Officer Dodd. This..." Marlene paused and looked down at the body below her and then glided an upturned hand over it, as if presenting it to an audience for the first time. "This is not how it will be done with Gretel and her mother. You know that, of course."

"Who is it then? And why?"

"Because they were here!"

Dodd reached for his sidearm and pulled it from its holster, pointing it at the woman. The rage on her face was terrifying, unlike anything he'd seen from any perpetrator during his time with the System. Her face appeared to stretch, as if made of dough, and her eyes, smiling still despite the fury going on around them, seemed poised to fall from their sockets.

Dodd's hand wavered, but his training kept him locked in time and place. Nothing had killed more officers over the years than a lack of ability to focus on the situation in front of them. Too often they thought of the potential outcomes, and that was fatal.

"Calm down, Marlene. I just want to know who they are. That's all."

"Do you think I'm an animal, Officer Dodd? Is that what you're thinking right now?" Marlene's voice was calm, inquisitive.

"All I'm thinking now is that I need you to calm down, show me your hands, and let's go inside and talk about what's happening."

"You see, Officer Dodd, you may think I'm just an old lady, one who has found some secret that I've grown to treasure, yes? Some hermit who prefers to be alone, baking pies and biscuits and things. Perhaps does a little knitting! Is that it Dodd?"

"No."

"Cakes and pies aren't enough, Officer Dodd. As I told you, I crave. I crave the young ones most. Even outside of the concoction, I have an urge for them."

The long syllables poured past her jagged teeth, spittle flying. Dodd swallowed hard.

"I'm not the weakened prey of you and your ilk, Officer Dodd. I'll never be that again."

"No, you're not, Marlene. The fact that we're having this conversation tells me there is much more to you than that." Dodd was still now, his composure fully regained.

The woman narrowed her eyes and nodded, a gesture that indicated she, perhaps, beyond the obvious madness, understood Dodd's logic. He saw this as a small advantage, a hint that maybe the eroding situation could be turned around.

"Yes there is," the Witch of the North whispered, and then, as if a great vacuum had been positioned beneath her, the woman dropped from sight, disappearing into the ground cover of burned grass and tall weeds.

Dodd was momentarily stunned, almost skeptical of what his eyes had just communicated to his brain.

He was brought back to reality by a brushing sound to his left, and he flinched in that direction, just in time to see the weeds shake in a wave as something scurried through them toward the house. Dodd could only see the arched back of the woman's cloak, but he shivered at the grace and speed with which she moved. It looked like he had disturbed a wild boar in its shelter.

With his sidearm still brandished and locked in the direction of the house, Dodd sidestepped his way toward the mutilated body. As he did, he listened closely for the opening of a door, either to the cabin or his cruiser, as well as for any rustle of leaf litter out beyond the perimeter of the property. But he only heard silence.

When he reached the spot where Marlene had been standing only seconds before, he looked down reluctantly at the carcass beneath him and then vomited directly on top of it. It was an embarrassing reaction, not to mention an egregious violation to the crime scene. But none of that mattered did it? If this body was ever discovered by the System, it would mean Dodd was already dead.

The head of the man's body was missing, and the torso faced down, with two separate holes dug into the back where the kidneys had been dug clean. Blood and sinew puddled everywhere around the body, and a section of the man's spine was exposed in a prehistoric skeletal smile.

Dodd put a clenched fist to his mouth but held off any further spew, and he continued to scan the property for any sign of Marlene.

"This can be worked out, Marlene," Dodd called, trying his best to sound friendly.

Tone and Command was a training course all System officers were required to take when they first came on the force, and though Dodd always thought it was a bit of a silly class and one not practical to the field, he now searched his memory for some of the techniques.

"Look, I know this is who you are. You're strong—magical even. That's why I'm here. Remember? You just caught me off guard a bit."

Dodd stopped and thought about what he'd just said aloud. *That's why I'm here.* His System instincts had taken over, but the truth was that he still wanted to be a part of this deal. His brief foray into the world of witchcraft and sorcery—which thus far consisted of little more than a vague conversation and becoming an accomplice to kidnapping—was enough that he still wanted this life. He wanted it more than he'd ever wanted anything. There was nothing in his life thus far that had come close to this feeling. He could still salvage this scene. He felt sure of it.

And besides, he'd come too far to go back now. His old life was over; the secrets that he'd kept hidden were enough on their own to send him to the gulags.

Another sound, this time opposite the house, out by the tarp. It sounded as if something had fallen from the trees.

Dodd turned and pointed his gun at the truck, then quickly lowered the pistol, trying to display his interest in bringing back a dialogue. If she was watching him, he hoped to reel in the mad woman and bring her back to the shores of sanity.

"Is that you, Marlene?"

There was no answer, and Dodd began to creep his way toward the truck, keeping his head on a swivel, back and forth from the house to the tarp.

Dodd reached the side of the truck and placed his hand on top of the tarp where it covered the left fender. He peered over the hood and checked the opposite side of the truck facing the woods. Nothing. He walked around to the front of the vehicle now, and then to the passenger side. Still he saw no one. Dodd then walked the length of the passenger side until he came upon the bed of the pickup. He walked to the back and stood frozen as he stared at the covered bed.

There she was.

With the tailgate dropped, Dodd could see the toe of a shoe sticking out of a gap between the tarp and the truck, just beyond the fringe of the dried canvas.

He stepped back from the truck bed now and raised the gun once again. "I see you there, Marlene. You don't have to hide from me. I don't want to hurt you. Remember? I just want our deal. I just want a little bit of what you have. We can talk through this. Renegotiate."

Again, there was no response. Something was off with the scene. Something beyond the dead body in the yard. Dodd couldn't have said exactly what it was, but the stage was definitely wrong.

He moved closer to the edge of the flapped open tailgate and pushed the shoe that was peeking out from the tarp. It fell to the side with no resistance, and Dodd knew instantly what was wrong: this wasn't Marlene.

He quickly moved back to the side of the truck and grabbed the tarp in one motion, pulling the fabric up and back toward the cab.

The body of the young girl was seated in the bed, legs stretched forward, her back against the outside of the truck's cab. Her face was blue; her eye sockets were dark, empty voids at the top of her face, and a large chunk of flesh had been ripped from her neck. She couldn't have been older than sixteen.

Dodd closed his eyes and threw the tarp back down over the girl and then doubled over, trying to catch his breath. "What have I done?" he said aloud, and two tears dripped down to his shoes, leaving clean, empty circles in the dirt that had collected on the top of his boot.

"You've done nothing, Officer Dodd. That's why you don't belong here."

MARLENE WATCHED THE stone sail perfectly through the air, and then heard the sound as it landed in what must have been a crisp pile of dead leaves. She had failed to hit the truck, but the thickness of the tarp would have likely dulled the sound too much anyway, so it was probably better she missed. She almost released a laugh at the man's reaction to the noise—his face so stunned and filled with angst.

Marlene watched in delight, drooling at every step the man made toward the truck, watching him as she would a mother watching her child about to open a birthday surprise.

And this surprise, she noted, had been prepared especially for Mr. Dodd.

As he peered over the hood and then shuffled to the opposite side of the truck, Marlene left her station next to the house and pattered quietly through the brush to the woods on the opposite side of the yard.

She positioned herself behind a large oak and peeked around it, smiling, almost exploding in applause as Dodd flung back the tarp to reveal the young friend of Gretel Morgan. Marlene closed her eyes and breathed in deeply, imagining the smell again.

She opened her eyes now and saw the System officer vulnerable, hunched over, no doubt wearied with pain and regret. She moved along the tree until she was only a foot away. And then she waited.

"What have I done?"

She moved behind the officer now, her wooden cane raised, looming. "You've done nothing, Officer Dodd. That's why you don't belong here."

She swung the cane like a bat across her body, as if she was beating the dust from a rug that had been hung out on a line. It connected perfectly on the wrist bone of the officer, and he dropped his sidearm, the scream of pain exhilarating in her ears. It was loud enough that even her heavily drugged prisoner may have heard him.

The second strike of the cane caught the officer near the right ear at the top of his jawbone, splitting his cheek open like a peach. He buckled to the ground, his one good hand still grasping his broken wrist.

"Please," Dodd choked out, blood popping from his cheek on his loose 'P' of the word. "I've come to tell you something. It's about Gretel." He winced as he spoke, using every crumb of energy to get the sentences out.

Marlene rolled her eyes.

"She's home. Petr Stenson told me."

"I know she's home, Officer Dodd." Marlene closed her eyes and drew in a long breath. "Can't you smell her?"

Dodd's face warped into a look of puzzlement.

"I can smell her, even now with the body cold and rotting. But that's one of the gifts it gives you. Enhancements, I suppose you would call them. That's how I have always thought of them."

"There's more though." Dodd's voice was descending into defeat.

"Oh?" Marlene's eyebrows quivered slightly.

Dodd said nothing, and Marlene could sense him reconsidering, internally debating whether to give her this secret with his demise almost certain.

"Tell me, Officer Dodd, what more is there?"

"You have to promise you'll let me—"

Marlene smashed the cane down on Dodd's ankle with all the force she had. She could feel the bones give as they shattered into pebbles under his skin. His scream this time almost certainly woke the Klahr woman.

"What more is there?" Marlene asked again, her tone of politeness intact.

Dodd coughed and spat, barely able to breathe through the pain. "Anika," he managed finally. "Anika is on her way."

Marlene was genuinely intrigued at this news, and she waited patiently for Dodd to reach a point of relative coherence. When he was breathing regularly she asked, "When?"

"A few days maybe. I don't know exactly." Dodd's eyes widened, and he flashed a deranged smile. "But you were right, Marlene. She's coming home. Just like you said."

Marlene had seen this look in men many times over the centuries. The submissive smile of appeasement, followed by words of flattery in a final plea for mercy.

"And...and I brought back the book. Just like I told you I would."

It was Marlene's turn to smile now. She had temporarily forgotten about the book, so preoccupied was she with feeding and defending her home. She truly felt like an animal, but she rationalized there were worse things to be. "Where is it, Mr. Dodd?"

"You can't kill me, Marlene. We have a deal. I'll help you. I'll keep them away from here. You need me."

Marlene ignored Dodd. "I can see you're not carrying it with you, and I doubt that you would be lying to me now in your position. So, that means that it is in your car. Am I right?"

Dodd stayed quiet.

"It's okay. I'll find it, Officer Dodd."

Dodd began to speak again, and as he opened his mouth to announce the first word, Marlene smashed the tip of her ironwood cane through the back of his throat.

CHAPTER THIRTY-FOUR

"GRETEL!"

The oars hit the water just as Gretel heard her name called, and for a moment, she thought her mind had invented it in a combination of the wind and water and imagination.

She and Hansel had finished cleaning the basement with a few hours to go before sundown, and Gretel had seized the opportunity to get back to her canoe and the lake on which she had grown up. Now more than ever, rowing was the only thing that made her feel fully healthy, completely outside of herself; it was the only escape from her life of chaos.

She had found her oars behind the shed where she had stored them before leaving, and though they had splintered a bit through the damp and cold of the winter, they were still usable for a few more loops on the lake.

"Gretel!"

It was Petr. They were back from the System station.

Gretel had only been on the water for ten minutes, maybe less, but she was already tired, embarrassingly out of shape from where her fitness had been less than a year ago. Petr's return was a good excuse to stop for the day, though she would have relished another thirty minutes just to drift along the banks of the orchard and then down to Rifle Field.

Gretel u-turned the canoe back toward home, and within a few long strokes of the oars, she could see Petr standing on the bank of her property. He was so tall now, she noticed, so filled out compared to the boy she remembered standing on the opposite bank only a summer ago, when the harvest was ending and Gretel's life had settled into some semblance of normalcy.

Before her mother had returned.

That day and those that followed were the most joyous ones of Gretel's life. Of course, they were. And there was never anything she wouldn't have given to have that first moment when her mother finally came home safe and relatively unharmed.

But the price of that return had been the new life Gretel had carved out for herself. That life had ended the day her mother resurfaced. The life of the Klahrs and of Petr, of complete independence and adulthood, was to be destroyed, uprooted in a quest to find the answers to ancient questions in a strange world. It was a small price to pay, Gretel knew, but it was a price nonetheless.

"Petr, what is it?" Gretel steered the canoe toward Petr and stepped to the shore as the bottom of the boat nipped the muddy bank.

"It's done." Petr smiled.

"So he knows I'm back then, this Dodd person, and he doesn't suspect that you're up to anything?"

"It didn't go exactly as we planned, but I'm pretty sure he believed me. Believed us. Ben was pretty cool."

Gretel frowned and leaned into Petr, hugging him gently. "So I guess we'll know the truth soon. If the System is conspiring with the witch in some way, then she could be coming any day."

"There is no 'if,' Gretel, it is official. Officer Dodd was in his office reading that book you told me about. Your book. *Orphism.*"

"What?"

"I saw it up close. I saw the name."

Gretel was speechless but knew instantly that Petr was right. The officer had stolen the book from the cabin and was now bewitched by the promise of an everlasting life.

But he was reading it?

"So they'll almost certainly be coming, but we may have a day or two longer than we thought."

Gretel was stilled stunned by the *Orphism* revelation, but she let it go for the moment. "Why is that?"

"Thanks to Ben. He told Dodd your mother was on her way here but that she wouldn't be coming for a week or so."

How Gretel wished that were true. "That should work. It's my mother she really wants, I think." Gretel paused and then swallowed hard. "But what about Mrs. Klahr, Petr? How can this go on?"

"I don't know, Gretel. I just know that we have to trust this plan. This is what we decided, so we need to see it through. We have to trust that the woman will keep her alive. That she'll come out of this okay. Somehow. We stay the course, at least until we see it isn't working."

Gretel nodded and grinned. "When did you get to be a man?"

Petr shrugged, and then the two teenagers walked back to the house where Hansel gave Petr a tour of the newly cleaned home. They hadn't quite figured out a full plan for how they would kill the woman once and for all, but each of the kids pointed out a few places where potential traps could be laid.

When nightfall arrived, the three kids sat on the deck, awake but quiet, listening to the sounds of the forest.

"Petr!"

It was Ben, banging on the outside door, frantic.

Gretel quickly sprang to the front and opened the door. "Ben, what is it?"

"Where is Petr?"

"I'm right here, Ben," Petr said, stepping next to Gretel. "What happened?'

"It's Sofia and her brother Claude. They've gone missing."

"Missing? What? How do you know?"

"I went to check on Sofia, to see how she was doing after yesterday. I wanted to make sure she was okay and that she still understood that she wasn't allowed to talk to anyone about what we discussed. I just never had a perfect feeling that she was committed to her promise."

"And she was gone?"

"Her mother said they left to go check on someone. Someone they were concerned about. She pressed them, but they wouldn't tell her who it was. Her mother said Sofia looked very concerned. 'Like she had seen the devil,' she said."

"Oh no. Oh my god." Gretel felt a surge of guilt well up from her belly and she teetered on the verge of crying.

Petr instinctively put his arm around her.

"They went to look for her, didn't they?"

"I don't know, Gretel, but I can't think of anything else. I didn't know what to say to her mother, but I think she suspected that I knew something. I must have turned completely white."

Hansel came from the porch now. "Why did you go over there, Ben? Why couldn't you leave it alone? Look at where we are now."

"I went to check on my friend, you little brat!"

Hansel moved in toward Ben, and Petr stepped in between them.

"Stop it," Gretel snapped, her voice short and low. "Hansel, that's enough. We have to figure this out, but not by ripping each other apart."

"She's dead, Gretel," Hansel said. "And her brother too."

Gretel couldn't have imagined the words her brother had just spoken being said with any less emotion. She stayed silent, a tacit acknowledgement that what her brother had just stated was probably true. With that understanding, Ben let out a short cry of despair.

"There's nothing we can do now."

Hansel walked back to the porch and resumed his darkened meditation.

"She may be coming sooner now," Petr said finally, allowing his friend to gather himself first. "This could change things."

"If she does, we have to be ready," Gretel stated flatly. "We have a lot of work to do tomorrow."

"What do we do about Sofia?" Ben asked, swiping the streaks of tears from his cheeks. It was a question of logistics.

Petr took control. "I'll go to her house tomorrow and speak with her mother. She doesn't know me, but I'll tell her my father used to work for the System."

"So? What will that mean to her?"

"If she hasn't already, I'll tell her to call the System and file a report on her children. And then I'll tell her to make sure she asks for Officer Dodd."

CHAPTER THIRTY-FIVE

AMANDA KLAHR WOKE WITH a scream and stared at the red streak smiling across her window. It looked like the residue from a clown's kiss but was, in fact, the dried blood of the young victims who had attempted to help her. Who were they? Where did they come from?

She looked at the shadows on the wall and judged it late afternoon; she had no idea of which day. She couldn't depend on the quality of her assessments about much of anything anymore—the drug dosages had been substantial over the past week—but she judged that it had been several days since the kids had been there.

She had heard the returning voice of Dodd, and his departure again the next day, and she was positive she had also heard the coming and going of at least one other vehicle.

And she specifically remembered the hovering presence of the woman, standing above Amanda the moment the sun broke through the bedroom window.

"They know you're here, Amanda. They know you're alive. Just as I suspected." The glee in the woman's voice had been like that of a young girl who had just heard the secret of a school yard crush.

"I don't know them," Amanda had managed, her voice drugged and dreamy. "That isn't them."

"Oh, I know that's not young Petr, and the pretty girl with him certainly was not Gretel. But they're acquainted. Somehow. Especially the girl. I could smell it on her."

"So kill me. Kill me now. They know you're here. Those kids will be missed. They'll be coming for you."

"Kill you?" The woman's squawking made Amanda cover her ears with her hands. "Why would I do that now?"

"I...because..." Amanda's voice trickled off into a low groan.

"Because they'll be coming for me? Who? The System?" The cackling again. "Not yet, Amanda Klahr. Not yet. But when they finally do, I will be gone. We're leaving in the morning. We're going back to your home in the Back Country. And on the way, I'll make my decision about whether I want Gretel and Petr to watch me kill you, or you to watch me kill them."

CHAPTER THIRTY-SIX

"YOU SHOULD BE TENDERING to shore by morning, Mrs. Morgan. The voyage was about a half day longer than I anticipated. For that, I apologize."

It was less than six days since she and the crew of the *Kugel* had departed the docks of the Old World, leaving her new mysterious allies Oskar and Noah, behind. She hadn't looked back at them when she walked to the pier, wanting to remember them without tears in their eyes.

"Well that simply won't do," Anika joked. "I've got a tea with the queen at midnight."

Captain Hemmer looked at Anika quizzically and then smiled, catching the sarcasm a little late.

"I didn't know there were boats made that could go so far at such speeds." Anika sat on the bridge, staring out at the dark water before her.

"There are many, but most people cannot afford to take them across the great seas. But you are the great friend of my friend Noah, and you are privileged."

"I thought you owed him a favor."

Captain Hemmer kept a straight face and continued staring forward over the wheel of his ship. "Yes, there is that too."

Anika bellowed a full throaty laugh. It was a sound she couldn't remember having made in years.

But she would be home soon, and though her future—her very life—was dangling like an overripe cherry from a tree, Anika felt she had landed for a moment inside a small circumference of peace.

"Thank you, Captain Hemmer."

The captain nodded and stayed focused on the horizon. "You should sleep, Mrs. Morgan. And be ready for the day ahead."

It was great advice, and Anika decided to heed it. Tomorrow could be the longest day she'd ever known.

CHAPTER THIRTY-SEVEN

AMANDA KLAHR WAS RIGHT: they would be coming. And sooner than Marlene would have liked.

Perhaps she would have had more time if she had only taken the children's lives. She had smelled Gretel on the girl, that was true, so the children clearly hadn't stumbled upon Marlene's cabin accidentally, but that didn't necessarily mean they would have been missed immediately. Back Country folk were wanderers—often becoming transients and runaways—if she could have located the vehicle that had taken them to her, she could have hidden it with the others. It would have given her an extra day, at least. Even longer if no one talked with Gretel and her gang of misfits.

But none of that mattered now. Dodd was dead. And that changed everything.

Marlene walked to the cruiser that she moved beside the covered truck at the line of her property. It wasn't completely hidden from view, but anyone who casually approached the yard wouldn't have seen it without focusing on it. She opened the trunk and was struck immediately by the smell of a decomposing Georg Klahr. His body was gone—Marlene didn't try to imagine what Dodd had done with it—but the odor remained. She guessed that even someone without her abilities would have smelled it.

She closed the empty trunk and then opened the back passenger door and looked on the floor where she saw the thick corner of something peeking from under the seat. There was no mistaking what that was.

Orphism.

She slid the book into full view and brought it to her chest, embracing it as she would a lost pet that had been found alive. She opened the driver's door of the Klahr truck and placed the book gently on the seat, preparing it for transfer.

She closed the door and then walked to the front of the truck and pulled the tarp completely from the vehicle and draped it as best she could over the police cruiser. The cruiser was slightly too long and bulky for the canvas, but again, in a few days, none of it would matter. By then, she would be gone. By then, she would be headed for her homeland.

But before that, there would be a reckoning. At least for Gretel Morgan. If her deliverance to Anika Morgan had to wait, then it could, but she wouldn't allow them both to go unpunished.

As much as she detested having to do it, Marlene made the decision to keep Amanda Klahr alive. She figured the woman could have some use gaining access to the Morgan home, if that was, indeed, where they had taken refuge. Perhaps the Klahr woman could spring any traps that had been laid in wait for her. Gretel was smart, and Petr seemed to have some wit to him as well, so Marlene would tread gently once she reached their lair. If she was wrong and the woman was proved to be a liability, Marlene could easily kill her at any moment.

Marlene pushed *Orphism* to the passenger side and sat in the driver's seat. She grabbed the steering wheel with one hand and started the ignition. With not much protest, the truck fired up. She drove to the front and got out, leaving the engine running, and walked in the front door of the cabin.

Amanda Klahr was sitting in the lone chair like a life-sized doll. Her head bobbed to her chest, but she was awake, moaning. Just enough medicine, Marlene thought. I just need you to walk.

"Get up!"

Amanda Klahr grunted and got to her feet, the protest of her mind and body dwarfed by her broken spirit.

"We're going home, Mrs. Klahr. You should be thrilled."

Through a haze of drug and slumber, and with her eyes still closed, Amanda Klahr extended a broad smile that made Marlene's face twitch into a sneer.

Marlene guided Amanda into the passenger seat and then walked around to the opposite side.

"Let's go kill your family."

Amanda Klahr's smile broadened, and then she lifted her left hand into a fist and thrust it toward Marlene, striking her just below the ear.

Marlene screamed with fury, a sound born of frustration as much as anything, and then she raked her icy nails across the face of her prisoner.

The blood from Amanda Klahr's cheek splattered the side window and windshield, and Marlene grunted at the potential attraction this would cause.

"It is with the smallest of margins that you are still alive. One more movement that I think is out of place, and my nails will slice your throat."

CHAPTER THIRTY-EIGHT

GRETEL WOKE THE NEXT morning with the premonition of Mrs. Klahr lingering in her mind. She knew it was a positive sign that her friend and mentor, her surrogate mother for almost a year, was alive.

Gretel always considered the possibility that Mrs. Klahr would be in tow with the witch when the evil hag eventually came, a hostage to hold off any potential ambush. And thus, the traps they had laid were considered carefully, established with Mrs. Klahr in mind. A woman as mad as the witch would waste no time disposing of her captor, especially if she believed she, herself, was about to die.

No, they needed to let the witch arrive onto the property safely, unencumbered; and as she made her way toward the home, they couldn't give away their strategy or position too early. They would have to rescue Mrs. Klahr first, and once she was safe and the witch was isolated, then the real battle would begin. And Gretel knew it would be mostly hers to fight.

Gretel had let Petr take command of the planning; it was, after all, he who had stayed and investigated the witch for almost a year, discovering the cracks in the System's work and calling them to account for it. And the woman had killed his father. His vendetta ran deeper than hers, she supposed, so the least she could do was allow him the lead at this stage.

But the next stage was hers.

The lessons she had learned in *Orphism*, on her own and from the elders of the Old World, would be realized soon.

Or perhaps not. Either way she would know in the next few days. Maybe sooner.

She had studied the words in the book carefully, not only out of respect to her heritage, but from a true love of the lessons inside. She began to feel the power of them, not just on an emotional level, but physically as well. She never actually believed the time would come to summon the power though, since such strength was only needed against someone as dreadful as the witch, and she, everyone knew, was dead.

But she wasn't dead, and soon it would be time to act.

"How did it go with the mother? Are they calling the System?" Ben ran toward his own truck as Petr brought it to a stop in front of Gretel's house.

Petr got out of the truck and looked down toward the ground, not making eye contact with Ben or Gretel.

"Petr, what's the matter?" Gretel asked.

"I don't think she believed me."

"Why? What did you say?"

"I told her who I was. And that my father worked for the System. And that she should call them if Sofia and Claude didn't come home soon. She had already called the local police and was a little suspicious about calling the System. Folks here don't do that very often, apparently."

"No, they don't."

"Anyway, she walked me out when I was leaving, and she noticed the truck. She asked me if it was yours, Ben, and I said no. I'm not sure why I said that, but I thought it would seem suspicious that I was driving your truck. She gave me a funny look. I don't think she believed me."

"It doesn't matter, Petr. Let's just get back to work." Hansel stood at the top of the porch stairs. "She could be coming any second. You all understand that, right? We have to have the attitude that she's right around the corner."

"I told you we stalled her, Hansel. She's going to wait for your mother. And she doesn't think your mother is coming for a few more days."

"Or maybe she just killed a couple of kids on her property and now she's a little concerned that word will get out. Maybe she's been spooked. Have you thought of that, Petr?"

This is Hansel now, Gretel thought. A shift had happened within him. Some kind of psychological break. And it was as much her fault as anyone's. Maybe it was all her fault. Two years from now, if they were still alive, she'd probably feel sorry for him and what she'd instilled in the boy, but in this moment, she was relieved.

"He's right," Gretel agreed, "it doesn't really matter what Sofia's mother does. What we need to do now is prepare."

"What are we going to do?" Petr asked. "We don't have the time to build some elaborate trap."

"No," said Ben, "but we do have guns."

Gretel chimed in. "This one pistol isn't going to be enough for her, Ben. Believe me."

Ben snickered. "I'm not talking about your great-grandfather's gun, Gretel. Or whatever that thing is."

Gretel frowned, slightly insulted.

Ben jogged over to his truck and dropped the tailgate, and then pulled himself up inside the bed. He walked to the front and then stopped at a dusty red blanket that covered something long and rectangular. Ben pulled the cover toward him until it dropped to the bed, revealing an old wooden box that ran from one sideboard to the other.

"What is it?" Petr asked.

"It's a gun box. And it ain't empty."

Ben unlatched the top and reached down and grabbed a rifle and a double-barreled shotgun, holding them up over his head like a soldier whose platoon had just won the enemy's high ground.

"A gun box? This would have been a nice thing to know about when we were back at the witch's cabin. We might have done things differently."

"Look Petr, I've never even seen you fillet a fish. And I had just met Gretel and Hansel. I didn't want you or me or Mrs. Klahr getting shot by a bunch of kids who don't know the first thing about guns. And that wasn't the time to give a crash course. And there was Sofia too. I just—"

"Okay, okay, I get it. What do you have in there?"

"I've got these two," Ben said holding the guns higher, "a shotgun and a rifle with a scope, and a pistol a little more modern than the soaked out one you have there, sweetheart. The rifle is mine. Distribute the others as you see fit."

"So we're just going to stand out here with our guns and unload on the woman when she drives up? What about Mrs. Klahr?" Hansel's tone suggested he wasn't completely against the plan, but he was skeptical of how they would pull it off.

"We'll hide. The four of us. One of us will have the angle. I know there's risk, but that's always going to be the case." Ben was becoming annoyed that his friends weren't as impressed with his arsenal, that they couldn't see that this was the answer they'd been looking for.

"No, Ben," Gretel said. "That plan won't work. Not like that."

"Why not?"

"You're right about Hansel and me. We were never hunters, not really, and we couldn't be counted on to pull off what you're talking about. But I also think you're wrong about Petr." Gretel looked over at her friend and nodded. "From what I remember, this son of a System officer is quite skilled with the iron. Pistoleer award when you were ten, if I recall correctly."

Petr grinned and blushed. "I told you about that?"

Gretel knew Petr pretended not to remember. She could see it in his face. In fact, she suspected Petr remembered every moment they spent at Rifle Field. The day of Gretel's first kiss. "You did."

"Well, hell, Petr, you never told me that." Ben seemed genuinely hurt by this biographical omission.

"You never asked."

"How would I know to ask that?"

Gretel refocused them on the task in front of them. "So that's how it will be then, Ben; you and Petr are going to do the shooting. One of you will have to kill her."

"What about you and Hansel?" Ben asked.

Gretel grabbed her brother's hand and squeezed it tight. "Hansel and I will be the bait.

CHAPTER THIRTY-NINE

MARLENE DROVE THE INTERWAYS at a speed that was just fast enough not to be stopped and ticketed, but not so slowly that she would draw suspicion from some stray backwoods constable. The sun was still a couple of hours away from rising, so there was still time to make it to the Back Country unseen; she hoped to arrive before most folks began their day's work.

Amanda Klahr slept beside her, a fresh dosage of sedative working in her bloodstream.

Marlene had originally intended to head directly to the Morgan property, where she would confront and kill the Stenson boy, along with any other recruits they had brought on to fight in their battle. And then she would take Gretel. Brutally if necessary, but alive.

They would be waiting for her—of course they would be—but that was to be expected. This renewed chapter of the Morgans was always going to end in confrontation. It was true that events had moved more quickly than she'd expected, and that she'd been somewhat outmaneuvered by her enemies, but those truths were never going to stop her from coming. She would be ready for the trap, the ambuscade, protected by the vulnerable flesh of the Klahr woman. She, and the feelings Gretel and Petr held for her, would be Marlene's shield, just as the nurse Odalinde had shielded Marlene from Georg Klahr's shotgun.

But Marlene's mind was clouded now, unable to focus fully on her mission. It kept drifting to the letter. The letter Anika had left for the Klahrs, with the itinerary and destination of the Morgans in the Old World. The details of the journey didn't matter anymore as far as the Morgans were concerned, but Marlene's interest was still unwavering. She had to know. In case she never made it off the Morgan property, she had to be reminded once more of the places she had once known intimately.

The Morgans had gone off to the Old World, that much she had learned since her awakening, but to which region and specific town was a mystery, and that is what continued to tickle the back of her mind. So, at just a few minutes past dawn, just as she was coming up on the dirt driveway where she had planned to steer Georg Klahr's truck toward the Morgan farm, to head directly into the ambush, Marlene pivoted her plan and continued straight on for a half mile more until she reached the unmarked road of the Klahr orchard. It was the letter that she thought of as she drove, but it was Life that drew her there.

"We're changing our plans slightly, Mrs. Klahr. I hope you don't mind."

"They'll kill you," Amanda mumbled. The words were dry, breathy, clearly dialogue from a dream. Still, Marlene was mildly unnerved by how poignant they sounded in the moment.

Marlene nodded and replied somberly, "Not without killing you too. Now let's go have a look at the old cottage."

Marlene backed the truck in so it was facing the road—in case she needed a quick escape—and then walked to the passenger door and opened it in a way a chauffeur might after arriving at a sophisticated party. Then, in amazing contrast to her door gesture, she grabbed Amanda by the upper arm and slung her over her shoulder like an old carpet. Marlene felt strong, energized, perhaps a result of her proximity to Gretel and the prospect of a returning Anika. Or maybe it was a sense that the end of her time in this world was coming soon. The Old World beckoned. In any case, she had so much to repay the Morgans.

Amanda Klahr grunted as her abdomen fell across Marlene's spindly shoulder, but the woman offered no real resistance, and Marlene quickly carried her inside and up the stairs to the secondary quarters across from the Klahr's main bedroom.

She placed her on the bare mattress that laid on the iron bedframe and began to tie her down. Marlene realized there probably wasn't any urgent need for the restraints at this point, with the Klahr woman nearly comatose, but the thin drapery that hung next to the bed seemed like a sign not to be ignored and an ideal fabric for tying Mrs. Klahr's hands to the bedpost. If it took her longer than she expected to find the letter, she would come back and reinforce the job with more proper shackling.

But within a few moments of searching, Marlene knew that wouldn't be necessary.

She strode across the hall and into the main bedroom—the arena where she had done battle with the Klahr woman not so many nights ago—and was immediately drawn to the destressed white vanity that sat in the corner of the room, obviously Mrs. Klahr's side of the bed. She opened the long thin drawer positioned just below the main surface of the vanity and immediately saw a white envelope with GEORG AND AMANDA KLAHR handwritten in the center.

Marlene took the envelope out and smelled it, and then ran her long fingernail under the fold, splitting the paper casing, careful not to destroy the contents. She pulled the wrinkled letter from the envelope and unfolded the paper and began to read:

Dear Mr. and Mrs. Klahr,

Thank you for respecting my wishes not to read this letter upon delivery. When you do read it after we are gone, I pray that you are doing so only out of concern, or perhaps burning curiosity, and not because something dire has occurred. I can never repay you or thank you enough for what you have done for my family, so please do not interpret my secrecy regarding where we have gone as anything other than extreme precaution on my part. You are the only ones I trust, and it is why I have written this letter at all.

In the event you must contact us, we have gone to the town of Hecklin in the ancient region of Jena. It is located just at the base of the Koudeheuvul Mountains. This land is the ancient region of my mother and her family, and my belief is that there are secrets there that can help explain the origins of my family, as well as the reasons behind the trauma we recently endured.

And perhaps more fully explain the powers that exist in my daughter.

Our family name is Aulwurm. It is a rare surname, so we should be easy to locate should you need us. Please be prudent, however, and contact us only if there is no other choice.

I fear for us still. Please be careful.

We will return.

Anika

Marlene placed the letter down on the vanity and stared out the window across the lake at the Morgan cabin where all was still and dark. The sun not yet risen above the canopy of the property. A new darkness will be coming soon, she thought.

She sat on the edge of the bed and closed her eyes, attempting to clear her mind, to force her thoughts back to her life in the mountains. The Koudeheuvul Mountains. It was a name similar to the one her family had given to the range thousands of years ago, but it had been bastardized over the centuries, by kings and settlers, to its current iteration. But the name still rang powerfully, and just reading the word elicited energy in her blood. Marlene felt her heart race, and she took a giant breath to calm herself.

Jena. It was the land of Orphism, both the book and the religion. It was where she would flee when this was over, when she had concluded her task with the Morgans. When she had once and for all taken their lives for her own.

She was in a reverie now, and she smiled at the image of her home, the image of a fire burning brightly beyond the hearth, her mother giving a tired simper as she set a basket of wood on the stone floor. There was no father in this image; perhaps she would never remember him.

Marlene could have chased this scene for hours, but she was wrenched from the dream by a woman's voice screaming from the front of the cottage. She sat still on the bed, eyes wide and searching.

"Petr Stenson!" The voice was desperate, almost sobbing. "Come out here! I know this is where you live! You will tell me where my children are!"

AMANDA STUMBLED FROM the bed at the sound of the screaming, like a farmer conditioned to rise at the crowing of a rooster, but she was yanked back to the mattress by the sheets wrapped around her wrists.

"Who is that?" she whispered to herself, her intoxication still heavy, creating doubt as to whether she had heard anything at all.

"Petr Stenson!" the woman called again.

Amanda got to her feet again, slowly this time, and leaned her body forward toward the window as far as possible without falling, the sheets keeping her from collapsing.

She could see the shape of the woman standing still in the driveway—based on her voice and posture, Amanda guessed she was in her forties—and then she started walking toward the house, her stride purposeful.

"No!" Amanda called to the closed wall of glass in front of her. "Run!"

With a heavy tug, Amanda tested the curtains on her wrists and could instantly feel the loose wriggle of fabric. Compared to her imprisonment at the cabin, these restraints hadn't been tied with any real purpose. She flailed her arms now, flexing all the strength in her biceps and forearms; she must have looked like a mad woman, she thought, or a drowning victim.

But the motions paid off, and within a few more desperate twists and yanks, Amanda managed finally to get one hand free, which she then used to untie the other. She was free.

Amanda immediately ran to the window and opened it. "Go away!" she called to the woman. "She'll kill you! Go! Please!"

"Who are you? Are you Petr's grandmother?" The woman's pitch was angry, accusing.

"You have to listen to me." Amanda was desperate now, almost crying. "Get away from here. Get in your car and..."

Amanda never heard the woman enter her room, and she never saw the cane that struck her in the back of her head just above her neck.

And thankfully, she never heard the tortuous death of Sofia Karlsson's mother as she was torn apart on the dusty driveway at the entrance of the Klahr orchard.

Amanda saw only a flash of light, followed by a voice that said, "I'll deal with you later." And then she lost consciousness.

CHAPTER FORTY

GRETEL WALKED OUT TO the front porch and looked up at the darkening sky. It was still early, but rain appeared imminent.

"Hey, Gretel," a voice called in the distance. It came from the trees at the top of the driveway where the road to the Interways began.

"Ben?"

"That's me. Can you see me?"

"No, where are you?"

"Up here."

Gretel descended the porch stairs and then followed the sound of Ben's voice until she came to a thick chestnut tree that stood about ten yards deep in the woods. She looked up and saw the boy smiling, his face and shirt smeared with dirt. He gave a silly wave and then looked through the sight of his rifle, practicing his aim, a motion Gretel guessed he'd probably done a hundred times already since establishing his position.

"So how good are you with that thing?"

"I'm pretty good." He paused. "I'm not bad with the rifle either."

Gretel laughed despite herself. "You're gross."

Ben laughed and then almost instantly turned somber. "Hey, Gretel?"

Gretel nodded, waiting.

"I am good with a gun, and I promise I'm not going to let anything happen to you or your brother."

Gretel smiled. "Not even Hansel, huh?"

"Well...no, not even him."

"Thank you, Ben. I need to go check on Petr." Gretel turned to the house and started walking and then stopped and looked back. "And Ben," she said, "I'm really sorry about Sofia. I know she was your friend. She should never have been a part of this."

"Thanks, Gretel. I'm sorry too. But it was my fault."

There was no point in debating the blame. Maybe later, Gretel thought, but not now. Now was a time for preparedness.

Gretel was pleased with Ben's readiness, camouflaged and poised like a soldier. She sensed that kind of strength and will in the boy from the moment she met him. It was an attractive quality, the feeling that he was a protector.

Petr, on the other hand, was still balking at the plan, unsure of their decisions to this point. Gretel sensed he was doubting himself, doubting his ability to perform his role once the horror was at hand.

Gretel walked down to the back of the house where Petr had been standing for several minutes now, staring out at the lake. She stopped beside him and gazed in the same direction.

"I'm scared, Gretel."

"I am too."

Petr turned to Gretel now, a look of confusion on his face. "You don't understand, Gretel. I'm not scared for me."

"Then who? What?"

Petr shook his head and snickered, seemingly irritated at Gretel's naiveté. "For so long, I wished for you to come back. I thought about it every night, the moment when you would just appear without notice, to tell me that you were here to stay. And then it happened. You were just floating in the lake in front of me. A mirage. That was a miracle for me, Gretel."

Gretel felt flush at the admiration being poured upon her.

"And now? Now I wish you hadn't come back. I wish you were still in the Old World and that I had no idea what you were doing because then I would at least know you were safe from her."

Gretel let the words land. She didn't want to step on his thoughts by responding too quickly, diminishing his feelings. Finally, she said, "I'm here, Petr, and there's nothing that is going to change that. We can only turn into this problem now, face our crisis as the imperative that it is. It's the only choice we have."

"But what of this magic, Gretel?" Petr's face was pleading, not giving up on the possibility of something divine coming into play.

"What are you talking about, Petr?"

"You have these powers. Like Hansel was speaking of. Powers like the witch, yes? Perhaps you're even stronger."

Gretel wasn't going to argue or downplay her abilities to Petr, so she instead decided to be direct about what she believed her potential to be. "If I wanted that, then yes, I think one day I could be that powerful. Perhaps. But that day will never come to pass. I'll not live a thousand years, Petr. I'll never have the luxury of endless time in which to hone and develop whatever heritage has been placed within me."

Gretel could sense a shame bubbling in Petr. "I'm sorry, Gretel, I just thought—"

"You don't need to apologize, Petr. Do you think I haven't thought of that? Of course, I have."

Petr nodded in understanding. "So what are we doing, Gretel? Are we going to die?"

Gretel placed her arms around Petr's neck and focused his eyes to hers. "I don't know, Petr, but my hunch right now tells me that we are exactly where we should be. It's true that I may never be as physically strong as she is, but my feelings and insights—my natural instincts—are no less resonant than hers. I believe it's true. I believe it like I believe I need air to breathe."

Petr smiled and pulled Gretel toward him in a hug. "It's because you're a good person, Gretel. It's your reward from the world. It's your defense. And I trust you. I trust whatever you decide we should do."

Gretel pulled away and kissed Petr on the mouth. She held her lips on his for several beats before unlocking and then went in for another short brush of his mouth. "Good. Where's your gun?"

Petr hesitated, flashing a proud smile at the gift of Gretel's mouth, and then walked under the porch stairs and picked up the shotgun with the indifference of a bank robber.

"Is it loaded?"

Petr broke open the barrel, peered inside, and nodded; it was a three-part move that Petr pulled off almost simultaneously, and Gretel was comforted by his obvious aptitude with the weapon.

"There's no range on this gun, Gretel. If it's going to be me, if I'm the one that's going to kill her, she'll need to be right in front of me. If I'm not close enough, I can't risk it. No one can shoot and miss."

"So you want to have the pistol too?"

Petr looked down, as if holding back.

"What is it, Petr?"

"That goes for you too, Gretel. You have to be sure. You can't pull the pistol unless you're sure. You have to understand that."

Gretel did understand it. She'd thought intensively about her role as the lure, the magnet that would draw the witch in, freezing her for just long enough that one of the boys could get a shot on her. But for all the trust she held in Ben and Petr, Gretel was intent on insuring the plan by keeping the pistol in the back of her pants, under her shirt. She hoped not to need it—of course she hoped that—since that would mean that the blueprint of their plan had been destroyed and desperation was at hand; but if the situation did devolve into a level of chaos, she wanted a chance.

"I won't panic, Petr, if that's what you're saying. If you and Ben are as good as you think you are, we can end the day on the right side of life."

"Is Hansel ready?"

"I'm ready."

Gretel watched her brother as he walked past them, not making eye contact, his chest full and his shoulders high.

"Are you?" Gretel asked.

Hansel stopped and turned to his sister, his eyes narrow, voice challenging. "Do you think I'm not?"

"Are you at your post right now?"

"Are you? Because it looks to me like you're down here snogging with your boyfriend. Hardly ready, I would say."

"Ben is at his post, which is at the front of the property. He'll see anyone coming from that direction a mile before they're here. You're to be at the lake's edge pretending to be unaware, drawing her to you if she comes from the Klahr's."

"She's not coming from the Klahr's, Gretel. We were there just yesterday. And how would she come from the lake, anyway? The canoe is here."

"The Klahrs have boats, you nit. She could come easily."

"I know why you put me there. You've stuck me on the lake to keep me out of the way. To hide me. You know she isn't coming from the Klahrs. Not on a boat. She would be too vulnerable."

"Just get there!"

Gretel was fuming now, and Petr stepped in to bring down the temperature. "Hansel's right, I think. About us getting ready. And Hansel, your sister is also right. You should get to your station. We agreed on this, remember?"

"I don't remember, Petr. I remember you all making the plans and me contesting them and then my sister saying that was the final word on it. I wouldn't call that an agreement."

"Yes, but Hansel—"

"Forget it. I'll be at the lakeshore fingering my arse if you need me."

And with that, Gretel had enough, and she stepped toward to her brother, intending to grab him by the back of the shirt and pull him to the ground for a wrestling match, the kind they probably hadn't had since Gretel was in grade school.

But it was too late for that.

The witch already had him.

CHAPTER FORTY-ONE

ANIKA RODE SILENTLY in the back of the taxi, taking in the sights of the New Country. The buildings and lights and signage that were routine to most were things Anika had rarely seen in her life. The Back Country—and a few years of riding to the Northlands to visit her father—were the extent of her travels for most her life. Until this past year. Until her incredible journey to the Old World. She considered now the prospects of returning there someday, perhaps even permanently, but something inside her resisted it.

She reached into her bag for her pocket watch and suddenly felt a shriek ripple through her head. She made a sound like, "Ouoh!"

"Are you okay, ma'am?" the driver asked with a peek toward the mirror and then back to the road, not wanting to be too intrusive.

Anika shook her head quickly, not having the energy to reply.

"Ma'am?"

"Yes," she managed, and then put her palms to her temples. "May I lie down?" she asked, and then did so before the driver could answer.

"Sure, ma'am. I'll let you know when we've arrived."

Was it the sickness or the mystery orange pill of the villagers? Anika couldn't have said, but either way, the pain was ferocious. It was a few more hours to the house. She would sleep until then. And when she arrived, she would find her children. And then find the book.

CHAPTER FORTY-TWO

AMANDA KLAHR AWOKE to the staring corpse of the woman from the driveway.

Amanda was again tied to the bed, this time with thick strands of burlap rope that cut her skin and brought rings of blood to her wrists and ankles.

The corpse was situated in a chair on the side of the bed, upright, eyes crooked and terrified.

Amanda barely flinched at the dead body this time; her nerve endings apparently having died somewhere back at the woman's cabin.

She did, however, regain a small bit of comfort from being back in her home. She had always assumed she would die at the hands of the abominable witch—Marlene, she'd heard the officer call her—so if that were to be Amanda's fate, then let it happen in her own home.

"What are you looking at?" Amanda said to the dead woman, not the slightest tone of amusement in her voice. "We'll try, right? That's all we can do. We'll try to help them. They drew her away from there. Petr and Gretel. They brought her back here. I have faith in them. You should have had faith too. You should have stayed away from here. This wasn't your fight."

Amanda now looked in the woman's face and began to cry. "I'm sorry for you. And if those were your children."

Amanda gave a moment of respect to the dead family and thought of God and heaven; she prayed they were all there now. And then she silently pled for their forgiveness.

"Now let's start trying, Amanda. Let's start trying."

CHAPTER FORTY-THREE

"GRETEL?"

Hansel's voice wasn't loud enough to be considered a whimper, and Gretel had to use all her restraint to keep the gun in its resting place at the small of her back. From the corner of her eye, she saw Petr twitch just a bit, and Gretel held a hand out, backing him off, signaling him to bury any instinct he was about to follow concerning the shotgun in his hands.

"If that gun is still in your hands three seconds from now, I'll bury my finger deep in this boy's eye."

"Petr!" Gretel called, and then watched the gun bounce impotently on the gravel in front of her.

"Gretel Morgan and Petr Stenson," the woman sneered, her voice like some ancient insect, a beetle that had gained remedial vocal abilities over the hundreds of millions of years of its evolution. "The great untold love story of our time." She laughed now, and Gretel's stomach burned with anxiety and hate.

"If you let him go, I'll replace him," Gretel pled. "You want me. And I can bring you to my mother. Just leave him."

Gretel's breathing was shallow, and she almost crying now, in disbelief that they had ended up in this position. With all their precaution, with all the danger they had left Mrs. Klahr to face, they had still been outmaneuvered.

But this was the moment now, and she had to turn into it, just like she had advised Petr only minutes ago.

"He doesn't have what I have. What we have. You know that I'm right."

"He's an Aulwurm. Maybe not with the Orphic instincts you possess, but his blood is your blood. Although, about your instincts, I'd be remiss were I not to point out how dulled they were just now, eh?" The woman looked at Petr before shaking her head slowly, grinning. "I will have all of you in the end, anyway. You've always known this, Gretel."

"You can't make it away from here..." Gretel paused, chasing a name that flashed in her mind for an instant. She'd never heard the woman's name, or seen it written, but she sensed it somehow. "Marlene? Is that your name?"

The witch gasped, almost choking on the oxygen in her throat, her jaw hanging loosely in awe, a look of fear glazing over her eyes.

"You can't get away, Marlene. The System knows about you."

The spell Gretel had cast on Marlene at the utterance of her name was broken at the mention of the System, and the witch threw back her head in a gregarious, taunting laugh. "Yes, the System. They know all about me."

"I'm not talking about Dodd."

Marlene stopped her cackle and stared with interest at Gretel.

"I'm talking about the overseer of your case. Conway." Gretel could tell by the look on her face that Marlene didn't know about this person. "Yes, Marlene, it's not all covered up like Dodd wants you to believe. There are other people at the System, good people, and they'll be coming for you."

Gretel paused, allowing the witch an opportunity to join in the dialogue if she wished. Instead, she remained silent, listening.

"But I can make it go away. Petr and I."

Marlene's eyes shifted to Petr, her grip on Hansel's neck tightening, causing a groan from the boy.

Gretel stayed calm, despite her brother's suffering. "Petr has known that you were alive this whole time. He tried to convince the System months ago, and everybody else for that matter, but nobody would listen. It's been his quest to find you."

"What is this to do with me?" Marlene finally said, humoring Gretel, the impatience in her voice obvious.

"If he says you're dead, if he tells the System he saw proof of your dead corpse at Rifle Field, or floating in the lake or something, they'll believe him. And then you can go. You can escape back to the Old World."

The witch raised her eyebrows just slightly and tilted her head to the side at the idea Gretel had just presented. Gretel thought she even detected the faint trace of a smile.

"But you have to let go of Hansel. You have to take the truck, the truck that's here, and drive it to the docks. You can get on the first steamer headed for the Old World. It's your only chance."

"But there are no more Aulwurms in the Old World," Marlene said to herself, as if now considering a point she'd failed to earlier. "My potion would not—"

"There's no more potion!" Gretel growled, the fury in her voice as potent as any she'd ever delivered. It felt almost divine.

Marlene looked at Gretel confused, almost hurt by her words. "But there will always be my potion. That is what this is all for." She turned now to Hansel and studied him curiously. "I don't need this one really," she said. "In the end, you'll be far more trouble than I need."

Marlene's expression turned wickedly twisted, like the face of a rotting jack-o-lantern, and she raised her hand high above her head, nails pointing toward the top of the boy's skull.

"No!" Gretel screamed, and then reached at her lower back for the gun tucked in the waistband of her pants.

As her hand touched the handle, before she could brandish her weapon, Gretel heard the report of a rifle followed by the scream of Marlene.

"MARLENE? IS THAT YOUR name?"

The sound of her own name landed like a boot in Marlene's gut. How could a girl this young have developed the skill so quickly? It had taken Marlene generations to finally acquire this ability—which wasn't quite mind-reading but was something akin to it—and Gretel apparently now possessed it as a mere teenager. And it seemed she was more adept than Marlene, who rarely landed on the exact name.

"You can't get away, Marlene. The System knows you're coming."

Marlene's fascination with the girl was broken, diminished by the ineptitude of the System. She laughed. "Yes, the System. They know all about me."

"I'm not talking about Dodd. I'm talking about the overseer of your case. Conway."

Marlene didn't quite know what an overseer was and had never heard of this Conway person before.

"Yes, Marlene. It's not all covered up like Dodd wants you to believe. There are other people at the System, good people, and they'll be coming for you."

Dodd was dead. Marlene had thought little of him since she'd skewered him with the point of her cane, but the mention of him brought her back to the reality of her situation. They would be coming. Again. And there would be no cover-up this time. No hiding out in the ground, hibernating until the trouble passed.

"But I can make it go away. Petr and I."

Marlene felt Hansel squirm and pressed lightly on his neck. How easily she could crush him. How easily she could crush them all.

"Petr has known that you were alive this whole time. He tried to convince the System months ago, and everybody else for that matter, but nobody would listen. It's been his quest to find you."

"What is this to do with me?"

"If he says you're dead, if he tells the System he saw proof of your dead corpse at Rifle Field, or floating in the lake or something, they'll believe him. And then you can go. You can escape back to the Old World."

The image of Marlene's mother appeared in her mind again, and she was taken back to her youth during a time when her life had relative normalcy. It had been centuries since those days, and her memory was almost certainly cushioned as it pertained to the comforts and stability of her childhood. But her memory was all that mattered now.

"But you have to let go of Hansel. You have to take the truck, the truck that's here, and drive it to the docks. You can get on the first steamer headed for the Old World. It's your only chance."

The Old World. The Old World had nothing for her. The sudden realization was like a blast of sunlight through a dark room. "But there are no more Aulwurms in the Old World. My potion would not—"

"There's no more potion!"

If the sound of her own name earlier was a punch to the gut, Gretel's words this time were a knife to the heart. The potion was all she had now. There was nothing else. There would never be anything else.

It was time to move forward with this encounter. She was being stalled, and it was time to cut her losses. "But there will always be my potion. That is what this is all for. I don't need this one really. In the end, you'll be far more trouble than I need."

The pre-destruction ecstasy was already flowing through Marlene as she anticipated the feel of her bladed nails sinking into the boy's soft scalp. She inhaled as she raised her hand high and then screamed in terror as her hand exploded above her.

"HANSEL, RUN!"

Despite the fountain of blood shooting from her hand and wrist, the witch made a fervent grab to retain Hansel as he spun away from her grasp. Marlene's face was a tapestry of expressions, the most dominant of which, Gretel thought, were hatred and disbelief.

"I will kill you all!" Marlene roared at the trees as she ducked into the woods next to the house, dodging the one round Gretel was able to get off from her weapon. Her feet reacted quickly to the turn of events, and she strode with deer-like quickness into the deep brush, disappearing.

Petr was a little slower than Gretel getting to his weapon, but he was armed now, the shotgun chambered and ready; Gretel could see by the look on his face that he was still confused, stunned, trying to figure out what had just happened.

But Gretel knew. It was Ben, from his perch at the front of the property. And he was in the same woods the witch had just entered.

"Ben!" Gretel called. "Ben, watch out! She's gone!"

Gretel assumed Ben understood that her warning was intended to be a one-way conversation, and that he was not to answer and give away his position. Besides, it was likely he saw all of what happened in his scope following the impossible rifle shot.

"Hansel, come here quickly," Gretel called.

After a second or two, Hansel appeared at the front of the house, having gone all the way around it from the back. "Is she gone?"

Gretel motioned to the woods.

"We have to go after her, Gretel. This has to end here. Today."

"Hansel, listen to me, and I don't want any argument."

Hansel stood motionless, his eyes locked on his sister.

"It's Mrs. Klahr. I think...I know she is at the orchard. Get to her. She's in the house somewhere, and she could be in grave condition. When you get there, find her, and then use the phone to call the System." Gretel looked to Petr, her face intensely serious. "Overseer Conway. That's right, isn't it Petr? We can trust him?"

Petr nodded, understanding the impact of his answer.

"Tell him what's happened. Tell him to come with only his most trusted officers."

Hansel stood, and Gretel could see him wavering, reluctant to exit the fray.

"Go! The canoe is on the bank."

"I guess there are two now, right?" Hansel confirmed, a sorrowful look in his eyes.

"Two what?"

"Canoes. That's how she came here. You were right, Gretel. I should have kept to the plan. I should have been there watching."

Gretel calmed her tone, eager to bypass having to reassure her brother that he wasn't at fault. "It doesn't matter, Hansel. Everybody is okay for now. But you have to go. Go save Mrs. Klahr and call the System. Remember, only Conway. If he isn't available, then—"

A scream from the front of the woods interrupted them. It was in the direction of Ben.

"Hansel, go!"

MARLENE RAN INTO THE woods far enough that she could no longer see the Morgan cabin. She sat and rested at the base of a large oak, hidden from the direction she'd just come. She studied the void in her hand where her last three fingers should have been. This was a terrible loss, she thought, just as her eye had been, but not fatal. Not if she could stop the bleeding.

"Ben! Ben watch out!" Marlene heard in the distance. "She's gone!"

There was another one then. Of course, a sniper. Marlene had always suspected there would be others to contend with, but she had apparently underestimated them, having seen none upon her arrival at the property. She had been right to attack them from the shore of the Klahr's, but she hadn't considered a sniper.

Marlene moved deeper into the woods by at least a hundred yards, trying to get distance from them in case they decided to hunt her immediately, and then started to make her way up toward the road that led to the Morgan's property. It took her less than a minute to reach the point where she could see the road through the trees—at about fifty feet or so— and then she began to backtrack in the direction of the house. If her calculations were right, based on the direction the bullet had flown and the sound of the report, once she retraced her lateral movement from the house, she would be just about at the location of the sniper.

The foliage was dense enough that she could stay hidden from view for most of the way, but with the twigs and leaf litter, there was no way to stay silent for long.

It was time again. It was time to fly.

Marlene crept slowly back toward the house on the latitude where she thought the shooter was and then closed her eyes and smiled. She opened her eyes and began to walk faster. At a small clearing, she broke into a light gallop for three or four steps before lifting herself from the ground.

She glided like a kite lifted by a sudden wind, rising about ten feet up and twenty feet forward until she landed on the sturdy branch of a thick white oak.

Marlene caught her breath, exhilarated by the feeling of flight and of her own powers. She took a moment to view the world below her before continuing her hunt. She couldn't see the shooter yet. She assumed he had camouflaged himself in some way—but she knew if she gave him enough time, particularly under these circumstances, he would reveal himself. They always did; it was almost as if they wanted to die, Marlene sometimes believed.

While she waited on the branch of the oak, Marlene thought again of the potion, as well as the option that Gretel had proposed. Perhaps the girl was right. Perhaps she should have left for the docks, stowed away back to Old World and the mountains of her youth. But that would mean an abandonment of the Morgan women, a violation of her commitment to Life.

Or would it? The Old World didn't mean the end. Not necessarily. There were other sources there she could pull from. They hadn't the virile potency of the Morgans—the Aulwurms—but they could sustain her for a time. Until she could recover and come back for them.

And even if the Old World meant an end to this life, was that the worst thing? Did she believe it was going to last forever?

The woman shook off this last notion and focused on the task before her. She looked straight ahead, searching for movement, but she only saw still foliage. She was too far away. It was time to move again.

She stood tall on the branch now and, never looking down, stepped forward as if walking from a bridge to her death. She felt the pull of gravity on her front foot and then pushed off the tree with her back, flying forward to another tree eight or nine feet straight ahead.

She landed perfectly on the limb she had aimed for, hugging the trunk to retain her balance.

And then she heard it.

It was just the slightest twinkle of a sound, the clink of metal combined with the cessation of a breath in mid-inhalation, but it was unmistakable and telling.

Marlene narrowed her stare as she looked up, adjusting her perspective, finally zeroing in on the shine of a boy's blue irises. Beautiful eyes, she thought.

"BEN!" GRETEL CRIED, chasing the sound of the scream that had come from the direction of Ben's perch. Petr followed closely behind, the shotgun raised in front of him.

Gretel looked ahead to the spot where Ben's nest had been and saw a violent ruffle in the branches that sent leaves and branches falling to the ground. Petr and Gretel stopped, and Petr aimed his gun at the commotion above him.

"Petr, you can't see anything. You can't just fire into the trees. You could hit Ben."

Petr squinted his free eye and kept the gun poised, his trigger finger stiff and steady.

"Petr!" Gretel yelled again, horrified at what the boy was about to attempt. She debated stepping in front of him, her arms flailing above her.

And then she heard a cry dropping from the trees, followed by a thick, gruesome thud.

"Ben," Gretel said softly, the defeat in her voice palpable. "Oh my god, Ben."

"Gretel look," Petr said, awestruck.

Gretel looked up. She saw an invisible wave ripple through the tops of the oaks, at least ten feet higher than where the scuffle had taken place, cascading away from the house, and flowing deep into the woods toward the Interways. It reminded Gretel of the motion the sea had made when their ship left port for the Old World.

"Is that her?" Petr asked, knowing the obvious answer.

Gretel swallowed, took a deep breath, and jogged over to the place where Ben's descending yell had come from.

Petr followed behind, saw his friend first, and sprinted over to him. "Ben, are you okay?"

Gretel came up beside Petr, almost too afraid to look down at the body below her, though the tone of Petr's voice had sounded optimistic.

"My shoulder is dislocated for sure," Ben said, "and I probably have a broken collarbone. So after we kill this fucking hag, I'm going to need to see a doctor."

"Oh my god, Ben." Gretel's grin was touching her ears, "I can't believe you're alive. How?"

"I don't really know. She came at me through the trees. Which, truth told, I hadn't expected. The fact that she can fly would have been a helpful biographical point."

Gretel looked away sheepishly.

"She landed right next to me and knocked me from the tree. I thought she was going to come down after me, pounce on me like a leopard or something, but she just flew off. Like she got spooked or something."

"She probably saw you with the shotgun, Petr. She sensed you were going to shoot."

"I was going to shoot."

"But what about Ben?" Gretel wasn't scolding, just curious.

Petr shrugged. "I saw enough of her. I thought I had the shot."

"You saved me, buddy." Ben said, pride in his voice at his friend's conviction. "We'll call it even on the borrowing-the-truck thing."

"Well, you and I are not even, Ben. Not even close." Gretel's voice was humorless as she and Petr helped Ben get to his feet. Tears of pain erupted from the boy's eyes the moment he lifted his arm of the ground.

"You saved my brother. She was going to kill him, and you saved him."

"It was quite a shot if I do say so myself."

Gretel put her arms around Ben and hugged him tight. "Thank you."

Ben let the hug linger for a few beats and then said, "You're welcome, Gretel. Anything for you."

"Yeah, well, we can't get too comfortable now," Petr said. Gretel detected just a touch of jealousy in his voice. "She could be coming back anytime."

"Oh no," Gretel said, turning toward the lake. "Oh god, no."

"Gretel, what is it?"

"She's not coming back here."

"Where then?"

"The Klahr's. She's going back for Mrs. Klahr. And Hansel is over there. We have to go. Now!

"All right then," Ben said, unable to disguise his weariness. "Let's go."

"Not you, my friend." Petr's tone was steel, and Ben didn't raise the immediate protest that was his typical reaction. "You're staying here. Take the shotgun and stay in the house, alert. I'll take the rifle. You're a decent shot, but you'll be no good firing this thing with one hand."

"I'd still be better than you."

Gretel was already in the truck with the engine rumbling. "Petr, let's go!"

Petr jumped in the bed, and Gretel sped down the drive and out toward the main road. They would be at the Klahrs in less than a minute.

CHAPTER FORTY-FOUR

AMANDA KLAHR LAY DEFEATED on the bed, her eyes closed, listening to the front door open slowly, the creaky hinges deafening in their finality. It was over now. The witch was back, and the children were almost certainly dead. She now prayed it would end quickly for her, not because she feared the pain, but because Amanda wanted as little time in this world as possible to mourn the children she loved so much. Amanda doubted that the woman would grant her even that level of mercy.

She listened closely now, the sound of the intruder moving through the kitchen to the base of the stairs. It could be one of the children. A lump of possibility formed in her throat; but her reasoning sprang to life and quickly killed the hope. Amanda knew if it was Petr or Gretel, they would have entered her house with much more urgency to save their beloved Mrs. Klahr.

No, it could only be the woman; the quiet, unsure footsteps that ascended the stairs were not those of her favorite children.

"Mrs. Klahr?"

Amanda's eyes exploded open. She waited a beat before answering, needing to register the sound completely, ensuring that what she'd heard was a true sound and not the invention of desperation.

"Mrs. Klahr?"

Hansel.

"Hansel!"

The bedroom door opened slowly, and Hansel Morgan walked in to find his neighbor tied to the bedposts, a brutalized corpse beside her in a chair. She couldn't have imagined how deranged and pathetic the whole scene must have appeared to the boy.

"Hansel, Hansel it's me. You're alive! And your sister? And Petr?" Mrs. Klahr tried to stay composed despite the flood of questions brewing in her mind.

"Yes, ma'am, they're alive," Hansel said, his eyes locked on the dead body. He turned his gaze toward Amanda. "But they're in danger. She's come here. She's..."

Hansel stopped in mid-sentence, and Amanda could see that he had recognized there was certainly no need to tell her about the witch's presence in the Back Country.

"I need your phone. I have to call the System."

Hansel was already next to the bed working on the restraints, and within seconds, he freed Amanda's arms. He reached down to her feet and unknotted the twine from her ankles, spinning the fabric away and freeing Amanda completely.

"Where is your phone, Mrs. Klahr?"

"It's in the kitchen by the sink. You call and I'll—"

Before Amanda Klahr could finish her directions to Hansel, thunder blasted from the ceiling above them, shaking the floor and the walls around them. It was as if a stick of dynamite had been detonated on the roof.

"What was that, Hansel?"

Hansel was already staring at the ceiling and said with no doubt in his voice, "It's her, Mrs. Klahr. She's on top of your house."

PETR WAS OUT OF THE truck before Gretel came to a full stop, keeping his eyes to the sky, looking, unbelievably, for a flying woman.

Gretel parked and moved quickly toward the house, crouching like a soldier. "Petr, if you see her, shoot," she said. "No matter what. I'm going in to find Hansel and Mrs. Klahr."

Petr wanted to protest, but instead just nodded, not knowing if Gretel could even see him.

But he would shoot. If he had even a sliver of an opportunity, he wouldn't waste a second in filling the woman with as many bullets as he could get off.

But Petr was beginning to think it wasn't his fate to kill her. That despite his superior claim to her life—Marlene having murdered his father—it wasn't his fortune to have it end at his hand. There was a connection between Gretel and Marlene that he didn't have, one of blood and ancestry. Petr realized now that if the witch were to die today, Gretel seemed destined to be the one to land the mortal blow.

Suddenly, the trees behind Petr rustled, and he turned away from the house and pointed the rifle in the direction of the sound, exhaling as he watched a golden eagle fly away over the lake. He tracked the bird in his sight for a second before lowering the rifle. That would have been too easy, he thought.

Petr focused a few more seconds on the eagle as it diminished into the blue sky, and for a moment, he was envious of how detached the creature was from the tragedy playing out below him. How amazing it would be to just fly above all the troubles of the world, to escape to the air whenever life became too burdensome.

Boom!

Petr snapped back to the moment and turned to the sound, his right eye already in the scope, searching. It had come from the roof, on the pitch opposite where Petr stood.

Petr took his eyes from the sight and looked over at Gretel, whose hand was frozen on the door knob as she was about to enter the Klahr house. She was staring back at Petr, eyes wandering, listening for the sound again.

She gave a pointing motion toward the house indicating that she was going inside, and then gave another to Petr instructing him to head around to the back. Petr shook her off furiously. They had to stay together, and he certainly didn't want her trapped inside.

Gretel pulled the pistol from her waistband and nodded. She was going in, and no look he gave was going to stop her. She gave Petr the five-minute hand sign, indicating that she would head in, get her brother and Mrs. Klahr, and be back in that spot in five minutes.

Petr frowned and nodded, knowing it would never work out that way.

AFTER GRETEL MADE HER decision, she moved quickly, entering the house in a sprint and ascending the stairs two at a time. At the top of the staircase, she ran headfirst into Amanda Klahr, nearly knocking her to the floor of the upstairs hallway. Only Hansel, who was standing directly behind her, kept them both on their feet.

"Mrs. Klahr!" Gretel blurted, and then lowered her voice to a whisper. "You are alive! I knew you would be."

Mrs. Klahr bear hugged Gretel and then released her in one motion. She then spun her and pressed her hands to Gretel's back, guiding her down the steps. "I know, my baby. I knew you would know. But now we have to go."

"Hansel, are you okay?" Gretel asked, looking over her shoulder.

The shattering of glass in the bedroom seemed to answer Gretel's question, and before she could scream, Marlene was standing in her line of sight. Her face was wild, smiling, and she was holding up her hand to show the nubs of where her fingers had been.

"Gretel, go!" Hansel screamed. He was at the back of their small pack, and he would have been the first one skewered by the nails of the flying psychopath who had just plunged in from the sky.

"Come here, boy." The woman spoke with a terrifying confidence, as if she were reaching to grab a lobster from a crowded tank.

As Hansel would tell it later in his life, after the images of the woman started to fade and he could finally speak about the events, that moment when he felt the woman's fingernails rake across the back of his head, down his neck and between his shoulder blades, just missing the collar of his shirt, he was as certain of his own death as he had ever been in his life. Even more certain than when she had held him as a negotiating pawn and Ben Richter had saved his life.

If she latched on this time, he knew it would be fatal. At that point, there would have been no more negotiation; Marlene was on a rampage.

Gretel leaped down the remaining four or five steps to the bottom, retained her footing, and then turned toward the stairs with the gun raised. She waited for Mrs. Klahr and Hansel to reach the floor and clear the way, and then she fired three rounds through the empty space into the wall at the top of the stairs.

Marlene was gone.

Gretel stared up the stairwell, allowing a moment for the terrible face to appear one last time. Just one more chance so she could shoot a bullet through the woman's cranium. But there was only silence from upstairs.

"Gretel, let's go," Mrs. Klahr said.

"She can't live, Mrs. Klahr. Not past today."

Hansel, Gretel, and Mrs. Klahr stood paralyzed in the foyer, waiting for the sound from Marlene's location to dictate their next move. She was fast, faster than any of them had realized, and she was capable of flight, so it wasn't as easy as just running out the door into the open space of the orchard. From there Marlene could pick them off easily, like grubs exposed in an opossum's den.

For now, they would stay huddled at the bottom of the stairs with gun in hand. That seemed like the safest play.

As if a test to the theory, the front doorknob began to turn, slowly pulling the latch from its casing. Preemptively, Gretel grabbed the knob and snatched the door open. She pulled back the hammer of the pistol and held it skull-high as she swung the door wide, and then pushed the barrel against the forehead of Petr, who stood on the other side of the threshold.

"Gretel!" Mrs. Klahr snapped a whisper at Gretel, who lowered the pistol to her side. Mrs. Klahr then pushed past the teenage girl and grabbed Petr by his shoulders, bringing him into her arms. "Thank you, God."

"Gretel was right, Mrs. Klahr," Petr sighed, the relief in his voice palpable. "She always had faith you would be okay."

Despite herself, Gretel basked in the credit and then allowed the reunion of Petr and Mrs. Klahr to last just a moment longer than she should have.

Finally, Gretel grabbed the bottom of Petr's shirt and pulled him fully inside the house.

"She was in here, Petr," Gretel debriefed, her voice barely audible. "At the top of the stairs. I don't know where she's gone. We didn't hear her leave, so she may still be inside."

Petr matched Gretel's volume. "I didn't see anyone outside. Maybe she's flown off." He made a flying motion with his hands, like a bat. "She probably wasn't expecting us to fight. Maybe she's decided to quit for now."

Gretel was quick to kill any hope in Petr. Complacency meant certain death. "No, Petr. She knew. She came to the Back Country fully expecting a battle. She surprised us by coming across the lake." Gretel avoided Hansel's eyes, not needing to call attention to his dereliction of duty at this point. "But she knew we would be prepared to fight. It's part of her nature. It's her disposition to engage this way."

Petr was shaking his head before Gretel finished speaking. "What? How can you know this, Gretel? How can you know her like that?" Petr was unsold, weary.

"Because it's how I feel about things. That need to always struggle, even when there are easier options. Even when the struggle isn't there at all. I can't explain it, but trust me, she's not gone."

"Maybe we should go before she comes back."

"Are you listening, Petr? She's not gone."

"So are we just going to stand here then? In a circle in the foyer? Our backs to each other, waiting for her to come down the stairs or through the front door?"

Gretel dropped her head, looking down at the floor, and then stepped to Petr until she was only an inch away. She stared up into his face, breathing heavily, her eyes fire. "Did you see her fly?"

"Yes, I saw her, but—"

"She could be waiting for you on the roof right above us. And the second you step back outside she'll collapse on you like an avalanche. And devour you."

Petr stepped back toward the window, holding the rifle next to him with the butt on the ground in a resting pose.

"Okay, Gretel. I'm with you. I want to get out of here as badly as you do. I just want us all to make it out of here alive."

"Death is coming," Gretel said to no one.

Petr, Hansel, and Mrs. Klahr let Gretel's words hang in the air for a moment before Mrs. Klahr finally picked up where Petr left off. "So what do you want to do, Gretel?"

Gretel sensed a bit of defensiveness from Mrs. Klahr for her adopted son.

"She was up there, and I haven't heard a sound since."

"Shhh!" Gretel whispered, stepping away from the group with the pistol raised, her gaze slightly upturned. "Did you hear that? It came from the kitchen, I think."

Gretel took a step toward the kitchen and stopped. She took another, all eyes on her as she crept toward the sound.

On the third step, the sound of chaos detonated into the house from behind her, inches from where Petr stood. The bow window that looked out toward the lake shattered inward.

Hansel and Mrs. Klahr stood in shock, showered with glass. The light refracted through the shards, giving them a dreamlike essence. Gretel looked past them, past Petr, and there she was.

Marlene.

She was standing at the window, her arm reaching through the destroyed frame, grabbing for the barrel of the rifle that was leaning against the wall next to Petr. She coiled her long fingers around the metal tube and pulled it toward her.

Petr's instincts were fast, and he clutched down onto the butt of the gun before Marlene could pull the rifle entirely through the window. He couldn't quite get his finger steady on the trigger, but he was holding his own in the tug of war for the weapon.

Gretel turned to Hansel and Mrs. Klahr. "Go to the kitchen and call the System!"

Gretel lifted the pistol and aimed several feet to Petr's right, eliminating any chance of hitting him with friendly fire. She squeezed off two shots in Marlene's direction.

The first shot missed, hitting the right frame of the window. The second was purer and struck Marlene just below her left shoulder, dropping her from the square of the window, her body disappearing as if the ground below her suddenly imploded. There was a delightful howl of pain left in her wake. Gretel knew it wasn't a mortal shot—unfortunately—but it was injurious. Maybe enough to give them the advantage they would need to finally finish her.

Petr pulled the rifle in and held it ready, looking at Gretel, wonderstruck. "Nice shot."

Gretel nodded, a bit surprised at her own acumen.

"I'm going after her, Gretel."

"No."

"Yes, Gretel. We're trapped in here. And you're out of bullets. Or close to it. And she's hurt. Now is the time. If we wait, we'll die in here."

"Petr, wait!"

But he was already out the door, and within seconds of leaving, she heard a round shot from the rifle, and the wails of Marlene's distress had turned to laughter.

GRETEL WAS NAUSEOUS now, and for the first time since she'd returned from the Old Country, she had no idea what to do next.

Mrs. Klahr ran back from the kitchen and stood next to Gretel, staring wide-eyed toward the window. "What happened? Where is Petr?"

Gretel was silent.

"Where is Petr, Gretel?" Amanda Klahr shouted at Gretel, her anguish unlike anything Gretel had ever heard from the woman.

"Don't you fret, Amanda. Petr is just fine." Marlene was as clear as crystal from outside the door, her voice dripping with disdain as she grotesquely drew out the word 'fine.'

Judging by the volume, Gretel estimated the woman was only ten or twelve feet from the house.

"His tender neck feels wonderful beneath my boot."

Hansel had now arrived back from the kitchen and stood with Gretel and Mrs. Klahr; the defeat on his face terrified Gretel. He didn't look afraid—that was the old baby Hansel—he had the more frightening look of disappointment. Whether it was directed at Gretel, she couldn't have said, but it was as clear to her as anything she'd ever known that Hansel's faith in the world had been broken.

Gretel hugged her brother. He kept his arms by his side.

She turned now to Mrs. Klahr. "I'm going to get him back, Mrs. Klahr. It's me she wants, not Petr. And not you either."

"Gretel, you will do no such thing!"

"This will be okay. I know it will." Gretel studied the woman's face for understanding. "Okay, Mrs. Klahr? Just stay here. There isn't anything else to do."

Gretel embraced Mrs. Klahr, kissed her on the forehead, and then walked to the door. She opened it, stepping out to a beautiful day in the Back Country.

As Gretel knew before she looked, Petr was in as desperate a position as Marlene described. His cheek was pinned down in the gravelly dirt of the driveway, and Marlene was leaning forward, her foot on the side of Petr's neck. Gretel could see he struggled to breathe, was begging for oxygen. Marlene stood like a hunter with a trophy kill below her, the rifle on her hip and a smile on her face.

"I'm proposing this trade, Marlene, and you will take it as it comes. You will let him go, and I will go with you to the Old World. With no resistance. I'm sure you have a sedative with you, so just to be safe, I'll take it and go quietly. You've won. Just leave him and my brother and Mrs. Klahr in peace."

"I don't need your deals anymore, Gretel, but I do need your gun. Drop it to the ground."

Gretel had forgotten about the weapon in her waistband. She had no intention of making a desperate play in this situation. Negotiation—the exchange of her own life—was the only hope she had of saving Petr. The System had been called, but they would likely take hours to arrive.

Gretel tossed the weapon to ground.

"Of course you need my deal, Marlene. You can't make the potion if I'm dead, and if you hurt Petr, that's the only way you will ever take me. But you have a choice: if you let him go, I promise you I'll come with you, and you can use me for your liking."

Marlene stared hard at Gretel, considering.

"It's not good enough, Gretel. Your deal, that is. There are two Aulwurms here. And another one, as I understand it, is on the way. My Source. I need all you. I need all of it. I could never leave that much behind."

Gretel closed her eyes, fatigued, her will as frail as talc. She now understood that this woman was mad beyond even the most basic logic. She couldn't possibly expect to take them all. Her mother too? And take them where? How? It would be nearly impossible to wrangle three people back to the Old World. Or wherever she was planning to take them. She hadn't shown the ability to maintain even one prisoner in her own home.

The situation trended toward hopelessness. The deal Gretel had offered was sincere—even fair, in a maniacal way—but it wasn't enough. It would never be enough. Her addiction, her dependency on the potion, was absolute.

"My mother isn't here," Gretel said.

Gretel hoped Marlene could at least reason as far as that. That she couldn't simply make a person appear from nowhere.

Marlene nodded and rubbed her chin, a motion suggesting Gretel had a good point.

"You'll just have to take me alone. I'm sorry. The deal I've proposed is fair."

"But your brother is here. Your young, delicious brother."

"Just me," Gretel snapped, landing each word solidly, leaving a pause between them. Her tone made it clear that notion was off the table.

"You haven't the leverage to hold such a strong position, my dear. And I've little more patience for this place. Hansel will be coming with me. As will you. Or your lover below me dies."

"No!"

Marlene lowered the barrel of the rifle until the muzzle was snug against Petr's temple, her finger hooked around the trigger.

Gretel began to cry. "No...please. Don't. You can't take Hansel. I..." She had nothing more to offer.

Marlene smiled now, displaying her infamous fangs. "So be it."

Petr closed his eyes in anticipation.

"I'll come with you."

Hansel stood at the door, his eyes as cold as iron.

"Just let him go."

Marlene smiled wider now and then broke into satanic laughter. It sounded so horrible Gretel wouldn't have been surprised to see the leaves behind her turn brown and drift to the ground.

Hansel walked over next to his sister and grabbed her hand. "Here we are. You have us as you asked. Now let Petr go."

Marlene's laugh ended abruptly and she snarled, "I don't think so."

She repositioned the muzzle on Petr's head and put her eye to the sight.

"No!" Gretel screamed.

And then a blast shook the air around her, and blood, bone, and brains exploded everywhere.

GRETEL CLOSED HER EYES and screamed, falling to her knees. She was coughing and crying into the dirt, blood from the blast dripping from her face.

"Gretel, are you okay?"

It was Petr's voice. How was that possible?

Gretel looked up and saw Petr on the ground, miraculously unharmed. Beside him was Marlene, half of her head and face gone. She moved her mouth as if trying to speak.

"What? How?" Gretel stared down at the scene on the ground in disbelief, shaking her head clear, making sure it was all true before forming any hope. She felt Hansel pull away from her and head in the direction of the lake.

"Mother," he said once, his voice squeaking on the first syllable. And then he started laughing like the child he was.

Gretel looked up. "What? What do you...?"

And then she saw her standing like an infantry soldier, the last wisps of smoke dissipating from the shotgun. Her hair and clothes were dripping wet. Mother.

"Are you all okay?" Anika asked.

Gretel just nodded and then ran to her mother, almost tackling her and Hansel to the ground.

"Petr? Are you okay?"

Petr stood and stared at Anika, his eyes captivated by the woman before him. He swallowed hard and nodded. "I think I am."

"Mother, how did you? I don't understand."

"Your friend Ben told me you were here. I didn't have a car or a boat, so I swam. Thankfully, he had a spare shotgun."

Gretel considered this explanation and asked, "So you're...cured?"

"We've a lot to talk about, Gretel. Not now though. Has anyone called the System?"

Gretel didn't like the deflection, but she knew her mother was right. Now was not the time. "We called them."

A gruesome liquid sound sputtered behind them.

"She's not dead," Petr said. "Look at her. She's still breathing."

Gretel placed her hands on the shotgun in her mother's hands, and Anika let it go with little reluctance. Gretel strode to the woman's damaged body and stood over her, assuming the position Marlene had taken over Petr just moments earlier.

"Gretel wait," Anika said. Her tone was unconvincing. "Think about this, honey."

Anika Morgan had blown the right side of Marlene's head out from the back; the witch's face was little more than a pile of smiling red flesh.

"You had a choice, Marlene," Gretel said, the pitch of her voice almost sympathetic. "You should have taken it."

"Marlene. Daughter of Tanja," Anika whispered. Gretel catalogued the words for later.

The witch made a grumbling sound, trying to form a word, blood and teeth falling from her mouth as she spoke. To anyone else, the word would have been incoherent, but Gretel recognized it at once. Aulwurm.

"That's right, Marlene. We are Aulwurms. And after today, there will be one less of us in the world. Turn away, Hansel."

Gretel didn't check to see if her brother followed the instruction before she pulled the trigger.

CHAPTER FORTY-FIVE

"THE CURE IS IN *Orphism*?" Gretel asked.

Anika lay on the bed, a wet cloth over her eyes. Gretel sat at her mother's vanity table, thumbing through the pages of the mysterious book. Her mother was still dying, and the cure was somewhere in the pages of *Orphism*.

Marlene was dead. For good. Gretel had left no doubt on that subject.

Gretel would later rationalize that the shooting was as much a mercy killing as it was revenge, but in her heart, she knew the truth. Marlene had killed Mr. Klahr, and that was enough for Gretel to have pulled the trigger.

Overseer Conway had come with his team of agents, who were followed by a team of medical examiners and detectives. The scene was quite spectacular for a few hours with sirens blaring and lights flashing, but between Marlene's history and the witnesses at the scene, there wasn't a need for more than a few questions. After all, as Conway himself pointed out, on the books, Marlene was already dead, so there wasn't much to investigate. Of course, Gretel interpreted this as an excuse to avoid what was sure to be an amazing amount of paperwork, but the conclusion sounded good to her. She had more important things to do. She had to find her mother's cure.

"I've read this book front to back a hundred times. I still don't understand all of it, but the elders taught me enough. There's no cure for cancer in here."

"It's not cancer. And it's not in your book." Anika shifted and grimaced, treading along the edges of consciousness. It was clear to Gretel that the sickness had returned and her mother was now symptomatic. "It's only in hers. It's only in that woman's book. That's what they told me in the mountains."

"Then we have to find her book. Petr said he saw one of the System officers reading it. The officer who was involved with Marlene. Perhaps it's at the System barracks still. Or maybe he brought it to her. It could be back at her cabin now. Yes, that's probably right."

"Maybe," Anika groaned, her tone as indifferent as Gretel's was panicked.

"Mother, you can't quit now," Gretel commanded. "Please. You've come this far."

Anika removed the cloth from her eyes and sat up. She looked at Gretel and her eyes softened. "It was a long shot, Gretel. I never believed I would make it back there. I just needed to come home. I needed to make sure you were okay. You and Hansel."

"What do you mean make it back there. You mean here."

"No, Gretel. I meant what I said. They told me—the ancient ones—that I had to bring the book back to them. Marlene's book. They said the cure was inside and that they were the only ones who could interpret it for me. Or something like that. I'm not sure exactly why they needed me to bring it to them. The translations weren't exact."

"They were lying, mother."

Anika smiled. "I thought that too."

"Marlene has been in the New Country for hundreds of years now. There's nothing in the Old World that we can't do here." Gretel was defiant, pride in her birthplace spewing from her lips. "They just wanted you to bring them the book. It was self-serving this instruction."

"That was a theory of mine also." Anika smiled wider now. "Maybe I have a little of that special power after all. What do you think?"

Gretel flashed a smile but then was back to business. "I've learned the language, mother. The elders were thorough. Once I learned the grammar rules, I was a quick study. I can translate the cure. I'm sure I can."

"Gretel, you need to rest now. Hansel and Petr are napping, and you should be too. I can't imagine how tired you must be. When did you sleep last?"

"I don't know. I don't care. I'm going out to visit Mrs. Klahr at the infirmary today. I'm taking her truck, and then I'll drive up to the Urbanlands after. I'll speak with Conway."

"You can't drive to the Urbanlands, Gretel. When did you learn to drive at all?"

"I don't know!" Gretel yelled, her voice breaking, closing in on tears.

"Okay, okay, Gretel, we'll go together. And I will drive. Later, though. You let me sleep for now."

Gretel watched her mother cover her eyes again with the cloth, and then Gretel quietly stepped out to the hallway. The house was a museum with Hansel in his room sleeping and Petr on the porch doing the same.

Gretel descended the stairs to the basement, the lingering odor of Marlene still present in the air, and then she stepped out the back door and walked quickly down to the lake. She picked up the oar and pushed the boat into the water, steering the vessel easily across the lake and onto the shores of the Klahr orchard.

She walked up the embankment to Mr. Klahr's old truck and opened the driver's side door. She was going now. There wasn't time to waste, and her mother was in no shape to drive several hours to the Urbanlands anyway.

According to Petr, he had 'borrowed' Mr. Klahr's truck from time to time—an easy enough task since Georg Klahr had always left the keys inside. But Georg hadn't been the last person to drive the car. Marlene had brought Mrs. Klahr back from her cabin in the truck, so the location of the keys now was anyone's guess. If there was a God, and if He was merciful, they would be somewhere inside the vehicle.

Gretel sat in the driver's seat and felt first around the ignition with no luck, and then she scanned the passenger seat, again finding nothing. The glove box was also empty, except for the truck's registration sticker.

And then Gretel reached under the seat.

There were no keys there either. But there was a book.

GRETEL BOLTED FROM the truck and ran inside the Klahr house, dropping the book on the kitchen table and opening it to a random page. She had learned her own book like a religious obligation, and after a brief scan of Marlene's book, it took Gretel only a minute to recognize the three pages at the back of this book that didn't exist in her copy of *Orphism*.

The symbols on the page organized in her mind like a handful of coins dropped onto a magnet—automatic, effortless—and by sundown, Gretel had deciphered the secret to her mother's sickness.

It was so obvious.

It was the potion.

The recipe that had been made of her mother's own body was the only thing that could reverse her sickness. It was obscene, this revelation. The cure for her mother was a type of self-cannibalism.

Gretel looked away from the pages of the book for the first time in hours and then stared off across the lake at her home. Her mother was there, dying, and Gretel now realized there was nothing she could do to stop it.

The book's addendum described her mother's sickness in a way that was cautionary to the creator of the potion. This cancer—for Gretel's lack of a better term—was an unintended side-effect that occurred when a source was prepared improperly or incompletely. The Source should be destroyed at this point, the text recommended, but if salvage is preferable, you must make the source ingest that which has already been prepared. This will normally restore the potency and suitability for blending.

It was impossible. If this was the only answer, then there was nothing to be done. And not just because her mother would never agree to undergo the torture of the blending again. And not even because Gretel would never be able to figure out how to prepare the blend or that there wasn't the time necessary to find all the ingredients.

It was more than that. It was technically impossible to save her mother because even if Gretel could make all those other things happen, the sickness was already inside her, and making a new batch of potion with a sick Source would do her mother no good. It was too late.

Gretel closed the book now, and her mind drifted now to Mrs. Klahr, who had been recovering at the infirmary since early last night. Gretel had promised herself that she'd go see Mrs. Klahr today, but her mother's revelation had altered those plans.

There was, of course, every excuse not to go now. The hour was late, and Gretel's prayers of returning her family to normal were effectively destroyed. But still, she wanted to see Mrs. Klahr tonight, and beyond the obvious reason that she loved the woman. Mrs. Klahr seemed to be calling for her, and Gretel knew too much about herself now to ignore those instincts.

Gretel drove the Klahr truck a little less than ten miles up the Interways until she arrived at the infirmary. Mrs. Klahr's room was on the second floor—a floor that seemed to indicate Amanda Klahr was in worse shape than Gretel first believed. God knew what poison Marlene had injected inside of her, and Gretel perished at the thought of losing her mother and Mrs. Klahr to the same evil woman.

Gretel pushed open the door to Mrs. Klahr's room and stepped inside, and there she saw Mrs. Klahr sitting up in her bed, a small glass container clutched in her fist.

"This is it, Gretel. This is what you came for, yes?"

"Yes," was all Gretel could manage despite the flurry in her mind.

"It was there, in her kitchen, sitting on the counter. I was alone there, for only a moment, feigning sleep, but it was enough time. It was supposed to happen. Just a moment before we left to come here. And I grabbed it and stashed it in a rather unmentionable place."

Gretel didn't even suggest a smile at Mrs. Klahr's attempt at levity; she just stood staring at the bottle, entranced.

"There's but a swallow left, Gretel."

"It's enough. How did you know?"

Mrs. Klahr paused now, considering the question carefully. "I don't think I knew anything, Gretel. I still don't. But I think that whatever gift you have, whatever signals you receive from the world, sometimes transmit outward as well."

"But I didn't even know about the potion. I didn't even know I needed it until less than an hour ago. How could you have known to take it?"

"Or perhaps you did know, Gretel. Without knowing."

"What do you mean?"

"I listened to that witch speak at her cabin while I was locked away in my own delirium. I heard her teaching that corrupt officer about the lessons she had learned throughout her life. About gifts bestowed upon her that she couldn't explain. As long as she had lived, she still didn't understand all the powers she possessed or where they came from. She just accepted them as they came. Unquestioning. The universe delivers, Gretel. You know this. Life delivers."

ANIKA GRABBED THE VIAL and swallowed what remained of the potion in one swig, not questioning the potential effects or the story her daughter had just told her. At this stage, there was nothing to lose.

"Delicious," Anika teased. "I can see why Marlene was so set on this recipe."

Gretel smiled. "I know this will work."

"I know it will too."

Gretel left the room and returned an hour later to find her mother up from her bed, straightening the room. "You're better then?" Gretel asked, the glee in her voice obvious.

"I feel quite wonderful," Anika said. "I feel as if I could swim the oceans."

Gretel couldn't hold back any longer and began to weep, a month's worth of pent up emotions flowing from her at once.

With purpose, she walked toward her mother and hugged her tightly, sinking her face into her shoulders to muffle the sobs. Anika stroked her daughter's hair and reciprocated the embrace. "I knew it would work," Gretel said. "It had to."

"Yes, dear. You were right. It seems to have brought me from the brink. I feel wonderful."

Anika now pulled away from Gretel and smiled with her lips, though her eyes suggested other emotions.

"Is everything okay, Mother?"

Anika chuckled in a way that made Gretel shiver. "Of course. I just, I feel so wonderful."

"Yes, you've said." Gretel's smile waned. She looked at her mother, wary.

Anika's eyes flickered at the sarcasm, and Gretel detected the slight curl of a sneer on her mouth.

"Mother, what's wrong?"

"I have to ask you a question, Gretel," Anika said stoically, staring in her daughter's eyes, the pace of her words unusually fast.

"A question? Okay, what is it?

"It's about the potion."

Gretel forced down a swallow and then took an enormous breath as she nodded.

Anika Morgan dropped her gaze to the floor for just a beat and then looked back to her daughter and smiled. Her eyes blazed, and Gretel noticed her teeth seemed a bit larger than before.

"What about the potion, mother?"

"I was just wondering," Anika said, her hands trembling lightly. "Is there any more?"

DEAR READER,

Thank you for reading Marlene's Revenge. I hope you are enjoying the series.

The story continues with Hansel. In Hansel, the evil witch's plague on the Back Country is over, but a new terror now lurks in a distant land.

Years have passed since Marlene's death, and Gretel, unable to cope with her mother's descent into madness, has fled the Back Country for the solitude and anonymity of the Old World. But one quiet day in the remote village of Stedwick, Gretel is taken by Gromus, an ageless mythical figure known only by locals, but whose reputation and power is steadily growing.

It is now up to Hansel to save his sister and the ancient land of their ancestors from a horror as old as the book that unleashed it to the world.

Hansel is a scary and twisted tale that will leave you asking yourself, "what would I have done?"

Order your copy of Hansel today.

OTHER BOOKS BY CHRISTOPHER COLEMAN

THE GRETEL SERIES
Marlene's Revenge (Gretel Book Two)
Hansel (Gretel Book Three)
Anika Rising (Gretel Book Four)
The Crippling (Gretel Book Five)

THE THEY CAME WITH THE SNOW SERIES
They Came with the Snow (They Came with the Snow Book One)
The Melting (They Came with the Snow Book Two)

THE SIGHTING SERIES
The Sighting (The Sighting Book One)
The Origin (The Sighting Book Two)

CHRISTOPHERCOLEMANAUTHOR.COM

Made in the USA
Columbia, SC
03 December 2019